RISE, TAKE FLIGHT

Sisters of Bloodcreek #3

MARY GRAY

CAMMIE LARSEN

Monster Ivy Publishing

Thrilling and captivating.

— CARL, AMAZON REVIEWER

Once you start reading this book you will not want to put it down even for a minute.

— BRITTANY, TEEN LIBRARIAN

I will definitely be getting the sequels. I like the different twist on ghost mythology in the story, the teenagers are authentic, and the humor is sly to add a little fun, the occasional smirk.

— GLENNA, GOODREADS REVIEWER

A good blend of mystery, paranormal, and romance. It is a clean read, nothing crude in it. I feel good about recommending it to my friends – a quality that many books in this genre don't possess.

— LORNA, AMAZON REVIEWER

I love the way each chapter is from a sister's point of view.

— BRENDA, KOBO REVIEWER

Totally fun and imaginative read. The sisters are relatable, the supernatural is thrilling, and the settings are true-to-life. I am so excited to have a new series!!!

—JENNIFER, AMAZON REVIEWER

The Chaldeans represent the Soul as originally endowed with wings, which fall away when it sinks from its native element, and must be reproduced before it can hope to return. Some disciples of Zoroaster once inquired of him, "How the wings of the Soul might be made to grow again?"—"By sprinkling them," he replied, "with the Waters of Life."—"But where are those Waters to be found[?]" they asked. "In the Garden of God," replied Zoroaster.
—Thomas Moore

CHAPTER 1 - FROST

One hundred meters of water plunges into the vaporous river, so deep.

The moon flares from a purpled sky, and I am in another land—where gravity is much lighter, and the air smells of tangerines.

Trees stand on tippy-toes, exposing ankle-like roots, and labyrinthine branches shield us from the ash fluttering from the sky. I am just about to move on—Leonardo would not linger so far away—when I spot a lone figure hunching on a bridge.

Downcast. And kneeling.

A spear lies discarded like a broken bone on the wooden planks, and as I approach, my chest twinges in gratitude. For I have found him. Leonardo has not, as of yet, been snatched to Our Brother's side.

Armor houses his broad chest, and a leather girdle covers his loins. Part of me accepts he came to be alone, but he must know I have come to help in any way.

A red cape dramatically swoops over one shoulder while his head bows as if in disgrace. But he is my dearest friend, and I know he feels the same way.

As I pick my way over the bridge's squealing planks, I worry the lumber will break. But my fear is ungrounded, for it isn't until we are in our mortal forms that we must truly grapple with gravity.

"I found you," I say. I am careful to retain the optimism in my voice. As I struggle with the thin grapevine railing, I cannot help wishing Leonardo had chosen another place. The water is so unpredictable here, sloshing and gurgling below our feet.

His ash-covered shoulders flex as he clutches something close to his breastplate. His boots, slightly scuffed, hint that he has been on the front lines, though we are not supposed to join Father's forces until later today.

I scan the river—the once blue liquid that, because of the ash, has turned a black-green. The cliffs, formerly grand overlooks, are covered with the sooty water Our Brother cast to form this thunderous grave.

Running my fingers along the hilt of the dagger on my belt, I keep my words as calm and measured as Our Father's voice. "Why are you not prepared to fight?"

Leonardo clutches his secret treasure to his chest as the river thrashes and snatches at our feet.

Perhaps he has been forced into a trance. One of Our Brother's soldiers reminded him of the illnesses we could endure in our mortal forms—both the physical and of the mind. They pretended to know some secret, a terrible ailment or obstacle no one could overcome, even with Father's aid.

But the Leonardo I know would not have trained so long, only to fall for the half-truths of Our Brother's side.

"Come." I stretch a hand toward him above the planks.

He doesn't budge, so I stretch just enough for my translucent fingers to caress the bracer on his arm. The cool alloy reminds me that all sensations shall be heightened once we enter mortal life.

When he still doesn't look up or respond, I bite my lower lip. "What won't you show me?"

Leonardo's face twitches with this horrible emotion I cannot place. His lips twist like he means to smile, but his eyes are welling up *like he might cry. If he already feels this plethora of emotions, what shall it be like for him when he gains mortality?*

I crouch to take his cupped hands in mine. If I can but share some of my hope and belief that everything will be okay.

He removes his hands, though, pigeon-holing me with his troubled eyes.

Making sure I am watching, slowly, ever so slowly, he removes his top hand to reveal the most astonishing creature I have ever seen.

Half the size of my hand, its wings have been kissed by our moon. It's thin as a leaf. When I stretch to feel the creature's unfathomable body, Leonardo flinches, startled by my action.

One of the wings—then, the other—flutters from his hands and drops down, down, down to the black, filthy water.

The water churns with greed.

I cover my mouth with my hand as Leonardo's eyes stretch wide.

Now, because of us, one of Father's delicate creatures has entered a premature grave. All spirits who enter the river's dark waters re-awaken as something dark and twisted. There is no saying what will happen to the mortal creature when it wakes.

I stare at the sickening water. "Did Our Brother force you to tear its beautiful wings?"

Thunder crackles in the distance.

The grapevine rails begin to shake.

I think Leonardo will find the proper words to explain, but an inexplicable danger lurks in the air—an aura of discomfort and agony—but I know why our world feels this way. More and more souls are falling into the water, and we knew *there would be a rebellion. But so many of Father's children have been drawn to the darker side.*

"Our Brother," Leonardo says, avoiding my eyes, "asked me to join him on an excursion to show me what life down there is truly like."

Terror creeps up my throat and wraps around my incorporeal being. But visiting Earth before our allotted moment is forbidden. Our Brother visits select mortals only to inflict pain.

I hold out my hand, trying not to tremble. While I do not know all regarding Father's plan, I do know I must help Leonardo move past this erroneous choice. "We shall forget the wounded creature. Let us take up our ranks."

Guilt, sharp as a cutlass, flashes in Leonardo's eyes.

The murky water splashes dangerously, nipping at the backs of my knees. I scramble back half a step. "If Our Brother tricked you, then you have even more reason to fight."

As Leonardo stares at the filthy water, my stomach dips. He has the same exact look as when he first admitted he wasn't sure he could endure what would happen in mortality. What if I make the wrong choices? he asked. What happens when I succumb to the temptations I do not foresee?

I endeavored to ingrain in him a thick layer of armored faith. I showed him all the good he had done—how he'd unwittingly taught a score of students to sculpt beautiful artifacts with clay. He didn't believe that his efforts were of any worth. It doesn't matter, he claimed.

Now, though, I can offer him the comfort and assistance he needs. "This isn't you." I step closer so we might finally embrace, but he scrambles back so fast, I am left feeling like the enemy.

The river tremors and convulses, a volcano about to break.

A sick, resolved look folds over his eyes.

He is accepting the lie that he belongs on Our Brother's side, but Leonardo is not evil; he has merely been confused by too many of Our Brother's lies.

Barely looking at me, he murmurs, "You will be everything I was supposed to be."

Slick, brown liquid latches onto his feet.

Grapevine unravels from the rails like twisting serpents, claiming his arms and legs.

The bridge groans as the vines constrict around his body.

I need to convince him. Convince him to break free.

With my trusted dagger, I slash and slice the grapevine, but it only grows thicker, as if it relishes the pain.

Leonardo grunts, but I cannot tell if he's telling me to stop or if he believes I should keep fighting.

The swirling plants pile over his head.

They dig into his ears; in, then out of his eyes.

He is going to fall.

Going to fall.

I yank my hands from Leo's on our unremarkable bridge back in Bloodcreek.

My pulse threatens to implode from the inside of my skull, and I can't do this.

Can't do this.

I can't breathe.

The air wraps around me like a suffocating blanket, and my arms sag from our world's sudden weightier gravity.

Leo steadies himself by grabbing the chain-link railing. I pulled us out of the memory, because I couldn't watch it.

Not when I know he left me.

The gnarled branches around us eclipse an ice-patched floor, reminding me that we're in the deadest part of winter.

Hope in Bloodcreek is impossible to find.

With sweat caking my chest, I lift my damp hair from my neck as I try to make sense of what Leo showed me. I close my eyes against the memory of that bridge—Leo's beautiful, red cape.

Seizing the chain links of this bridge, I shoot Leo a dark look. "*Stop* showing me the villain you used to be."

CHAPTER 2 - EVA

Spanish moss, cattails, and creeping vines. More moss in this here swamp. Another alligator glides by. Snore. We've been here for*ever*. It used to be all exotic and romantic, back when we were here together. We, as in, Raylan, Maggie, Frost, even Beau, and me. But thinking about them makes my body kinda radiate with a sort of guilty pleasure. Not the joy and love it should, so I slam the door on that thought. I know it's not my guilty pleasure. It's hers. Alora.

My body feels emptier in the aftermath of the takeover. Didn't know it was possible to suck any more out of me.

A long-legged spider scuttles by, and I recoil internally while my arm involuntarily reaches for it, like it's a long lost friend I recognize, but it doesn't recognize me. Either way, it's enough to rouse my consciousness from more than *I'm borrrred.*

Never knew I could be bored. Especially while being possessed. But seriously, all this chick likes to do is hover around in swamps, like she and her "sisters" find way too much in common with the cold-blooded gators. Like all they do is float around until a delicious meal trots by.

You pretty much look like a gator. I hurl the thought into the abyss. I don't really know how it works, but I know she gets the message loud and clear, because she immediately hurls an image at me. Raylan, back at Tess' house, at the bottom of her pool, minutes from death.

I do my best to not retreat from my own consciousness. Show her I've still got some fight left in me. It's the game we've played for—weeks?—now. I actually don't know how long it's been. That *may* be the one thing scarier than Mr. Furry-legs o'er yonder. I can't rightly recall every moment since Ms. Croc took over my body. As bored as I am, I'm glad I'm still conscious. Most of the time, at least. My stomach twists a bit at wondering what I—no—*she* has done in my absence.

Anyway, I'm pretty much the embodiment of passive aggression, now that I can't twitch a finger on my own volition, not for lack of trying. It's almost enough to make me want to exercise. Bask in the sheer appreciation of being able to control my own body. I'd prefer a nice long kiss with Raylan, though. Chased by a Diet Coke.

Frost, her leg seeping blood from where Tess shot her, flashes in my mind, and I back off. Not because I can't take the memory, but because I know my pain just makes Alora stronger. I'm saving my own strength . . . waiting for any moment. Any opportunity.

So, how to think about evicting this wench without thinking about evicting her? Can I make up a secret sign language for myself? I pretend to sigh an epic sigh that would make Mama proud. I miss my people. It's a conundrum. But I refuse to twiddle my fingers, waiting to be rescued.

A low hiss erupts to my right, followed by the sound of

bubbles forming and popping. An alligator must be going for a swim.

The shortest Despairity heaves, her black smudges of features contorting like pulsating black holes, all while sounding remarkably like that alligator. But I don't get a chance to tell her I don't speak Ancient Ugly. Instead, I'm like a toddler being sent to my room, my consciousness getting shut behind a door. The lock closes with a *click*.

CHAPTER 3 - FROST

*L*eo looks like a cardboard cutout of himself as we try to find our equilibrium back in Bloodcreek.

My throat's become a drought. My head's so full of sand, I could sleep for three whole days.

That must be nothing compared to what he's feeling. The truth is, the further Leo takes us back, the greater the toll it takes on him. Blood drips from his nose, and while he says it's a temporary side-effect, his moods have become rather bleak.

What I would do to see him smile again.

I tug the handkerchief from his pocket, wordlessly wiping away the blood pooling above his lips. "I told you I didn't want to see any more of your rebellion memories."

A muscle feathers along Leo's jaw. "It is important. You need to let me finish the memory."

I make sure the blood's stopped before balling up the dirty handkerchief. Squeezing it into my palm, I say, "I get that you have a checkered past, but this has nothing to do with freeing Eva from the Despairity."

"It is more related than you know."

I shoot him a look that says he has got to be lying. He's

never forgiven himself for becoming a Blurred One. He's throwing this in just to prove he's still not worthy of being saved.

He sees I'm not about to let up on this, and his cheeks slacken with an apology. "It has a happy ending."

If I understand the memory right, all that happens next is Leo's swallowed up by a bunch of plants before being thrown into a river that looks about as clean as a septic tank.

I don't want to witness that. But I won't abandon Eva, either, so I wait for an explanation.

Anything.

Though Leo's about as communicative as Raylan and Maggie have been ever since they started tracking Eva's movements.

Last I heard, they're still back in New Orleans.

It's been weeks.

Ever since we got back, Leo's and my relationship hasn't been great. Apart from these sessions, he never really touches me. I tried kissing him a couple of nights ago, but he pretended not to notice, and then when it was time to leave for the night, he vanished without so much as a goodbye. I don't want to complain, but Leo's *always* been generous with affection—even when we were kids, and it was childlike and platonic.

Something's wrong. Something else is on his mind.

Taking up my hand, Leo wordlessly absorbs each and every inch of my face. His gaze roves over my eyes, my nose, my lips, making me feel like I'm the most gorgeous woman in the world without him actually saying these things. Beneath his intense gaze, my neck prickles with little fireballs of heat.

He doesn't break eye contact, not even for a second. "You know I turned out evil eventually."

I drop his hand.

I think of all the other memories he's shared—the happy

ones, where we gathered as children around Father's knee. We learned about birth and His plan for us to fully experience joy, pleasure, sorrow, and pain. *You cannot escape the darkness without fighting for the light*, Father explained. He didn't want us to suffer, but coming to earth was the only way for us to learn who and what we needed to be.

"Okay." I force myself to believe Leo will finally show himself in a positive light. If he shows me how to find Eva and stop the Despairity, it'll all be worth it. I'll get my sister back, Raylan and Maggie will return, and we'll all play the Blue Bloods edition of Monopoly.

Tentatively, Leo wraps his strong fingers around mine. I grip his knuckles back, wishing it didn't physically harm him to take me back so far. But we need to do it.

For Eva.

For her, we will do *anything*.

I vaguely register the low roar of a fan boat nearby. The boats come and go, but my captor and her BFFs always stay put. Cowards. They're more into low hanging fruit, like tall, ugly, wrinkly vultures. Well, I guess this Alora's had a somewhat decent makeover since hijacking me, but the others are still ugly, ripe Despairity, and I know better. Their quasi-human shapes ain't fooling anybody.

My head cocks to the side, listening. I swear, my muscles groan like dusty rafters from lack of use. Why possess me if you're just gonna sit around?

The hum from the latest passing boat gets a lot louder. We fade a few feet farther into the marsh's thicket so we can watch like the cowardly predators we are. Gotta say, this chica's made me a whole lot more graceful, at least.

I guess being ancient has its perks, huh? I yell-think at her, then brace myself to not react to her punishment. Nothing comes. She's too focused on the boat, which is now just a couple yards away, but I can't see the passengers yet through the brush.

I expect us to retreat and find another spot to hover, but

the boat keeps getting closer. A man with a youthful, curly beard and a woman with the best-winged eyeliner I've ever seen are alone, beaming with the thrill of adventuring explorers.

My gut pulses with an inexplicable hunger.

What?! Tell me we're not cannibals, too? I scoff at her. I don't think even these chicks are that nasty.

As if in answer, my eyes focus on the couple, who seem to realize they're not alone. The man cuts the engine, and they peer through the brush, not seeing us. We study the woman, and I notice she's beaming with more light than her glitter-speckled shirt. I don't know much about auras, but I'd bet whatever that pinkish hue around her means she's in love. It's like we're seeing her soul.

My stomach pulses again with hunger.

Shoot. *No!*

My own face breaks into what I feel is a smile befitting a nasty, under-the-bridge type troll. One who's about to snag a tasty traveler.

NO!

Like we're all telekinetically connected, the other two Despairity and I lurch forward at the same time, gliding fast, toward the boat. I don't float like the others, though, with their phantom black rags flowing behind them. Instead, I drag waterlogged boots through the water, pulling giant clumps of weeds with me. It doesn't feel nimble, but we're moving quickly. The couple hears my splashing and finally spots us.

The girl's brow furrows at the sight of me, because what girl in her right mind goes tromping around in the swamp. I'm sure I'm looking purdy scary right now. But even scarier than me are the sisters flanking my sides, looming closer and closer to her. My deadly, demented bookends.

The girl instinctively leans toward her boyfriend, a soft

scream escaping her. Her boyfriend is smart. He immediately puts the boat in reverse, but of course, it's way too slow for these predators.

I throw my consciousness as hard as I can against the cage keeping me from accessing my own body. It's like running into a sadistic laser force field.

Don't hurt them! I shout.

The boy's muscles ripple under his ripped sleeves, itching to fight, but instincts rightly tell him there's not much he can do.

Shorty sister is on him like a rabid hyena. The smudge that was once her mouth drops impossibly low, like she's a python, and she breathes in his soul like he's oxygen and she hasn't breathed in her entire life.

Predictably, the other sister eyes the girl. I don't even know why, but something's always told me she's the meanest. She flies to the girl before the girl can do much more than throw her hands up. And dang it, I'm sprinting after her like if I don't hustle, I'll miss out on the best cake on the planet.

JUST STOP! WHY ARE YOU DOING THIS?

I feel my lungs chuckle a bit, but she's too preoccupied to bother with me.

A loud splash comes from the back of the boat. The guy's fallen overboard. This seems to delight my hijacker, and we leave the girl to the sadist and join Shorty.

You're nothing but a disgusting vulture. We should have killed you along with Knox.

I try to think of more insults to distract her, but I'm pretty horrified at the moment.

The Razorback mascot on the guy's shirt floats up through surprisingly clear water, and the guy's eyes bulge. Arms and legs flail. But he's not able to make any contact with the ground. Shorty's pale, pocked arm lazily holds him just under the water. Bubbles escape his mouth as he looks imploringly at me.

My face grins, which feels remarkably equal to what Knox looked like back in Mags' guest room.

The poor guy's eyes loosen from asking for help to sadness. A faint, green glow emanates from him, but it's fading fast. He looks for his love, but I'm sure he can't see her through both of us. He coughs again, air only going out. Water going in.

I push against my cage as hard as I can, but it's excruciating, like the time I accidentally grabbed an electrified fence back home in Missouri.

Just leave him alone! I'll do anything! I go to lunge against my mental cage once again, only bracing myself for a half moment for the upcoming pain.

Instead of the jolt of pain, my body inhales, deeply, and I breathe in the most precious substance I have ever seen, touched, or could have possibly imagined. I almost don't notice the man's terror as we suck out his soul.

CHAPTER 5 - FROST

The difference between them and us is they cover their faces.

Scraps of cloth swaddle Our Brother's soldiers' heads like executioners on execution day, and meaty clubs swing from fists as they rain from precipices, tall as the sky.

Their mission? To shove us into the river, so we emerge on Our Brother's side.

We wear the bronze helmets Our Father gave. Quills sprout from the tops of our heads, proving our allegiance to a Higher Being. While we clutch onto shields, we are safely cocooned between alloy-like steel and breastplates.

Our mission is the antithesis of Our Brother's: to protect our essence and the essence of our allies.

The spirits who have neglected to pull on their armor are easily snatched and dragged into the water. How foolish are they, for once the river swallows them whole, they emerge as newborn Blurred Ones, come alive.

When I first spot Eva, I almost do not recognize her. Bronze wings are etched into her helmet, and twin battle shooters mark off both her thighs. But, all at once, I know who she is.

She is our General of the East.

Surrounded by a trio of Blurred Ones, tar still clinging to their barren bodies, Eva raises her fireball shooters. She blasts them with unnatural speed.

Their jagged clubs fall to the ground like heavy stalactites, and their spirits burst into powder—irregular clouds of black smoke that can be neither created nor destroyed.

They will return in the water.

Always in the water.

It can take several days.

As Eva fearlessly shoots one after the other, more Blurred Ones rain.

Resembling demented crows, they soar from the sky.

I watch the black pool for Leonardo to wake, but instead, orc-like souls stretch and clamber from the water as newly hatched Blurred Ones.

Tar stretches from their lips as they attempt to open their sticky mouths wide.

A Blurred One raises a club to strike me from behind, so I spin around and stab him easily enough through the nape of the neck.

His essence shoots in particles, puffing into my eyes.

When Eva nods at my victory, I am amazed how, during battle, her fun-loving nature becomes so grave. We are not the only ones who trained together when Leonardo was nowhere to be seen. An entire battalion of soldiers follows her, eager for her expertise.

When a Blurred One drags a pair of wiry-looking brothers toward the river, Eva tosses a pistol to a somewhat dazed soldier so he can blast the enemy. The Blurred One snaps at Eva's throat, but she waits for the soldier to act, trusting everything to be okay.

The soldier's eyes narrow as he finds his purpose. He shoots the Blurred One through the apex of the jaw, and Eva knocks elbows with the soldier in a congratulatory exchange.

The soldier beams, and now he will follow his fine General all the rest of his days.

As I look up to the craggy rocks lining the sky, I survey the routes Leonardo and I used to take. The mossy boulders provide the foundation for the Goliath-sized trees, and the moon shines, too stubborn to hide.

Perhaps Leonardo is up there, waiting for me. Maybe he fought his way out of the river before I came?

Grasping at my slippery strands of faith, I fasten my daggers onto my bracers and sprint for the cliffs.

I trample over vegetation that used to be a fuller shape.

Dodging several masked soldiers, I scurry over weathered earth that's become as empty and barren as moonscape. Stems of greenery nod at us from rocks, and I am just cusping the hill when a familiar figure with a partially askew mask catches my gaze.

The mask infinitesimally slips over his straight nose, and the somber expression tells me it's Leonardo.

My Leonardo.

He has not raised a club to fight.

The field is littered with so much carnage, broken rocks and trampled plants alike. I dive between a pair of Blurred Ones, losing my shield along the way.

This was supposed to be our moment—when we fight, back to back—him with his spear, me with my knives. We would sing the song we learned during practice, about the long-overlooked warrior being brave.

But I am too slow, for Leonardo is already refastening the mask over his eyes. His fingers are coated with tar, and there is this terrible sunkenness about the shape of his head.

From the vines.

When a Blurred One suddenly dives for my legs, I stab him through the back of the neck.

His essence scatters, dirty pollen from a tree.

Leonardo's slitted eyes meet mine.

And I know that expression.

Recognition.

I know it.

I know it. He still remembers me!

So I smile back, beaming at him the way I have only a multitude of times.

A tall, sinister-looking female with slicked-back hair sidles up to his side.

Black-spiked armor lines both sides of her spine, and her territorial stance reminds me of something I have seen in my future mind.

The female analyzes me with the same stoic disregard only Our Brother's original followers claim. She casually points a sturdy-looking bow in my direction while affixing two soulless eyes on me.

Leonardo will take action. He will plunge his spear deep into her side.

But he merely stands there.

In a trance.

As she takes aim.

She nocks her arrow, quickly glancing between Leonardo and me, before sending it straight for the center of my being.

I will soon be a pretty little explosion of dust, white on white.

A shield of bronze emerges out of nowhere, and the arrow bounces off with a clink.

I look around.

The fierce, bronze etching on the shield reminds me that, just like the other soldiers, I am not alone.

For we have our fine General of the East.

*E*mpty, glass-like brown eyes are fixed on a tuft of clouds in the sky, ironic beard gathering flecks of silt —our first victim. I can't even cry about it. I wish I could punch myself in the face. His girlfriend floats face down on the other side of the boat, her hair still partially bound in a gorgeous ponytail that floats higher than her head.

I murmur a silent prayer to myself, but it's answered by an arrogant huff. Accompanying the huff, my uninvited guest still hums with an excitement she didn't have before. Thrill of the hunt, I reckon, but then there's a twist of my neck. A cock of my head, and she makes us look at her even uglier sisters.

They stare back, hazy features vaguely pulsating. Whaaa —I've never seen them look so animated. They almost actually look alive. Shorty and Middle Child snap next to me like a released rubber band, and they're doing that weird heaving sound, as if they didn't *just finish* killing someone and they're about to pounce on new prey. But no one else is around.

Why do y'all look so happy, besides being successful at being psycho killers?

I brace myself for whatever torturous reply she's going to

slap back at me, but it's radio silence. Ms. Croc skipping a chance to rub me in something awful? That's definitely enough to worry me.

Before I can think much more about it, Shorty and Middle Child are off, and I'm forced to follow.

We're sloshing through the swamp, straight toward what I think I recall being the docks, but I could most definitely be wrong. Either way, we're booking it like there's a run on fresh meat.

Okay, so, small confession. It is kind of awesome how fast I am with this chick possessing me. Like she's a supernatural battery or power-up, and my feet don't even feel pruney, even though we've been in the swamp for ages. Wish I could just get rid of the whole evil part.

Before too long, and amazed that I just ran super far and I'm not even winded, the docks we used back when meeting Tess come into view. I expect us to stop and hover awhile, stalking victims like these chicks love to do, but we keep going. In no time, I'm grabbing the splintered post of a pier and hoisting myself out of the heavy water, bounding up after the sisters.

They speed up.

What is going on?

The tiny hairs on the back of my neck raise, and I know it's not her doing. Something's wrong. Even more wrong than the whole killing two innocent people we just did twenty minutes ago.

The image of a cream-colored envelope with beautiful calligraphy forms in my mind. "Eva," it says, and in my mind, I'm pulling out the card. The wench is trying to tell me something.

It's painted in gorgeous hues of blue and yellow and a color I've never seen before, somewhere on the spectrum of orange and pink, but not. It's even warmer. So warm it screams of kindness and love. But considering the source, my gut twists impossibly tighter.

The colors come into focus, and I see a beautiful tree. Its symmetrically twisted branches and massive trunk are breathtaking. But I don't get a chance to take it in, because my hands are opening the ominous card. Inside, in the same gorgeous calligraphy as the front, it says, "Thank you."

What the heck? Thank you for what?

Just the image flashes, quicker this time. "Thank you."

Heck no, you don't get to thank me for anything. I'm not helping you with jack.

The vision disappears, and a neon sign flickers, grabbing my attention. We've traveled pretty far while I was distracted by my morbid thank you card. The main road rolls out before us into two swamp-filled directions. The neon sign of "Canoes for Yous," the shop we rented our canoes from last summer, squats on the other side of the road.

A handful of cars line the parking lot, and a group of frat boys in neon muscle shirts holds the shop door open for a super conservatively dressed religious group. Surely that's too many people for Despairity tastes, but to my horror, we don't stop and hover. No, they glide and I march across the road.

The first person spots us. A middle-aged woman who reminds me of Ms. Sanders, with faded blonde hair and a neon green shirt and a dog's face with sunglasses on it.

Come on, you just ate or whatever. Leave her alone!

A younger man, probably in his early thirties, with short-cropped hair the color of asphalt, steps out from around the back of their large SUV. He angles himself, casually protective, between the woman and us. Her son, maybe?

The group at the door spots us and scurries inside, slamming the door behind them. I expect these two to do the same. Or try.

They could shriek and run in fear, or at the very least,

start crying, but today is not following the rules. The young man's dark brows crinkle, like he's trying to place my face, and his mother looks up at her taller son for a cue on how to react. Could Frost and Raylan have put my picture in the news?

The three—four?—of us regard them for a moment, but we don't pounce, to my relief. Instead, we prowl toward the packed shop.

Not tasty enough prey? Are you worried they'd actually be able to fight back?

The crunch of gravel behind us would have me swinging my head around if I could, but I have to just listen instead. The faint sounds of Shania Twain singing, "You're Still the One" drift from the rental shop, and I continue to hear their hesitant footsteps.

Um, they're following us? At a bit of a distance, but still.

Don't tell me y'all can mind control now, too?

Ms. Croc ignores me. We climb the rickety wooden stairs up to the store's door, kitschy signs covering its every inch. Goodies like, "Don't try to teach a pig to sing. It wastes your time and annoys the pig," and "Hipster Jesus loved you before you were cool" cover the outside walls.

A beefy, ex-military type, giant of a man pushes the door open from the inside and steps onto the front entry. When his sunglass-clad eyes spot us, he does his background proud and doesn't run or scream, but immediately swings a punch at Shorty, the nearest of our trio. His fist sails right through her, but he corrects and doesn't lose balance.

The door swings closed behind him, and he nobly shouts a warning.

"Lock the door!" he yells, face beet red, but Middle Child reaches a hand toward him, and he's wilting in no time. No doubt she's feeding him the memory of when his favorite dog died, or showing him what it'd be like to be skinned alive. He's drained of all color within a handful of seconds.

Through the glass, I glimpse a woman with gorgeous black skin and a bracelet I recognize from a voodoo book Mags showed me. She bolts the door. I want to scream that it won't do any good, but of course, I can't. She locks eyes with me for a second.

My hand flashes for the door handle. Thank goodness Alora can't sail through walls while she's hijacking me. The second my skin touches the metal, it's burned like the handle has been roasting in a fire. The woman's smooth lips move, but I can't hear the words through the glass. Her eyes pulse like there's fire inside her. She must be chanting a spell.

HA! You can't get in!

My victory is short-lived, though. We turn back to the fighter, who has fallen to his knees and looks just moments from death. He screams, eyes wide, like he's reliving the horrors of a past war.

We inhale deeply, and that supernatural battery inside me warms even more. I feel like I could run three hundred miles and not get winded, except for the fact that I would want to shoot myself in the head the entire time.

The man slips fully to the ground, and a strangled breath cuts off suddenly. He's gone.

What have we done?

Turning away from the door and the chanting woman like we didn't want to go in there anyway, we face back down the steps again. The lady with the neon shirt is still standing there, clutching her son's arm. He's wearing a long-sleeved, button-up shirt, like he's just come from work, sleeves rolled up to below his elbows.

"Christian?" the woman questions her son. It makes me think of my own mom, the way she's so sweet but passive. It dawns on me—I may never see my mom again.

Instead of looking terrified or even sad, Christian just tilts his head, like he's deep, deep in thought.

Again, we leave them be and glide back down to the road. I shake inside my internal cage as hard as I can, welcoming the pain as punishment for my compliance with these murders, even if I know I can't help it.

What do you want and WHAT is going on?

The thank you card and tree flash in my mind again, and I wish she would just freaking talk to me. We twist briefly to see the man hug his mother, then walk away from her and follow us instead. Does he have a death wish?

What, are you taking groupies now?

Of course, she doesn't answer, because she's about as talk-ative as an angry porcupine. Instead, we saunter while the sisters glide, back into the swamp, but not from where we came.

CHAPTER 7 - FROST

Heavy purple circles rim Leo's eyes.

I imagine I don't look much better since I haven't eaten a proper meal in weeks. As I grapple for a piece of jerky from my bag, Leo catches my hand, trapping me in his gaze.

"I want you to know," he says with bloodshot eyes, "not reacting in that moment to save you has haunted me for a very long time."

I lick my dry lips, unsure of what to say. I believe him, but the tall girl with the slicked-back hair had to be the tallest Despairity. I recognized her baleful aura, her stance. *She's* the one who stole my sister from me.

Leo swallows hard, and I can feel his internal pain. He holds his hands behind his back, and his stiff posture proves, even now, he feels shame.

"There are things" —his voice breaks— "that happen in that water, which make it difficult to hold onto who one was from the beginning." He squeezes my hand with a fleeting strength. "It is hard for me to describe, but, in that moment, I wasn't truly me."

I think of the scriptures, and how they talk about hell being a lake of fire and brimstone. That black water was definitely charred and sulfuric. The sour taste in the air still lingers at the back of my throat.

While I don't know how long Leo was in that water, I still can't believe Eva was the General of the East. I mean, I can, but if Eva were here, she'd grab the popcorn and rewatch that little battle at least thirteen times—while making fun of it, because she wouldn't believe it could be true.

But of course, it is. My sister is noble, even if she questions that sometimes.

And she was a crack-shot, even back then.

Oh, and we had guns in premortal times!

I can't wait to tell Eva who she was in The Before. But I still don't understand why Leo felt the need to show me the tallest Despairity.

"Why show me *her*?" I lace my voice with enough disgust that Leo will know I'm not referring to Eva.

His gaze finds the bottom corner of my bag of beef jerky. In the wind, the metal bracers of the bridge squeak. "You know why." Vacantly, he looks to the wraith-like trees. "Alora wants nothing more than to destroy you and your family."

I think he'll say something more about how the two of them hunted together for a time before he figured out she was *The Exorcist* creepy, but instead, he reaches down, grasps the thin straps of the backpack, and asks, "Gatorade?"

A lump curls up my throat. What's going on? What is he hiding? I want to drill him with questions—just how well does he know this Despairity—but I also don't want to make things between us even more strained. He *has* to know we're worth fighting for—Eva, Mom, Maggie, Raylan. Us. After all this time, surely he knows he can confide in me.

He turns to leave the bridge, and I know I'll have to press him another time.

all red rock walls line the trail as Leo and I amble back to the parking lot where Beau waits.

The winter air bites at my nose, and I shove my freezing hands in my pockets, wishing Leo and I were still in a "hand-holding" place.

We shuffle over patches of ice and palm-sized rocks that must have broken off from the walls from weathering. I try to think of something cheerful, but having Eva gone is like missing my arm. I would do anything to hear her laugh again, and brush our teeth in our stupid, synchronized way.

A few paces ahead, Beau leans against his green, banged-up truck, wearing the very same cowboy hat he's worn since we met last July. Being human looks good on him, which he's been ever since we lost Lindy. While we don't know why he lost his powers after her death, the boy hasn't missed a beat. Thursdays, at the diner, he cranks up the karaoke, and an hour before the customers come, he lets his brothers and sisters downstairs to sing their favorite rendition of "Down to the River to Pray."

He's not a bad guy.

He just pales in comparison to Leo.

Just like everybody.

Root beer bottle in hand, Beau stuffs something in the back pocket of his Wranglers. "Did ya divvy and skivvy and call it good?"

Leo's masked gaze slides to mine.

"Ya sure must trust him a lot," Beau prattles on. "I wouldn't want anyone rootin' around in this pretty little head o' mine."

Not wanting to draw attention to Leo's and my troubles, I grab Beau's root beer and take a giant swig. Mind travel makes me thirsty. He probably backwashed, but I'd rather risk it at this point.

"You wouldn't believe how incredible Eva was in The Before," I say. Beau deserves to know a little bit about what's going on, considering he's been waiting out here for hours. "She led armies."

Beau pauses from spinning his hat on his pointer finger. "Well, butter my biscuit."

Leo leans his head against a wall of red rock nearby. "If a Blurred One ever turns Eva, they will have a general in their ranks."

"Not that Eva will ever turn." I find the need to reassure both boys. Actually, it kind of bothers me that Leo would even consider the idea that Eva might turn "dark side."

And now the root beer definitely tastes off, so I dump it out as Beau squeals, "Hey!"

I give him back what's left before patting the tassels on his sleeves. "We better get back. We still need to check on Maggie's place."

Sighing, Beau climbs into his truck bed, showing off the battered paperback—Maeve Binchy?—in his Wranglers' back pocket. He grabs another root beer from the cooler before hopping down and slamming the tailgate.

". . . Pours out a perfectly good drink . . ." he mutters before sauntering over to the driver's side.

He runs smack-dab into Leo, who doesn't budge or step out of the way.

Hands in his pockets, Leo silently appraises the cowboy, with his scruffy facial hair and red hair that flaps chaotically in the breeze.

"I believe," Leo says with authority, "it is time for Beauregard to tell us what he knows of Bloodcreek."

I'm pretty sure these chicks took The Proclaimers to heart and have decided to walk five hundred miles for whatever it is they've decided they want. We've been walking forever. But at least we're not killing people. Tiny victories . . .

I'm thankful at least for my new-found, super-duper healing powers, so my feet don't fall off as bloody blisters. We still keep to the woods, but I spot a sign about Memphis being eighty miles away, and I know I must have missed a big chunk of the trek here. The sign grabbed my attention because it has a Buccee's beaver sticker on it.

So, *hopefully*, we haven't been killing people. Ugh. I do have an idea, though. I just have to be careful not to actually think about it so chica doesn't catch on. We've reached a new swamp, and I'd be okay with blacking out for this crossing and all its accompanying critters.

A woman appears in front of me. Literally, she was not there one second, then she was. Another Blurred One, I suppose, since I can still see the trees through her. She's not nearly as far gone as these "ladies." She's still got pretty pale skin and straight, honey blonde hair that reminds me of Frost's.

The thought is like a noose around my windpipe. I miss my sister.

She flies right into my personal space, up to my face, and studies me like *I'm* the spontaneously appearing spirit.

"Alora?" Her voice is clear but amazingly sad. I feel my body bristle like I just got called a mean name or something.

My mouth, my lips open, and in the first time in who knows how long, I begin to speak.

"Zillah," we say.

You can talk? Since when?

Radio silence from the warden.

Shorty and Middle Child, as I will continue to call them until I know their names, and maybe even after, stop gliding but don't come closer. I picture mean girls eyeing prey.

"Nice body," Zillah coos and backs away to a stump covered in so much moss, it looks like just a lump of fuzzy green carpet. "Who's the extra baggage?" She peers behind me, and Alora turns to look. Holy smokes, the rental shop dude, Christian, is still there. His cheeks flush faintly, and he suddenly becomes really interested in examining the bark on the tiny tree next to him.

"An influenced man," we say, and Alora has us look back at Zillah.

Zillah gives Christian an appreciative once over, possibly noting his tall, lean frame and strong chin. But seriously, why is he following us? Is he like one of those vampire groupies, but for Blurred Ones?

He starts humming, of all things, "Never Let Me Down Again," one of the many songs Raylan and I used to rock out to with Mags. Dude's got good taste.

We step up to a mostly weed-free patch of swamp water and kneel before it. I catch my reflection, and it's a small comfort to see I still look like me, just a little extra rough around the edges. Like, uh, is that my hair or an amusement park for gnats?

We scoop up a handful of cool water and splash my face. If I didn't know better, I'd think Alora is getting a kick out of the simple physical pleasure of it.

Zillah drapes herself across the mossy stump as if exhausted from the three-sentence conversation we had. She closes her eyes, her cocoa eyebrows standing out against her pale skin.

"You all seem more energetic than normal." She slurs the words like she can barely be bothered to stay awake, even though she's the one who came to us. "Do share, because I just don't really see the point anymore." She sighs, and her barely green eyes fade even further, like someone turned the saturation way down in a photo of her. "I'd try to kill myself if I was actually alive." She shrugs as if it doesn't actually matter either way, but I've seen enough tormented people to recognize the void in her movements. Like her spirit will stop being a cohesive shape any minute.

Is that how you become the Despairity? I question Alora, hoping she senses my sincerity. That I'm not judging. But I don't expect a response.

An image seeps into focus instead of the *slam* of the horrific things Alora usually shows me. A gorgeous, tall, statuesque woman the likes I'd imagine in a comic book, all slim but with muscles on muscles. Power with a short mane of midnight hair.

Me, Alora says in my mind, and I jolt.

Did you just talk to me? I can't believe it one bit.

She doesn't speak again, but just like Zillah, her features slowly fade and smear. She lets me observe for a long moment, then, like a time-lapsed photo, her face dissolves until her eyes, nose, and lips are just the smudge she was before she wore my face. Between the honesty of the image—the fact that she's actually communicating with me—and the unmistakable tinge of regret, I reckon I'd shed a tear if I had control over my eyes.

I'm sorry.

A new image slams into my mind—Dad's severed arm falling on me, blood smearing my shirt.

No! Why? I just said—

"Things will change." I sound weird. Like an accent, maybe? Or like I've been smoking five packs a day.

Zillah blows a fallen hair out of her eyes and lays back on some lily pads, floating on them like a bed, but her navy blue dress doesn't take on any water at all. "And how's that going to happen?" she asks, sweeping her arms above her like a stretching cat.

"This one's influence," we say as we straighten up and stand.

Whose influence?

"And the tree," we continue.

Zillah stops stretching along the lily pads and pulls herself into a sitting position. "Tree. What tree?" Her cheekbones catch the moonlight, and I realize she is stunningly gorgeous when she doesn't look mostly dead.

Shorty and Middle Child draw closer, looking kinda like bullies about to steal her lunch money, and Alora and I stare at the latest member of our entourage. Like she's being pulled up by a puppeteer, Zillah snaps to her feet, smashing a lily. "The Tree of Knowledge of Good and Evil?" She spools the words like a poem but still manages to look pathetically bored.

My brow cocks in confirmation.

Like in the Bible?

Alora rewards me with a picture of a mass of people, spread over miles, all in varying states of despair. Some crying, others screaming in desperation, or is it pain? Some look completely resigned, like Zillah. And lots and *lots* of monsters. A werewolf, jinn, Chupacabra, some creepy lizard-looking dude, and way more I can't identify right away.

This is your plan? What does it have to do with The Tree?

I know a smug grin when I feel it, and having Alora being the one putting it on my face has my stomach flipping like a pancake.

Zillah swirls slowly, arms high in the air, as if she's feeling her limbs for the first time in a century, spinning the lilies with her. "Even I think I can dredge up some excitement for that. How'd you find it?"

FOR WHAT? JUST TELL ME WHAT IS GOING ON!

"Trades," my strange voice says flatly. "We get many souls to eat the fruit. The rest of the souls, we eat."

CHAPTER 9 - FROST

*L*ittle fish-shaped pieces of cat food rattle into the bowl as I shake the Purina bag to feed Maggie's strays.

To be honest, I'm grateful for the noise. Ever since Leo stepped in front of Beau in the parking lot, there's been this awful silence between us.

It's just as well Beau's baby sister called and insisted he come home right when things got weird between Leo, Beau, and me.

"What makes you think Beau knows anything that could help us?" I set the Purina bag on the concrete. I'm still not sure Beau *could* know anything. From what he said about Lindy, she "raised" him and his siblings by placing them in boxes and spelling them to sleep with her magic for decades. She didn't even let them out until they moved to Bloodcreek.

When Leo doesn't immediately answer, I buy him some more time by scanning Maggie's backyard for her kitties. The fire pit lurks in a corner, and the nondescript beige shed where Maggie keeps her weapons lies on the other side. I'll never forget when Maggie and Raylan put that screw in Leo's face to make sure that was how to bind a Blurred One to a mortal body—and block the Blurred One's powers. I remember how Eva held me in her arms as we waited on the gravel, and she sang.

Eva, where are you? How could you *not* be okay?

Leo sets down a fresh bowl of water for two approaching cats—one with black fur, the other a tabby. "Remember, I have lived a very long time."

Like I need to be reminded. "I believe you. Trust me. But if you or Beau are holding secrets, why won't you tell me?"

Anger—or pain?—flashes in Leo's eyes. "Beauregard prefers to hold onto his secrets almost as much as I prefer to hold onto mine."

What in the heck is that supposed to mean?

Tears pool in his eyes, and I don't like seeing him upset. It cuts me like a utility knife. The wind slices into my sweater, and a nearby screw-and-washer wind chime clinks loudly.

Wandering over to a broken crossbow that Dad and Maggie worked on repairing together but never finished—wasn't enough time—I casually dig for a backdoor connection to Leo's mind. If he won't tell me what's going on, maybe I'll just have to figure it another way . . .

I lift a tendril of my consciousness—aim to tap into his incorporeal Blurred One mind—but as I approach the cerebral cortex of his vessel, mental shutters fall, blocking my way.

"*Perhaps*," Leo says testily, "you should speak to Beauregard alone since you no longer trust me."

"I wouldn't have even tried that if you would talk to me!"

Leo's tone deepens. "There is nothing to say."

My cheeks flush. I stumble backward. Why is he lying? Is it because he still thinks there's something between Beau and me? Leo has to know I was desperate. I was grieving *him*. Tess had Leo locked in that basement; I didn't even know he was still alive.

"I've already lost Eva." I grit my teeth. "*Please* don't act like we've ended things."

The screw-and-wingnut wind chime spins with a musical jingle.

Feathers of wind tousle my hair, and I should have freaking brought earmuffs and a parka, it's so freezing out here.

Without a word, Leo shrugs out of his jacket and settles it on my shoulders.

He's gotten really close. His hand grazes the side of my neck as he gently lifts my hair from beneath the jacket's collar. Warmth rushes up my neck, and *oh me, oh my, I am so starved for intimacy*.

Tenderly, Leo cups the side of my face. *I do not wish to hurt you,* he says into my mind.

You hurt me by not *explaining*.

He pulls me into his arms, and we fit so well, it's like we never took a break. His arms curve and hold me in all the right places, and I lean my head on his shoulder. I know he wasn't born into this vessel, but we fit so perfectly, and I can *feel* how he loves me.

Softly tucking my face into his chest, Leo murmurs, "I wish I could turn back the hands of time." He rests his chin on my head and just holds me there.

It feels so good, so right.

He kisses the top of my head; little bitty fireflies flutter and glow against my hairline. His lips trail my ears, and I'm pretty sure he's going to keep going when a smattering of bootsteps echo from inside Maggie's house.

Reflexively tightening his arms around me, Leo holds me tight—as something inside the house crashes.

I seize the grooved handle of the dagger up my sleeve.

"Not today, Satan!" comes Beau's unmistakable, twangy voice.

Leo and I look to one another as the shadow of a smile fills his face. Beau. Just Beau. Everything's okay.

Another clatter of bootsteps rings throughout the house as Beau runs head-on into every loud spot in Maggie's '40s flooring. He flings the squeaky door wide.

Panting for breath, Beau rubs the back of his head. "Antlers get me *every* single time." Innocently glancing between Leo and me, he adds, "I heard a little sumpin' sumpin' on the radio you wouldn't believe."

Panic rises in my stomach. Eva? Please tell me she's okay.

"Death toll's been a risin'." Beau's antsy fingertips tap the doorway. "All the way from New Orleans to Mississippi."

Another gust of wind bites through my sweater despite Leo's jacket while Leo's met by another one of Maggie's strays. Bending down to scratch the calico behind the ears, Leo asks, "Drownings?"

The cat affectionately nudges Leo's hand. *Please* tell me Eva is okay.

Beau twirls his hat on his finger. "Some are sayin' they've made it as far as Tennessee."

My heart rate begins to race. "But Memphis is only five hours away!" That means the Despairity are getting close, but that also means I'll see Eva sooner than I thought.

I don't know whether to grab the C-4 or pull out the champagne.

Leo gives the calico a final scratch before standing up straight. "Blurred Ones possess an unparalleled power over water."

I pull the cuffs taut on my sweater, remembering all too well how the Despairity tried to drown Raylan when he was a teen. How alone and vulnerable Eva looked when she was possessed in that cemetery. "Why are they coming?"

Dramatically leaning his head against the door, Beau sighs like I've just asked him to unload the dishwasher for the thirteenth time. "I suppose now's good a time as any to come clean."

CHAPTER 10 - EVA

*L*ike someone pressed "play" in the middle of a movie scene, we're suddenly looking at a gorgeous, deep green lake house that makes the one we stayed at in New Orleans look like a broom shed. Six gables painted a burnt brown arch above windows that reflect the moonlit lake. The crisp air carries surrounding cedar pollen to my nose, and I feel like we must be getting close to home. It's both comforting and terrifying, because these witches *better* not be going after what's left of my family.

"You woke her," A guttural voice scratches. Alora has us face who's talking. Holy crap, it's Middle Child! She still looks smudgy and terrible, but like she's more than a heaving pile of hunger now. More solid.

You're all talking now?

My body chuckles softly. "The petulant child is perturbed," Alora makes me say about myself. "She wants to know our thoughts, but cries when we speak them." I'm gonna need so much therapy if I ever get out of this. Then, she speaks in my mind.

Your body brings us back the humanity we lost. You were once a mighty spirit. Now, we use your might for ourselves. Enjoy.

We stride toward the gorgeous house when an older, heavyset man steps out of the front door. His hair's so blond it looks white in the moonlight. He hasn't seen us yet. Maybe it's not too late.

I was mighty? Leo did tell me that once. Maybe I can distract her before I get another murder on my conscience. *I thought he was crazy.* I feel my body bristle again. Encouraged, I continue. Let her take her craziness out on me.

You know Leo, right? My sister's Blurred One boyfriend? Y'all need boyfriends. Maybe you'd lighten—

$\mathcal{I}$ open my eyes and meet another pair of lifeless eyes staring back at me. White-blond hair hangs almost to his bushy brows.

STOP SHUTTING ME AWAY! AND STOP KILLING PEOPLE! As terrifying as it is to kill, it's more so not to be awake. To not exist. I am dying to pull my hair, screaming, while running headfirst into a freaking tree. Anything for an ounce of control over my own faculties.

Alora ignores me and stretches our neck from side to side. Christian bounds out the front door, a Diet Coke in each hand, like he owns the place and he's just happy to chill and have a party. He bobs his head a couple of times, like he's jamming to his own reggae song.

"Nobody else home," he announces with an easy smile. Like Leo's, but more mischievous. His pale red shirt is untucked now with a couple more buttons unbuttoned, and I notice the darker hue of his skin for the first time. I wonder what kind of job he ditched to come hang out with us. He seems like a smooth talker. Like he could give inspirational speeches and, depending on his character, sway people to do really good or really bad things.

"Next place," Shorty shrills, darting every which way, like a kid with a sugar rush. I want to pump every last one of them full of rock salt.

At least stop putting me away like that. Please!

A car drives along the road through the trees, stereo blasting metal. My heart twinges. It's the song Raylan and I drove to that night after Dad died. My lungs pump like Alora's about to tell me what she thinks of me missing my man.

I just miss him. I'm tired of fighting. *Just let me at least be awake. And feel?*

No punishing image.

Thank you.

A humming sound carries through the trees, raspy and low. Electricity buzzes in the air. I feel a crackle on my wrist, where my triquetra used to be.

Salt and pepper dreadlocks untangle themselves from grasping branches. A marigold vest clinging to a dark chest emerges from the thicket.

"'Ello, ladays," Dominick sings.

Look, someone else I'd love to use for target practice. I wouldn't be in this mess if it weren't for this evil witch doctor. "Things a' goin' well. Many bodies ready for the takin'." He jabs the ground with his cane and stands squarely, both hands gripping the handle.

"Dominick," Alora has us say. "Plenty of more playthings to come. We'll get you one now."

A light turns on in the next house over, creeping through the trees. Something shifts within them, and my eyes fixate on the moving shadows. There are six or seven human-like shapes, but something is off about their heads. A flash of bone-white catches the light, and I make out the lines of antlers crawling from one person's skull. The monsters bob and weave through the trees, back out of sight, lurking in the shadows.

With a casual wave to Dom, we start toward the next house—the Despairity, Zillah, Christian, Dom, and whatever those things were in the trees. I hope Frost is finding more hunters to work with.

Dom scrutinizes Christian, who tries to hand him one of the Diet Cokes. Dom turns away with a growl.

We glide up to the house, which complements the first. The same green trim highlights an A-frame that looks like it should be up in the Rockies somewhere.

I need to come up with a plan. What would Leo do? I can't believe he used to hang with these fools.

My chest tightens again. What is that? I don't ask, though, realizing it's probably an involuntary reflex, and I just might be onto something here. We climb the steps to the house. I brace myself for the upcoming carnage, wracking my brain for whatever I can do to stop it. But the three Despairity freeze, with Dom and Christian right behind. Shorty and Middle hiss.

"Trapped!" Shorty wails.

Dom laughs his dead, musical laugh and starts chanting something that sounds just like what he was saying back in the Metairie Cemetery.

"What's wrong?" Christian asks Dom.

"Devil's trap," Middle Child snarls. "Someone is going to die."

It's like I can hear the *click* in Alora's head, and I steel myself to fight against being shut away again.

It wasn't me!

Before she can shut me out, another porch light flips on. Boots crunch on the gravel driveway, and we whip around.

A dark figure with a shotgun trained on Middle Child

emerges from behind the side of the house. "Y'all messed with the wrong family."

I'd recognize that voice anywhere.

Maggie!

The front door creaks as it swings open, and we twirl to see the other part of the trap. Eyes the color of the ocean reflect the porch light, and my heart leaps.

Raylan.

CHAPTER 11 - FROST

*B*eau holds onto one of the gazebo's pillars and spins round and round it while his hand squeaks.

All I can do is stare at the gazebo's narrow steps. How did I ever put myself in a situation where Beau would propose to me?

"I guess it bears mentionin'," Beau says, mid-hand-squeak, "that this here creek's as magical as my possum 'n' sweet potato pie."

Wait, there's magic in Bloodcreek?

Leo impatiently paces on the lawn, seeming to accept whatever Beau says. It also appears that Leo's found his suspenders again—he always takes more care in his appearance when he's stressed about something.

"It's why Mama insisted we move here." Beau slows his spinning. "For the creek 'n all. It's said that herein lies the tree."

"The . . . tree?" I prod him to go on.

Beau slaps the pillar nearest him. "Why, the Tree o' Knowledge o' Good an' Evil, Froster."

I push off from the pillar I'm leaning against. Wait . . . the Garden of Eden was *here*?

Leo gives a crisp nod, still accepting whatever Beau says at face value. "Where?"

"Yer standin' on it."

I raise my hand in question, feeling an awful lot like Eva at the same time. "You're telling me that you proposed on the very location where you believe Adam and Eve ate the fruit?"

Beau sticks a toothpick between his teeth. "You can't say it weren't a romantic idea."

Leo's eyes widen infinitesimally as he glances from Beau to me, then back to Beau, and crap, oh crap, oh crap. I never told Leo that Beau proposed!

Shame, hot and sharp, flares across my cheeks. Despite the cold, the entire park flares to ninety degrees. I *will* Leo to look back at me, but he runs his hand down the back of his neck, spins away, and stalks toward the woods.

I need to stop him before he thinks I cared that Beau wanted to marry me.

But Beau slaps his pillar again, completely oblivious to what's going on. "I'll grab the jackhammer."

I fight the tears threatening to tear from my eyes, my nose burning. The last thing Leo would want is for me to talk about this in front of Beau. I force myself to stay planted where I am. "How did you hear about this place, Beau?"

"Honey, I never 'heard.'" He chuckles darkly. "How do ya think *I* became a whore-ghoul?"

I can't remember how ghouls are created. All I can think of is an emaciated, E.T.-looking creature, working under the full moon and digging up his grave. "Uh . . . wrong place, wrong time?"

Beau frowns. "How da you think we got other creatures like me?"

So he's saying he and a bunch of others ate the forbidden fruit?

"It's not exactly a secret I'm one of the foundin' fathers," Beau adds.

At the edge of the woods, Leo stops walking. Spinning on his heel, he strides toward us, stoic eyes locking on mine.

"*That* is why she is coming," he says. "She intends for more humans to eat the fruit. Alora is building an army."

CHAPTER 12 - EVA

*N*ever in my entire life have I been so elated to see someone. Raylan is *here,* on these porch steps, looking ready to kill a T-Rex. And Mags, too? But things haven't gone well in the past when we've tried to fight the Despairity. And now they've got a small gang of circus freaks on their side to boot.

A blast shatters the night's quiet. Maggie's shot Middle Child with salt, and the Blurred One disappears, although, if these Blurred One battles have taught me anything, they never stay away long. Mags swings her weapon toward Christian, who raises his hand before taking a few steps away from the fight, all like, *I'm just here for the popcorn.*

I keep my thoughts as quiet as I can, determined to stay awake for this and help if I possibly can. Raylan's got a sawed-off shotgun trained on Shorty and me, and a flask I know he keeps holy water in bulges from his chest pocket.

"Let her go," he growls at Alora-slash-me. Mags charges closer to the wooden steps, keeping her eye on Dom, but her weapon trained on us in the trap. The trap pulses like a wall of static. Their powers can't reach outside the rim.

"What do you mean, baby?" I find myself saying, complete with head cock and hair twirl.

Raylan's body sags with confusion for just a second. He ain't gonna like that they can talk now. Evolving bad guys can't be good.

We blow him a kiss and add, "I'm actually useful with my well-fed sisters."

Middle Child reforms next to Shorty. Never one to waste words, Raylan shoots the other two spirits, who are close enough together to both feel the blast. They fade, but only for a second. The triquetra on his forearm glows faintly. Dom's melodic chanting intensifies. He must be trying to wear it down like he did mine.

"Mags," Raylan calls over my shoulder.

We twist to see Mags nod and slide the AR-15 around from her back to lay into Dom. Dom throws out a hand, launching a hatchet at Mags' gut. She jumps out of the way, the hatchet tearing her shirt and possibly more, but Zillah pounces on her like a hawk.

Mags throws her weight to the ground, grasping a salt grenade from her belt. She shoves it into Zillah's face. It releases with a pop, and Zillah fades.

Dom continues his chanting, more loudly and urgently than before, and the monstrous shadows from the woods emerge. Dark, white-less eyes glisten in the artificial light. They're animal heads, but so unnatural. Masks. The people scamper to Mags, their clothes nothing but tattered rags. They're all carrying rudimentary weapons—rusted garden shears, a metal file—and they all fall upon Mags.

"Haven't you tried this before?" We laugh at Raylan, but he grabs the flask from his shirt and throws the water on me. I *screeeeeam* like I'm being boiled from the inside out. His brow furrows, guilt stamped all across his face while his jaw twitches.

"Learned a new trick for a stronger trap from Rupert," he barks, swinging his gun barrel shut, ready to fire again. "Oughta hold for awhile. Let us go."

I hold my proverbial breath. Could this possibly work? I grimace at Mags' cries, which grow more faint, like she's moving further away, as Raylan pulls another flask from his back pocket and waves it at Alora.

"We'll even leave you alone," he says, eyes so open, even these crazed creatures have to see there's no deceit. "If you let us go. Now."

"No," Alora says, calm as death. She twists within me like a diabolical baby, and she's feeding on me. Drinking my spirit. It feels like I just got plunged into the deepest, farthest crevice of an arctic sea.

For the first time since she took me over, she allows me my voice. And I scream. All the sounds are muffled, and yet loud, and every single fiber of me screams for air. For life. It's excruciating, but I gather all the wits I've got for one word. "Run!"

Somewhere, seemingly miles away, I hear laughing. The other two Despairity. It hurts so much, I can't even be mad. I have no idea how I look on the outside, but I catch a glimpse of Raylan's face, completely rigid with fear and worry, so it can't be good. He glances at his tattoo and sees it's fading. This could turn into a whole other layer of bad.

He splashes the next flask on me, and I didn't know my body could make that sound. Dang it, he has way too much faith in me. I *cannot* fight her. The pain switches from the extreme cold to boiling from the water Raylan threw at us. He reaches toward me, and all I want is to curl up in a ball with him somewhere and never leave.

"Raylan!" Mags yells behind us, a desperation in her voice I've never heard before. He unloads six shells, one after another, on the other two Despairity, and they slump for a bit. A couple of feet from Mags, Christian purses his lips, like for the first time, he's considering this might not be the best crowd. I kinda want her to shoot him for not helping out.

Raylan glances at Mags, the veins in his forehead pulsing. "Let her go!" He yells, and I'm not sure if he's talking about Mags or me, but the masked people are dragging Mags into the woods. I can barely hear her screams.

Middle Child reforms again, and Raylan immediately shoots her right when Zillah throws herself against the trap. The invisible barrier crackles, and she screams, but she falls back for a moment and does it again. Shorty shrieks with delight. Zillah throws herself against the trap again.

What is she doing? I can't stay silent anymore. Alora shows me a picture of Knox throwing himself against the sigils on Mags' house, over and over, until they weakened over time. That's how he got in . . .

Raylan's reloading as Dom slithers across the yard's stone path to Christian. He reaches up to Christian's height and whispers in his ear before Christian nods and runs off toward the back of the house. It's so dark back there, Christian disappears within seconds.

Leave him alone! Please!

I'm pretty sure I just rolled my eyes at myself.

A crash like breaking glass comes from the back of the house. Did Christian break in?

Zillah, shaking her head from the blows, thrusts a hand at Raylan. Pulling the gun from his grasp, she holds him like a statue. Turning the shotgun in the air, she points it so the muzzle is directly below his chin—the chin I love to trace with my finger. Raylan's eyes flash, and his breathing becomes hard. Right behind him, a pale red shirt peeks out the door, and with a shove, Christian pushes Raylan into the devil's trap.

With no barrier between them, Shorty and Middle Child

crawl onto him like twin anacondas, lazy but hungry for their next meal. My face smiles, but something about it feels less than genuine.

PLEASE! I know you don't listen to me, but PLEASE don't hurt him.

The two spirits breathe deeply. The man I love is a fine wine they've been saving for years.

Use me as your Energizer Bunny. Whatever you need. I'll help you. My head pounds from the pressure, the fear, and the remnants of the pain, but I try to think clearly so I can save him. I *have* to save him.

You said I'm powerful, right? Leo said the same thing.

I feel my face freeze. A tiny hesitation.

Let's see how powerful I really am. Then, with enough willpower that, I swear, I could close the Grand Canyon, I say, *But only if you stop them.*

"Sisters, stop," Alora coos. "We have a willing partner. We'll have plenty of souls from now on. Possess the men. Enjoy the beauty of having bodies."

Her true voice—not the one she uses with my body— echoes in my head. *The rural Mardi gras followers have your friend. Her hunting prowess will have to save her. Submit, and save him. If not,* she switches back from words to imagery, showing Christian and Raylan, but focusing on Raylan. She knows he's the leverage she needs for my compliance. Her threat takes the form of an internal movie this time.

In the vision, I skip up to him, elated to see him and to finally be free. I throw my arms around him, like it's the most natural but wonderful thing in the world. I kiss him, long and hard on his delicious mouth.

Pulling back, I nuzzle his neck to appreciate his apple, maple scent. It's everything.

I kiss the strong tendons, savoring the taste of faint salt, the feel of the ridges of hard work and hard times.

His muscles tighten around me, pulling me closer, breath getting heavy.

I breathe more. I can't get enough of him. I might cease to exist without his scent in my lungs.

He groans quietly and kisses my temple, breath hitching.

Feeling this good, this connected . . . it's such a surprise, my eyes sting with happy tears.

But I sense another presence.

Alora sighs in my mind with sadistic pleasure.

I'm breathing Raylan's essence. His soul.

I immediately try to push him away from me, but she takes full control.

Raylan's real-life hands slide up to my arms to gently pull them off. But I don't let go. My arms are steel chains, and I *breathe*, heaving and relishing every particle. It's the most wonderful substance in creation. But I'm killing him.

He struggles in my arms.

"Eva," he gasps, his tanned skin quickly losing color.

But Alora and I don't stop.

I don't stop.

CHAPTER 13 - FROST

The jarring of the jackhammer makes me miss Eva so much, I can almost see her grabbing it from Beau and demanding a turn. Beau would shout something ornery, and Eva would call him something ornery back.

"We have to destroy the tree!" Beau shouts over the gravelly motor's noise. His goggles squeeze his eyes so much, they double in size.

Leo, of all things, mans the extension cord, but I imagine my Blurred One's biding his time, laying low. He wants to know exactly what we're dealing with before he commits to a response.

It makes me wonder what else he knows about this "Alora."

Of course, the stupid Despairity who is possessing Eva has to have a gorgeous name.

From the bottom of the steps, I gather the rest of the C-4 Maggie and I made last summer. Before meeting Beau, she and I made gallons of it on Friday nights. She stirred while I added the gelatin and petroleum while blaring The Cure the entire time.

The plan is, once the jackhammer breaks through the gazebo concrete, Beau, Leo, and I will have access to the tree. We'll destroy it—prevent "Alora" from changing more humans into creatures for her army—but I still can't wrap my head around the fact that *the* Tree of Knowledge of Good and Evil is here.

As the jackhammer pounds away on the concrete, I set down the last canister of C-4 on the ground to text Maggie.

Heard anything about drownings?

I wait for her to text back, but nothing comes. Doesn't surprise me. She and Raylan have been deep undercover for weeks. I just hope they can keep their chins up. With any luck, they've infiltrated Alora's army.

This weird hiccuping noise reverberates from the jackhammer, and when Beau cautiously moves it over a few inches, orange smoke flutters up through the cement cracks.

Leo snaps the extension cord as Beau mutters, "Oh, pucky!"

"What's wrong?" I cry.

Sparks and fireworks fly.

Flicking off the jackhammer, Beau yanks off his goggles like he's seen this maybe a hundred times. The cement cracks and rumbles before bursting open, almost as if it's been punched from the other side.

As Beau falls backward, I try to find a sense of balance by crouching on the balls of my feet.

Leo glances around for who knows what when Beau scrambles back to his wobbly feet. "Looks like the seraph don't want no visitors today!"

"Seraph?" I yell as Leo and I lock eyes.

The mound of broken-up cement grumbles so loudly, it masks Beau's reply.

Well, of course, there's a seraph. The Bible says a seraph with a flaming sword guards the tree.

I'm about to ask Leo where he stashed the ARs—not that I exactly *want* to shoot a celestial being, but we need to do something—when an iron-hot hand bursts from the cement, grabs me by the ankle, and pulls me to the other side.

CHAPTER 14 - EVA

*A*lora's internal horror movie ends, and I search for Raylan outside that A-frame that looks like it belongs in the Rockies. He stands just inches away from me, but he may as well be on Pluto.

Raylan's neck twists unnaturally far to the right. He raises his hand to eye-level, inspecting it, clenching and loosening his fingers. A scuttle like a bug crawls up his cheek, his eyes flit to black, and he licks his lips as a mesmerized smile takes over his features.

They. Didn't.

Before I can finish the thought, I lurch forward and shove him *hard*, elation surging through me for this momentary power. He stumbles backward against the barrier of the devil's trap, and like an instantaneous skinning, his body falls to the porch steps outside the trap while the intruding Despairity is left behind, captured.

For half a breath, everyone freezes. Raylan comes to and, ever the soldier, immediately twists to grab a weapon. My heart soars! No rotting for Raylan—he's free again! Also, I just moved my own body. I did it! Maybe now is my chance?

I steel every single freaking speck within me to tear right after Raylan and get this thing out of me. I bolt, one glorious step of my own free will, bracing myself for the barrier that I know probably can't feel too good, but I'm ready for delicious freedom. The trap is small, five or six feet wide, max, and I've only got two to go, but everything feels like slow motion. A black tidal wave nips first at my fingers, gulps up my arms, my calves . . . my stomach drops like I'm on the free-fall of a tower roller coaster.

My lungs fill with air, and I cough like I'm drowning.

I can feel my face and my neck, barely. I glance down, and with the emptiness that the blackness leaves behind, I half expect my body to be disappearing. But it's still there, though it's frozen.

Why can't I overpower her? Why am I so weak? Surely my spirit can be stronger than this stupid premortal wench? Maybe Raylan has an idea?

I search for him and meet his eyes. His brows fall as I lose more and more control, and his eyes aren't black anymore, but they're every bit as bleak. His gaze darts to the woods, where Mags was dragged away. Will he go after her? I wouldn't blame him. She's much less of a lost cause.

Raylan flips his pistol around in his hand, disarming himself just as I lose control of my face.

"Don't hurt her and I'll help," he says.

And everything goes black.

As the cherub pulls me through the gazebo's cement, I land on rocky ground so fast, it's the sound when billiard balls break.

I try to find a sense of balance, but the rocks shift and roll below my feet.

The air hangs heavy as the stalactites, not to mention the winged, hooded figure hovering before me.

He's six, seven feet tall, with large, alabaster feathers, which spread out like a beautiful Japanese fan. His robe jostles as his wings flap, causing a heady wind to splash against my face.

I've never seen a more magnificent creature in my life.

When the seraph lowers himself to the ground, a loud *clank* echoes throughout the cave. On impulse, I creep my hand toward the dagger up my sleeve, just in case.

Opaque crystals shimmer from the cave's dark ceiling, and an amber, phosphorescent tree branch gracefully extends toward me, like it's beckoning me.

The Tree of Knowledge of Good and Evil.

It's really been here all this time.

It's incredible that the tree is alive at all. With no daylight or rain, it's another testament that God can grow things in any time or place.

"YOU," the seraph says, his voice filled with the timbre of a chorus of beings, "ARE NOT THE THIEF."

I don't know whether to bow or cower. If Eva were here, she'd offer a Diet Coke and a chance to play charades.

Above me, though, the cavern soars maybe thirty meters high. Other parts of the cave look like it would only fit a toddler. I would love to watch the seraph move around, but he's obviously not in the mood for showmanship or play.

So I begin with what I know, a common ground. "Did Beau trap you down here?"

A waterfall trickles somewhere in the distance as the seraph stoically appraises my face. Wrenching a sword from behind a pillar formed of stalactites, he asks, "WHY DO YOU CONSORT WITH THE THIEF?"

Eeee. That isn't any ordinary sword. Totally forgot whatever sword the seraph has would have flames.

Not really sure what to do, I slip my finger under the hilt of my dagger. I could tell him Leo, Beau, and I think it might be best to destroy the tree because Alora plans to create more supernatural beings. But couldn't she just make more zombies or werewolves or whatever *without* coming down here?

Why, again, does she want the fruit of the tree?

"I haven't come to hurt you," I stall, feeling a little like a squirrel in front of a Philistine. "We aren't enemies."

The seraph rises triumphant, like an eagle, and I crane my neck to look up, up, up in his eyes. His hood casts deep and troubled shadows over his face.

"YOU HAVE COME TO STEAL THAT WHICH YOU SHOULD NOT HAVE."

There are certainly heat waves coming off that sword.

Sweat trickles from my brow, and I may or may not be having hot flashes. Should I really be down here, having this argument with the being God asked to guard the tree? How did I let Beau talk me into digging for the tree in the first place?

He should have told me he personally knows the seraph who guards the tree.

Okay, the real question is, do I tell this guy that we don't *want* to destroy the tree, but we're doing it for the good of us all? Something tells me he's not in the mood for listening.

I imagine the boys are hovering above the hole, devising a strategy to get down, but I can't rely on what they'll do. Leo's holding something back, and yesterday, Beau stuck hot dogs on a tuning fork to roast them in the microwave.

"He shouldn't have taken the fruit." I try to convince the seraph we're on the same side. "I don't want to eat it. Not really."

Palm-sized balls of fruit hang from the tree's skinny branches, and I don't know why, but I feel like it's talking to me.

Eat. Eat, Frost, it entreats. But I don't lift my hand. I can't be distracted this easily.

The seraph's wings flutter as he watches me with guarded eyes. "YOU FEEL ITS LURE, AND YET . . . YOU DO NOT REACH FOR IT."

I duck around an outcropping of musty-smelling stalactites as two low voices shout from above, "Frost! Froster!"

The seraph spins and soars up to meet Beau and Leo before I can say two more words. I think the seraph might converse with them, demand to know what they want, when a sharp yelp rings through the cavern as he yanks Beau's wiry frame through the huge crack above my head.

With his meaty fist, the seraph secures Leo next—not sure what happened to the sword—as Leo's black essence floats to the front of Leo's head and he punches the seraph straight in the face.

"RAWWH!" the seraph bellows in anger.

Wrenching the boys' arms half out of their sockets, he pulls them both all the way down to me.

There's a massive *thud* as the seraph hits the ground, rocks, pebbles, and boulders quivering. Triumphantly holding each boy like a newly won trophy, he grips them round their necks as Beau sputters to breathe.

Beau swats at the seraph's hefty fingers as Leo washes deathly pale. Beau grips the extension cord in his other hand, and *oh, crap,* what is he thinking?

"Uri!" Beau grins like they're old pals who used to rope steers together. Twirling the extension cord in his familiar lasso style, he says, "Sorry, pal, but I gotta tie ya up like old times."

Growling, the seraph swiftly reaches down, grabs Beau by the scruff of his shirt, and tosses him like a banana peel to the other end of the cave.

I don't know whether to run after Beau or try to face off against the seraph. "Beau!" I scream.

CHAPTER 16 - EVA

The first thing I register is silence. Not complete silence, though. There's a high-pitched ringing, like after I used to crank my music while Dad was gone, and then he'd come home before I expected. The sudden silence after I'd slam the stop button was so loud. Just like this.

Except, I can't hear my heart pounding in my ears this time. I can't feel *anything*.

Or see.

Like, Alora turned my consciousness off and forgot to flip it back on. Or, am I actually just dead?

The buzz burrows in, and if I could feel my lungs, I'm pretty sure I'd be neck-deep in a paper sack having a panic attack.

I've always believed in an after-life, so surely there'd be some sort of warm, flashing light or shiny bright angel to greet me if I were dead, right? No, I'm pretty sure I'm not. Or I'm at least gonna shove that thought deep into a box of ideas I ain't checkin' on for the next century.

So, not dead, but pitch-black darkness with no arms or legs. Sounds like a setup for a bad pun.

What the heck is Alora up to now? I hope Raylan and Mags got away. But those freaky antlered people and their hillbilly weapons . . . this is so messed up.

Think, Eves, think.

I'd much rather rely on my gut, per my usual M.O., buuut, seeing how I can't even feel my gut right now . . .

I sense something shift near me. I don't know how, but I know something is nearby, like a gravitational nudge. I can't hold my breath in fear in case it's some sort of ancient demon, and I can't shout out a friendly holler, so I wait. Ready to adjust in *whatever* way I can at this point. While not flexible, I am rather adaptable.

The darkness folds in, like a black cat on an even blacker street, but something is there, just feet away. If I could move, I could touch it.

It shifts again, and I reel my subconscious back, the only defense I have.

A warm, strong hand meets my cheek in the softest touch. The calloused thumb strokes my cheekbone, and I smell apples.

"Raylan?" I'm suddenly able to speak. His hand reaches behind my neck, and now I have a neck and a chest and legs as he envelops me in his arms and pulls me to his chest, like he just pulled me out of quicksand.

"I've got you," he murmurs in my ear, and I positively melt at the first comfort or kindness I've felt since that day back in the Metairie Cemetery.

"How in the daylights are you here?" I nearly squeal. "You're in my brain?"

He pulls back and kisses me quickly on the lips, but it may be the best kiss I've had in my entire life. "I don't know, but I'll take it."

If I squint as hard as I can, I feel like I can just make out the whites of his eyes, the vague silhouette of his messed-up hair. "Does this mean you're possessed too?" I ask. "What the heck are we gonna do now?"

He pulls me close in a bear hug again. "We need a plan."

"Most definitely," I say, burrowing farther into his chest. "Do you think Mags is okay?"

He chuckles softly, surprising me. "It'd take more than a few cowards in masks to keep her down."

The memory of their dead eyes and animal faces make me tremble. Their choice to take the beauty of nature, kill it, and combine it with their savage violence is just so wrong.

"I hope so," I murmur. Then, in case I haven't said it yet, I add, "Thanks for not giving up on me."

CHAPTER 17 - FROST

Beetles scurry beneath the skin on Leo's forehead, something I haven't seen on him in a very long time. He must not be fully in control. He must be worried.

"YOU ARE LUCIFER'S PROGENY." The seraph surveys the love of my life. Clutching Leo's collar, he gives him a not-so-gentle shake.

In a sudden cloud of black smoke, Leo bursts from his vessel's mouth. He tries to infiltrate the seraph's nose and eyes, but there's some sort of smokescreen. Leo bounces off at each and every entry point.

When Leo goes for the seraph's feet, the seraph simply lifts a massive boot and stomps Leo to the ground.

Like he's stomping a pile of termites.

Pebbles and boulders crackle as Leo's gossamer body shrieks; it's the sound of forks in a garbage disposal, which tears at my heart.

"We're on the same side!" I tug on the seraph's meaty arm to make him stop. "Please!"

The rock surrounding Leo burns white, and I hate seeing

him outside his borrowed vessel. He always seems less relatable, less human this way.

Leo screeches; the cave quakes. I wouldn't want to tousle with a Blurred One, but I really wouldn't want to tousle with a seraph, either. He has God's power on his side.

It isn't until Leo's shrieks soften to a dull whimper that the seraph seems to consider what I'm saying. Lessening his foot's pressure, he says, "YOU ARE HUMAN. YET YOU DEFEND THE DEVIL'S PROGENY."

"He is *Our Father's* progeny." I throw my shoulders back and wipe a tear I hadn't realized had fallen on my cheek.

Rocks scatter in the distance, and when I turn, I find Beau hobbling toward us, looking like he's taken a hockey stick to the face.

"For the love o' pearl, Uri!" Beau dusts off his hands on his pants. "Did ya *have* to go an' throw me clean to the other side?"

The seraph appraises the fresh cuts and bruises on Beau's face. "YOU ARE NO LONGER IMMORTAL." His gigantic wings flap once. "HOW?"

Beau waves the seraph's question away. "Thing is, now ya gotta let us destroy the tree."

The seraph lifts his sword so fast, he's going to decapitate us all if we don't explain quickly.

The flames grow brighter, closer. Shadrach, Meshach, and Abednego aren't the only ones who are faced with a thorough burning. I lick my lips, trying to find a way to explain our predicament. "Hundreds of Blurred Ones are on their way." I try to look up, but the fire is burning cataracts into my eyes.

Leo trickles up in a cloud of smoke, spinning over and around the seraph's leg.

"Not only Blurred Ones," I add, "but an army of humans." If what Leo said is right. "They want to eat the fruit of the tree."

In a gust of power, Leo fluidly sails back into his vessel's lips, which peel back in that same rubbery way as other times. Maybe Leo knows what to say, but the seraph shoots me a look that says his mind is made up.

Seizing Leo, Beau, then me, he cocks back his arms and tosses us out the way we came.

That's it?

That's it!

We get tossed out with no real chance at destroying the tree?

I land on my stomach with an *oof.* "We should go back down there!" My appendages feel like broken pieces of shrapnel as I scramble over the cement rubble to my feet, but Leo's confident hand wraps around my arm, stopping me in place.

"We need to regroup." The warmth of his gaze cradles me.

My feet are still scrambling toward the hole, though, and Leo grips my other arm with his other hand. "Frost?"

I pause mid-step, so hungry for the warmth he uses when he says my name and stare down at the hole with a sunken feeling in my chest. "Okay . . . okay."

I nudge myself deeper into the shoulder I love so much—the shoulder that, for all reasons my brain can come up with, cannot be here. But, we can think and plan while holding onto each other, right? If I let go, Raylan might evaporate.

"Listen, Eves." His voice rumbles through the dark, with his amazingly masculine brand of kindness. "Leo told me some stuff, about life before we all came to earth, that might help. Don't freak out, and I am just going to tell you this fast in case one of us disappears."

"Uh, that's encouraging," I say, heart sinking a bit.

"No, don't worry. It's totally in the past, but it will help us." He steps back, his hands sliding down my arms until he's holding both my hands in his. "Leo admitted you almost joined him as a Blurred One."

I jerk my hands out of his. "No way. He told me I was on the good team."

Raylan's hands bump mine in the darkness, and I don't pull away. "Eva, I'm so sorry to break it to you like this, but just listen so we can get you out of here. He told you that to make you feel better, and he thought it would help you stay on the good path now.

"But it's okay. You were on the fence because you were having so much fun up there, but Frost talked you into getting a body, and it's great because apparently, you persuaded a bunch of your buddies to come with you by saying you'd all find a way to make it fun."

He's talking so fast and saying so much. The buzzing silence comes back, if it even really went away, and it wasn't just because I was distracted. I drive the heel of my hands into my temples.

"What are you saying?" I sound like a tiny doll in a giant's dark toy chest.

"I'm saying, it doesn't matter that you weren't all that good back then, but that you were a great influencer and probably still are. Look how you've changed me. How you keep your Mom, Maggie, and Frost all sane and happy. I would bet if you can channel that in here, we could get people to come help us."

I mean, it's not the worst thing I've ever heard, but it certainly doesn't make me feel all warm and fuzzy. Like, okay, I joined the bright side because I was too chicken or bored to commit to the dark? And now I can be head cheerleader?

The buzzing amps up again, like there's actually a freaking buzz saw somewhere nearby.

"Leo said—" I shout through the noise, but Raylan cuts me off, pulling me back to him with surprising force.

"I'm sorry, Eves," he yells. "I'm sure he just wanted you to feel better about yourself."

The buzzing shrills and stutters slightly, like it's found its mark. Something warm and wet splashes my face, and Raylan's grip slides off my arm.

*B*eau takes another enthusiastic bite of his peanut butter sandwich, and I don't know whether to flog him or take his sandwich away.

He should have warned us about the seraph.

With two black eyes and a nose that's now solidly crooked, though, Beau's already had a thorough beating. But we need answers.

"I know I'm ugly as homemade sin," Beau says, taking a giant swig from a canteen, "but I'll heal. And be even *more* dazzlin'."

I rub the side of my temple. Does he ever take things seriously? "The seraph wouldn't be so distrustful if you hadn't stolen the fruit in the first place."

"Were you alone?" Leo paces on the grass, obviously not happy with how things played out.

"Lindy ate it with you." I fish for answers. "And . . . all of your siblings as well?" I don't know them real well, but they seem to be as clueless as their brother.

Beau opens his mouth to elaborate but seems to think better of it, because, instead, he takes another healthy bite of his sandwich. Around the peanut butter, he says, "We've *all* made mistakes, Froster."

"What I don't get is how you beat the seraph in the first place," I say.

Nonchalantly, Beau opens a bag of Wavy Lays.

I lean forward on the blanket Maggie quilted, pretending the gazebo isn't just behind us, and the seraph could come out and get us at any time. "You have to tell us what happened. You must have had *quite* the army on your side."

A look of guilt flashes over Beau's eyes as he stares down at the chips he only recently began to like. "Not an army . . . jus' a loophole, really."

He plunges his hand into the bag and tosses two potato chips in his mouth, and I can see he has no intention of explaining.

I look to Leo to see what he thinks, and as his warm gaze nestles into mine, heat flickers up my neck and across my cheeks. What I wouldn't give to break away from all this for a little alone time.

But Eva needs us.

I cap the lid to my Gatorade. "Everything would be a whole lot easier if we simply *saw* how you beat the seraph the first time."

I glance at Leo to see if he catches my meaning. *Let's extract his memory.*

But Beau's already crab walking across the blanket.

"It doesn't *really* hurt," I say. I don't bring up the fact that he doesn't have my special connection to Leo, so it'll probably hurt way worse for him than it does for me.

Leo stretches out his arm to seize Beau's hand, but Beau snatches it away.

"I'll tell ya what ya wanna know!" Beau scratches the back of his head with the hilt of his hunting knife. "It was a *long* time ago." He breathes out a weighty sigh. "Mama didn't really give us a choice. She had a plan. Figured a seraph could be stopped if children came to play."

I glance between Beau and his freckles to Leo's smooth, chiseled face. "What, you mean your siblings were like a distraction?"

Beau looks down at his hands—those long, calloused fingers that once itched to hold mine. "More like all-on-out warfare." He licks his lips. "Look, she learned that, because kids are 'innocent,' they can't be touched by other creatures."

"But zombies and werewolves hurt kids all the time."

"Well, seraphs don't," he says.

My mind flashes back to when his little sister exposed her undies while doing a cartwheel. How she and her brothers only know one song. "Down to the River to Pray." She and her other siblings were able to help Beau and Lindy get to the tree?

Beau shrugs, like he wishes it wasn't the truth. "They cast the stones while I tied up ol' Uri."

"So . . ." I try to fit all the pieces together. "We should get your brothers and sisters now."

Beau shakes his head, causing his hair to flop wildly. "No way Imma involvin' them again in this duh-rama."

"But if it means stopping Alor—"

Beau holds up his hand. "No." His voice comes out hard. "Jus' no. They've already been through enough, Froster."

"So how do we get past the seraph?" I cry. "Something tells me we *really* don't want Alora and her army to get to the fruit."

"We don't," Leo agrees.

"Maybe we could get some other kids?" I can't believe I just said that. Sending *any* kids down there when Alora's on the warpath is a bad idea.

"I don't know what to tell ya." Beau stands, dusting off his hands on his jeans. "But my siblings are off limits, jus' so you know where I stand on things."

"I'm texting Maggie," I say, secretly wishing she'd say gagging and kidnapping *any* kids would be a good idea.

But on my screen, I see I've already missed Maggie.

Her message is just two words: HUNTERS COMING.

Well, that's not enough info, so I click to call her back. We need to pow-wow. Plan what to do. She can tell me what's happening.

But when the call goes through, all it does is ring and ring until it hits her voicemail.

Come on!

I dial again.

I crouch like a deranged frog, both trying to find Raylan and stay away from the meta-buzzsaw. I throw my arms above my head, as if that will protect me at all.

Something makes contact, and I grit my teeth so hard, they might become powder until I realize it doesn't hurt.

"What are you doing?" Raylan's voice caresses me, and the intensity that is usually there when we're meeting a threat is completely gone. While thrilled he isn't roadkill, I'm so flippin' confused.

"Trying not to get chainsaw massacred," I cry, pulling myself deeper into my ball. The buzzing is so loud, I can't figure out why I'm not in pieces right now.

"There's nothing here. Maybe Alora's just playing with your mind?" The darkest gray blob that is him crouches next to me like we're just hanging out watching the grass grow now.

"Well, she's doing a really good job," I whimper, and I keep trying to melt into the ground. Something not super far away makes a metallic, groaning noise.

"That's probably it. She's messing with you. But she doesn't understand how strong you are. Turn it around on her. Show her who's boss."

"How the heck am I supposed to do that?" Though I love the man, his calm tone sort of makes me want to punch him in the face.

"She's trying so hard to wear you down. Just be you."

I scoff, but he continues.

"Really. When you are you, you have the force of a hurricane. So, just calm down and breathe."

"You know I hate it when you say 'calm down,'" I snap, but the buzzing does seem incrementally quieter, though I hear the metallic groan again.

How do I "be me" in this torture chamber of my own head? It sort of sounds like the stupidest thing I've ever heard. Pretty much my only useful skill before becoming a hunter was being so adaptable, people couldn't get to me. So yeah, I guess I don't even really know who that is. And I cannot believe this psycho-babble is going to save the day here.

The buzzing gets louder again and adds a piercing, vibrating ring. I think my ears are going to start bleeding.

Me. I was a fence-sitting party girl in the pre-existence, whose main accomplishment in this life is not dying and having an "awesome" extended family. But even if I was a total crap of a person back then, I'd like to think I could still be good going forward . . . so, I'm not loving the idea of being Alora's evil mascot or whatever.

Not that I'll do much good either way in here. Who knows what kind of situation Raylan's real body is in, let alone Mags or Frost or Leo. If I can just get conscious again, I can see what I can do.

The buzzing mercifully stops. But then I remember roller

coasters, and how there are all kinds of clicking and groaning before you plummet to what feels like certain death.

"Eva," Raylan says so suddenly in my ear that I jump. "Just let go. No one expects you to suffer this much."

"I can handle it," I say, a little annoyed but touched by his sweetness. "I just need a second to think."

He kisses my forehead, and it feels a bit lackluster. "I'm sure you can."

CHAPTER 21 - FROST

From my bed, a Pied Piper sneaks into my dreams. He weaves arpeggios into liquid gold, wandering, summoning . . .

I know I should ignore it, but the real-life piano music coming from downstairs needles like a claw inside my brain. It slinks down my throat, leaving a bitter taste.

I still can't believe Maggie's only communication with me was, 'HUNTERS COMING.' When? Where? What exactly does that mean? And this stupid, nonsensical part of me believes Leo's finally come to confess he's ready to talk—but, when *I* play the piano, he always pulls up a chair and straddles it backward.

Rests his chin on the tall, wood backing.

He doesn't play.

My gut says, whoever the musician is, he or she has come to talk to me. So I slip out of bed, pull on my gingham robe, and tuck a vial of holy water into my front pocket. Just in case.

Treading past Eva's room, I pretend not to notice how the door's ajar, like she's finally home and slipped inside. I wander past the family portraits hanging on the wall, careful not to wake Mom. If the music stays mellow, maybe she'll stay asleep.

Maybe Beau's come to show me that he mysteriously learned how to play? But his style's more Maple Leaf Rag, less Javier Navarrete.

Avoiding all the creaky spots in the floor, I grip the handrail, careful not to let my palm squeak.

Downstairs, bass keys hum; alto and tenor notes contend like they've been stuck together for decades. And the musician feels every measure, every single beat. Each and every silky crescendo, mezzo-piano, forte.

When I hit the bottom step, my foot hits the motherlode of all creaks.

I expect someone to lash out, but the musician trills a chord that parrots my heartbeats.

The piano light sets aglow the lone figure, and long, dark hair hangs like yarn down a slender back.

Eva?

Pasty hands eerily glide over the keys.

But every single time *my* Eva sat down to play, she performed a jaunty rendition of chopsticks before sliding her fingers to the top of the keys.

Even though it looks like her, that isn't Eva.

So I hold my breath. Watch and wait.

How many times could I stab Alora in the back before she would throw me? But that would mean I'd be stabbing Eva, so I must tread carefully.

The tallest Despairity emits the same melancholy grace Dad always said I had when I played. She doesn't pause, and she doesn't look up. She . . . just keeps playing, knowing she has an audience, choosing to make me wait.

Baritone notes rise and fall in big, dramatic waves, and for the briefest of moments, I can see that something about her spirit is breathtaking.

She is confident, yet quiet. Able, yet always improving.

I loathe the fact that I'm ten feet away from my sister, and yet I can't so much as ask if she's doing okay.

If Eva were in control, she'd wrap her arms around me and hug me for a full minute straight. Insist we go to Maggie's "to cook s'mores again, already."

When the demon strikes her final key, she hunches in this predatory way. Peering over her left shoulder, she huskily says, "I would offer to play a duet, but I suspect you would decline."

It's like I'm speaking to my sister and an alien at the same time. She *looks* like Eva. She sounds *similar* to Eva, and yet she moves and frames her words almost like an evil . . . me.

Insects scuttle beneath my sister's skin, and her lips are darker than boysenberries. Cocking her head to the side, she says, "You believe you can hide the location of the tree."

I didn't even realize she doesn't know the location. This is good. This can buy us some time.

Stalling on the largest of Mom's throw rugs, I try to figure out exactly what to say. Alora's here, so it's only a matter of time before she finds the hole in the gazebo and the tree. Please tell me she doesn't know we've been thrown out by the seraph already.

I take another bold step toward her, fingering the cool tip of the dagger up my robe's sleeve. But I can't stab her. I'd banish her, but something tells me she'd claw Eva up the second I tried. Could I cut her a little, maybe?

Ugh, I hate that I can't do a thing.

Eva. I try to sneak a message inside her mind. *Are you okay?*

A tendon quivers along my sister's graceful neck, and I

can't tell if it's because Alora heard, or if Eva is trying to reach me.

Taking another casual step toward her, I stretch out my hand like all I mean to do is play a few piano keys.

Leo showed me I have the ability to sneak into his and Knox's minds, so I attempt to slip a tendril of consciousness toward my sister . . .

A thick, black door greets me.

It's been bolted shut, with thick, black chains. Alora must have locked her up.

I mentally knock on the meaty lumber.

And wait.

Nothing.

From the piano bench, my sister's lips twist in a sinister smile, full of secrets and hate. "Your sister has been insubordinate, I am afraid."

Dad always used to say that Eva had some growing up to do when she didn't jump at his beck and call, but now I know it's because of her ingrained potential to be a leader. She is the General of the East.

I lift my hand to throttle the demon.

She raises a finger and throws me through the air like a broken paper airplane.

I slam into the horizontal mirror Mom just hung. Glass shatters, and please, please don't let Mom hear us and walk in at the wrong time.

I reach for the dagger up my sleeve, but with a swift tilt of the head, Alora sends that flying.

It embeds in the throat of a Nutcracker Dad bought Mom for her birthday.

Thick shards of glass slice into my toes as I scramble to my feet, and as I approach the demon, I wish I could push her eyeballs back in her face.

Grabbing the holy water from the front pocket of my

robe, I splash it at my sister. Eva's baby-soft complexion pops and sizzles like I just doused her with bacon grease.

Eva! I'm sorry!

The foul stench of rotting eggs pours over the room, and I cough up sulfur as my sister screams.

Alora grimaces as her nose crumbles into a giant crater in the middle of her face. She slaps her hands together, reminding me of my sister when she was five. "Splash me again, 'Frosty!'"

I dig my fingers through her greasy hair and pull the knots, remembering all at once, *I'm hurting Eva.* I release her and reach for the drill I keep in my back pocket. If I trap her, I can destroy her. Leo will help me find a way.

Biting back a cry, I steady myself on the partitioned wall —despite the glass that's wedged in my feet. All the while, Alora watches me. I'm an artifact in a museum—nothing but a great curiosity. Her nose and cheeks sizzle as they re-materialize, and the thin layer of my sister's new skin flushes with a dull, baby pink.

Somberly closing the lid to the piano, Alora says, "I need you to hate me." She pets the piano lid as if it's a starved child, searching for the perfect words to explain. "I need you to hate me almost as much as I have hated *you* since the beginning."

CHAPTER 22 - EVA

*A*ll I hear now is the sound of my own breathing. I can't even hear Raylan. How's he so calm right now? I muster up some courage and rap on the wall behind me, testing. Nothing happens. Maybe the queen bee is distracted.

I think I'll try to tiptoe around to see what's going on in here. But then, my meta cage rattles like a freight train is passing right outside the walls. That's new. My itty bitty spiritual self feels sweat gathering on my neck, like it's getting real hot in here. Maybe Alora's not distracted—maybe she's pissed. I reach around and snag Raylan's hand. It's equally clammy.

A hissing sound blasts from somewhere instead of the buzzing. If it's snakes, at least Frost isn't here. But the metallic groan joins the hissing, which grows louder and louder into a deafening roar. The air fills with a dank wetness, like a miserably hot and humid Missouri summer day.

Massive power rushes toward me. I realize too late that it's water, and I try to take a quick breath and turn away, right as I'm slammed by a giant wave. Water shoves itself into my nose and throat, and I fight, unsuccessfully, the urge to cough. My lungs instantly ache from the intrusion.

The wave throws me into Raylan, and we both get tossed like seaweed, pinning us against a wall.

The water recedes a bit, enough that our heads are out, and we sputter for air.

The wave rolls away from us, so the water's only at my waist.

"What do we do?" I yell to Raylan, barely audible over the sound of the water, which now rises like a rapidly filling bathtub.

"Maybe it's a test you need to figure out on your own," he shouts back. I wish I could see him better. It would help me think.

"What? No, she just likes torturing me." The water is up to my chest now, so I push off the wall to try to swim and see what our surroundings are, but Raylan's hand holds me back.

"Think about it," he says. "You were too powerful, taking over like that, so she put you in this box. Now you probably need to show her you're willing to obey."

I couldn't have heard him right. I pull my hand out of his so I can tread water more easily, and the motion splashes water in my face. "Obey?" I sputter. "Why would I want to do that?" I keep my head above the water so I can listen, but I keep swimming to look for options. The water is getting hotter, and although I know it's not even real, my body feels more and more tired by the second.

"Just so she'll let you out. How will we know when Frost and Leo come to help us if we're stuck in here?"

I keep swimming in the black water, breath getting harder to come by. He's got a point, but I *really* don't like it. *Obeying* just sounds like complying, just like Dad, Knox, and Tess were always trying to get me to do.

I swim till I hit a wall. I shove off that one with my legs

and quickly find another. At one point, my arm scrapes the ceiling, and I swear this room is getting smaller by the second.

Exasperated, I yell over the water again. "How would I even show her that I'm *compliant*?" The word feels so wrong.

"Just stop fighting?" He sounds like he doesn't like the idea, but I don't like him even going there.

"So what do we do? Just drown? How do we know we won't die for real?"

"I doubt she'd be able to use your influence if you're dead."

I really do not like this situation. "How do we know what will happen to you?" The water is so high, I hit the ceiling with my skull. Just a few more inches of air left.

There is nothing in this hell hole to use. No drain, nothing to stand on, nothing to shut off, open, or break. Why would there be? It's all fake, anyway.

"She needs me," he sputters, sounding weaker, "to hold over you." He is quiet again as I hear some splashing.

"Raylan?" I'm starting to panic. I'm likely about to drown anyway. How does that establish my subservience?

"I'll be okay," he yells. "Do it of your own choice!"

Ooooh. Make her drown me, and I'll probably get a new kind of hell. Drown myself, and she'll let me out. Great options, *Alora*. But I trust Raylan. He's been in way more of these scrapes than me.

Okay. I'll make the choice. Maybe it's better than fighting and having her win all the time. No time to dilly dally, gotta kill myself right away. The water is almost to the ceiling. I dive as deep as I can and pray I'm not about to meet a very stupid end.

CHAPTER 23 - FROST

The Current River's a rocket ship compared to the Comal—the river Eva and I floated down in San Antonio. To think how innocent we were those eight months ago—going on field trips and slathering on sunscreen, our biggest stresses being lectures from Maggie or the parentals.

I still can't stop thinking about the moment I splashed my sister with that holy water. How shocked she looked. How tormented.

I wish I could talk to Leo, but Alora's already taken me to her camp right on the river. If I'm lucky, I can find Maggie and see what she means by the hunters coming.

Between the decapitated lumberjack roasting on the fire and the gremlins sucking the juices from I don't know what kind of bodies, I'd say this isn't exactly the most peaceable place. And I've never seen the Current River so charged before, thrashing and bubbling. I'd say it's connected to the river in The Before, but I don't think that's really possible. Maybe it's from the same evil source.

Hoots and catcalls litter the woods everywhere, and it's clear Alora's teamed up with as many monsters as possible.

She can have any creature turn a human at any moment, so why, again, does she need the fruit?

An unnatural hiss comes from a nearby bush. No, a splash, and as I grip the leather straps of my backpack, I find a bearded guy down in the water. He yowls, "Help me!"

Thrashing and slapping the choppy current, he reminds me of what it felt like when Zombi bit me. How Beau pulled me out of the lake, and I never even thanked him, did I?

A slew of blue-black spirits hover over the bearded guy—not sure if they're other Blurred Ones or the Despairity. Grabbing strands of seaweed, they attempt to tie him down, and the man scrambles over a log, probably never more scared in his life.

One of the Blurred Ones clamps his mouth shut while the others kick him, over and over, in the head. The spirits watch, delighted, as the man flops face-down into the water. It bubbles, churning.

I start to tug off my boots. I need to grab him quickly, but Alora clamps an iron-clad hand around my wrist. "I would not interrupt my sisters when they feed."

I think she's going to throw me again to prove her point, like she did in my house, but she releases my arm as her nasty sisters suck the essence from the bearded man's brain.

They take his despair, his hope, everything he knows. His pride, visions of loved ones. Anything's possible.

Disgusted, I take another small step toward the man. Maybe I can save him before he's left with nothing.

A group of men with masks made of teeth and horns stand in my way.

Alora laughs at their presence. "The human won't interfere. Run along, Dominick."

Dom? The witch doctor who tried to erase my triquetra but settled for Eva's instead?

He's wearing a sleeveless vest, and warpaint dots his aged

face. He chants something low under his breath, which sounds an awful lot like the spell he used in the Metairie Cemetery, and I can feel that same greedy, oily octopus attempting to wrench its presence inside me, but I use my barrier gift and block him from my head.

Even from behind his mask, I can feel his hatred targeted at me.

"Relax, Dominick," Alora says. "We do not need to possess this one to succeed."

He grumbles a few more Cajun curses before stomping away, his posse trailing him silently.

"This way." Alora glides toward a swatch of cattails and purple weeds.

I follow, spotting a figure darting behind a cusp of trees. He's muscular and in a black leather jacket—Raylan? Please tell me that's you shadowing us in the trees!

Thankfully, Alora's still interested in what her "sisters" are doing. She looks at them before casting a conspiratorial look over her shoulder. "They can be a little dramatic for my taste." Sidestepping an old, smashed-up canoe, she adds, "But I learned long ago not to deny their true natures."

She makes it sound like no one's strong enough to withstand a bad choice.

"Everyone chooses the path they take," I say.

Amused, she cocks her head to the side. "Says the girl who won't accept the truth about what Leonardo chose from the beginning."

Fear bubbles up in my throat. Why is she bringing up Leo's choices from The Before? What is their history?

I survey my sister's battered Depeche Mode T-shirt and ripped jeans, her frizzy hair, and how her clothes hang on her so baggily. She probably hasn't eaten a proper meal since that night we ate pizza at the lake house outside New Orleans.

What I would give to see *my* sister, *my* Eva, dig into a plate of nachos with all the toppings.

Turning her back on me, Alora tramples over gravel toward a small, open-faced tent with a bedroll and a tree stump that serves as a work table. A quill and parchment lie haphazardly to the side, and an assortment of herbs hang in the doorway.

Not about to let Alora take the lead, I casually unzip my backpack and reach inside. It's probably a fluke that she let me bring it, but I pull out the Beaver Nuggets, anyway.

Eva? I hold it out for Eves.

Alora's tight smile proves Eva's still buried deep inside.

Time is limited, so I drop my sister's favorite snack and seize the aluminum can I stowed away. *You can't turn down Diet Coke, can you, Eves?*

Alora presses her lips together like she's trying not to laugh at my stupidity.

I know she doesn't want to let Eva come out, so I do the one thing I can think of, feeling foolish the entire time.

Locking my eyes on her, I pull the tab and take a long, slow drink.

As the carbonation sizzles on my tongue, I dramatically wipe my wet mouth with my sleeve.

It's so delicious, Eves.

Alora points at the tree stump, completely ignoring my charade. "Shall we play?"

Wary of falling for her trap, I scan the final two items in my bag: Eva and Raylan's favorite Smashing Pumpkins CD and Connect 4, Eva's and my favorite game. We'd play it for hours, or whenever Mom and Dad deemed that we needed more "downtime."

Alora must have been watching me pack if she's already offering to play. To think I thought I was being devious.

Primly taking a seat at the head of the stump, she extends a hand and waits.

I could tell her I don't want to play—it's Eva's and my game—but why else did I bring it if not to find Eves?

Pulling the smashed game from my school bag, I plop it on the stump of a table.

"I have never played." She folds her hands together with sickening formality.

What does she expect me to say to that? She behaves as if we're besties.

I open the lid, noting an old lady in a neon green shirt and flowers on her headband who paces by. She nods at me like we're secretly working together. Did Raylan send her over here? Not sure what to think.

"You can be red if you like," Alora says.

For all I know, she's poisoned all the red tokens, so I blurt, "I'll be black." I seize all the dark tokens.

Except now, Eva could succumb to whatever Alora's done to the red tokens, so I switch tactics. "Red! I'll be red."

Alora cocks an eyebrow, and I *hate* that she's using my sister to give me that skeptical face.

I snatch up the red tokens as Alora locks the bottom of the game's cage. When I line up all the tokens on the stump, Alora does the same. We're like carbon copies of each other, and I don't know if she's doing that on purpose, or if we're naturally similar.

Catching my eye, Alora smirks. "And how are Leonardo's kisses nowadays?"

I flinch so hard, I nearly knock over the cage.

"It has been a *very* long time," she purrs. My sister's long fingers tap the stump, and if Eva's really in there, she had better get out of the way.

I stare at the dead flies tucked neatly into my sister's hair, wanting more than ever to seize my battery-operated drill.

It's in the smallest pouch of the backpack, but I want Eva to be *free*, not make her stuck with the witch forever.

"Here's a thought." Alora slips a black token into the cage. "You tell me the location of the tree."

I'm not sure what's so hard about finding it—Bloodcreek's only a few miles wide—but maybe God's shielded it somehow. The seraph masked it or something?

I grab a red token and slip it into the cage. "I thought you said you wanted me to hate you. Mission accomplished. You can leave."

"But we have such a long journey ahead of us, Frosty." She drops her next token with a little more ferocity.

Plucking up my next token, I measure my response to be equal parts emotionless and terrifying. "You overestimate your life expectancy."

"What you fail to accept is, the only evidence you have *ever* received that Leonardo could be born was a lie."

I open my mouth to argue, but we both know it's true. Tess made up the lie that Leo could be born only to lure him to her place. All she wanted was to kill him, use him, and make him her trophy.

Regardless, I *know* we will find a way. Leo *will* be born. I refuse to give up that easily.

The amusement shining in Alora's eyes tells me she thinks I'm the biggest fool she's ever seen. She seizes my hand and squeezes it tightly. Digging my sister's fingernails into my skin, she glares so hard, a vein pulses below her hairline.

Sneaking a blue-black tendril of her spirit from Eva's head toward mine, she says, "There is something I wish for you to see."

I try to mentally block her path. I flinch. Left, then right.

But, quick as a lightning bolt, her dirty soul strikes directly into the cerebral cortex of my mind.

Briny sea air ripples against ill-tempered waves. Gusts of wind catch premortal Alora's thick, dark hair, and my stomach plummets. I'd rather be in anybody else's memory.

The armored spikes splayed on her back remind me of Kevlar; thin, yet reinforcing. And I want to close my mind when a masculine, athletic shape approaches her. He wears a long, red cape.

Metal bracers cover Leonardo's arms, and deep gashes line his armor from when he fell into that river, succumbing to the choking vines.

The light of the moon glints off his breastplate, and it's like our very world is rejoicing at my brothers and sisters' demise.

Clutching her bow, Alora delicately reaches out and unties Leonardo's mask. Like she's undressing him. I don't know how, but I can sense the lust and danger of her thoughts. Filthy.

Leonardo's mask falls to his neck, and his flat gaze tells me he's still caught up in the effects of the water. Doesn't know how to react, what to say.

Reaching a tentative hand toward his cheek, Alora says in her husky voice, "You are one of us now."

He doesn't respond. Doesn't bat an eye.

Seductively, she runs a graceful hand over the knots and crevices on his head and face. Securing both hands around the back of his neck, she breathes him in, wanting much more than a taste.

She's a huntress; he, her prey.

She slips one leg between his legs, and I try to wrench her greedy tendrils out of my head, but that only convinces her to hold on more tightly.

Her smoky voice echoes in my head. "You may not be able to be possessed, but you *shall* witness my grandest victory."

Leonardo doesn't retreat. He just stands there like he's made of plywood, and she's a much more experienced spirit. A spirit who swallows her mouth over his and runs her translucent fingers over his jawline.

Tousling his hair, she leaps into his arms and straddles his waist.

She licks the side of his face with her disgusting tongue, and I grip Alora's freaky tendrils and rip them from my mind.

It hurts worse than ripping out thirteen needles; sears with agony, but I can't look anymore. I have to put myself back together. Bar myself against her toxicity.

It seems I've sent her flying back—into the tent's fabric. Go me. One of the stainless steel poles slips from its former position as she laughs. I don't think she expected me to rip her out so easily.

Sheer cruelty smears across her boysenberry lips—lips that aren't supposed to be chapped, but relaxed. And pink. "I have wanted to show you that for a very long time."

I push off from the stump and, in a cloud of dust, tear away from the tent. Alora throws a tent pole directly at me.

My reflexes are freakishly good as I dodge it. Guess my adrenaline's working with me.

Another pole skims just past my hairline.

I grab the daggers in my boot.

Time to get out of here.

Time to find Raylan. And Maggie.

I wake up. Again. Well, hey, good news! I'm alive! And Alora didn't even make me prove myself further by dying an excruciating mental drowning death. I still feel like I want to sputter, but here I am, no longer in control of my faculties. Somehow, these days, that's a good thing.

No more Raylan in my head. I wonder where they're keeping him? And how is he helping them?

But Frost is here! I guess that's technically bad news because that means she's here in danger, but, by golly, I'm just so happy to see her.

Except, she looks so pissed. I haven't seen her this angry since . . . ever? I'm dying to show her I'm still here. I'd hate for her to give up on me and go ahead and annihilate my body in an epic act of revenge.

And is that Diet Coke I see? Beaver Nuggets and Connect 4? Frosty! She loves me! But . . . dang it! Holy crap, has Alora been playing Connect 4 with my sister? That just takes the cake on this whole mystifying situation. I'm sure Frost tried these things to wake me up. If I could just show her a sign. Suddenly bash my head against the table or something. Anything to ease those tightrope tendons in her neck, the pinch of her eyes.

But I just tried to prove my *subservience* to Alora. Subservience to end suffering. Ugh. I can't even bring myself to hope for freedom at this point. But letting Frost know I'm still here would go a long way toward that hope. Maybe Raylan could let her know without compromising my progress—if he's nearby. I'll pray for that.

"Run, little girl," we shout while Frost kicks a discarded tent pole out of the way. "Run, and spend what time you have left with Leonardo. Eva is gone. The rest of you will soon follow." Gosh, I'm annoying like this, but I try to keep my thoughts quiet, saving my strength for any opportunity to influence or whatever. Please, just don't give up on me, Frost.

She steals a look at me, but with no sign of recognition or searching. Like I'm truly just an enemy. And then she's gone.

Don't worry, Eva. I know how powerful you are, even if your own sister doesn't recognize it.

Thank you for letting her go.

There's a small shift in my vision, almost like someone just spliced two video segments together.

You hiding something from me? I probe.

Nothing of importance. The camp has grown much larger than my sisters believed. And you're not even trying yet.

Okay, I'll bite. *What do you mean? Or want?* I think back to her.

Help me gather my forces, and I'll let you go. I'll even let Frost and Raylan live.

And Mags? Do you have her?

No answer.

What do "your forces" want? 'Cause if it's the end of the world, that's not much of a trade.

We just want bodies. As weak as they are, I do appreciate the solid interaction with my surroundings.

Then you shouldn't have chosen the wrong side.

Mmm. Our older brother was convincing.

Why do you need so many people to make it happen? Can't you do it alone?

Insurance. I know if it's just my sisters and me, you hunters will have a chance at stopping us.

I can't help it; I'm a little proud she views me and my people as a threat.

That's right; accept that your spirit is powerful. Help me gather a few more people, and we'll leave you all alone.

All of us? Frost, Raylan, Maggie, Mom? Leo and Beau, too?

I feel a slight tremor in my chest, like she's dancing away from a blow I didn't even intend.

Of course.

She must be lying. But it's not like I have a lot of power to call her on it.

What do I have to do? I ask.

Stop fighting me.

That's it?

You're very powerful when you're just you.

Definitely sounds like a catch. Like it's the best in a list of all very terrible choices. But it's the most hope I've had since the hag took up residence inside me.

Fine.

My heart soars, and I'm going to believe that's not a sign I'm sealing anyone's doom.

Very good. Before we can get to work, you have an opportunity to show me some good faith. Otherwise, your boyfriend becomes dinner.

Christian's lithe form jogs into view, followed by his mom. When did she show up? They seem like themselves, as little as I know about them, so they're probably not possessed right now. Shorty and Middle Child must come and go. So why the heck are they here?

Your first followers, Alora answers.

What? They're here because of me? Unbelieving, I scan the unlikely pair for this situation. Hints of dark red smear Christian's tawny hand, and his and his mom's shirts are both soiled with bits of dirt and some kind of grime. I'm equal parts disgusted by them and mortified by my part in this. If Alora's right.

"Yes, dear," Alora replies. Wow, she's really upping her interpersonal skills these days.

"There are a couple of hunters taking out a bunch of your —our—people," Christian says, wiping his hands on his dark pants. Our fist tightening is our only response. Guess we're not too worried? "They caused a distraction. The girl got away."

We crack our knuckles. *"The girl?"* *Well, looky there,* I poke at Alora. *You tried to slide one past me, didn't you? Trying to pick on my sister ain't a good idea.*

Christian's mother puts her finger up to interject and fiddles with a giant costume ruby ring on her finger. We look at her, giving her permission to speak.

"Ma'am," she says with conviction, "one of them is a Blurred One."

"Show me," we say. *We'll finish this discussion later,* Alora tells me.

We storm out of the tent, and Christian jogs ahead of us, presumably showing us the way to, fingers crossed, Leo and maybe Mags? Raylan? The smell of smoke mixes with decaying soil and sage, and the slight bite in the air screams bonfire weather. But this is no time to think of pleasant things, right?

We stomp past a werewolf, moaning on the ground with a gaping hole in his side. Any smug thoughts I may have had stop at the sight of a cerberus munching on a creature with fangs the size of steak knives.

Shadows streak in all directions, some fleeing, some looking ready to fight. A set of antlers, the length of my arm and attached to a feathered mask, slithers forward. The rural Mardi gras people. This mask is worn by a petite woman, and the mixture of bone, feather, and skin demand to be examined. As she walks, her head turns toward me, more and more with every step, until her head is completely turned around while her body lumbers on. Her eyes are discs of black, the size of my fist.

But we keep walking, now obviously heading toward the screams of agony. Somebody's cleaning up. A lizard-type creature sails through the air toward us. Christian ducks, and it flies over his head. We throw up my hand and freeze the lizard guy mid-air. While I clench my fingers together, it starts to fold in on itself like it's in a trash compactor. Scales fall to the ground as it wails in agony, and when it finally stops, we drop it to the ground by opening my hand.

The perpetrator of all this violence stands some twenty feet away, and it's hard to make out his figure in the darkness, but the moonlight shines on his white shirt and ever-present suspenders.

Leo! I scream inwardly with glee, and I could swear Alora has a feeling of agreement about her.

"That's enough, Leonardo," we call, not conveying any of the happiness I believe we feel. "You allowed your pet to escape."

He stalks toward us, chest heaving, hair a mess. His eyes burn with an anger I've never seen in him before. He looks a bit like a mad man, but gosh dang it, I'll take it.

"I've been waiting for you to come," we say demurely.

"You know I'm not here for you." There's a foreign harshness to his voice. He storms down to the river's edge like he knows all too well we'll follow. Will we? Our heart twists, and I do believe Alora has a thing for Leo. Sure enough, we follow suit.

Christian lingers nearby, taking the scene in, always assessing.

When we're within earshot over the rushing water, Leo finally speaks again.

"Stop this, Alora." He turns completely toward us, the poster boy for openness and honesty, but his face carries every worrisome emotion in existence.

"Come back to me, Leonardo." We stand strong and proud, but I feel the insecurity dripping from her, because I know it all too well. She forces us to stare him down, searching his eyes. Feels a bit intimate for looking at my sister's boyfriend. "You used to be the best of us, *amare*. Leo, Who Gleans."

Leo breaks eye contact. "I no longer live like that."

"You deny your true nature." She shows me an image of her in The Before—the black spikes on her back and her toned arms around Leo's neck. His face is mangled, and he looks like a shadow of himself, but it's him. It's remarkable—his vessel looks *just* like him. "We were *great* together."

"We were dangerous."

We sidle up a little closer, delicately tracing his suspender strap with our finger. "I seem to remember a time when you accepted your path." We grab the strap and urge him closer.

He shoves off my hand. It feels terrible to have his anger directed toward me; it's getting harder to tell where she ends and I begin. I remind myself it's her who's the problem, and I definitely wouldn't want him getting too cozy with us.

"You don't know what you're doing," we growl.

"I never should have allowed you to influence my choice!" He takes a step farther away, agile on the slick river rock. The air feels colder.

Our expression hardens. "Remorse is an excellent companion. If you were a mortal, I'd drink up your soul."

Leo raises to his full height with the authority of a warlord. "I got Raylan out. Now free Eva."

Alora simmers with anger, but . . . yay!

Leo continues. "Free Eva by tomorrow, or I'll end you myself. Free Maggie, too, if you have her."

"Why do you care about that washed-out hunter?" we seethe. "About any of them? You have centuries of knowledge on them. You didn't blindly accept whatever fate Father wanted to hand out to you. Why do you want a mortal life?" Stepping closer, but not too close to seem threatening, we dig our fingernails into our palms.

"Alora," he says with a pinch of compassion, his brows arched. "This life is *right*. We were wrong."

"We can *make* us right. Even Eva is learning to accept her nature—that she's meant to control, not follow asinine rules." I feel us digging in our heels, both metaphorically and literally. "She knows she's meant to be here. Leave her be and go live your tiny existence with your girl. You'll come back when she's gone."

That's a pretty pessimistic outlook.

"Is that what you're telling Eva?" He suddenly seems to look deeper into my eyes, probing. "Eva, don't listen to whatever she's telling you. You are good. You were—"

"Eva has recently earned a measure of freedom," we interrupt, palm to his face and all. Goodness gracious. "Leave before I have to put her back in her place."

Leo's jaw clenches. "We will end this. You will not get the tree, and if you don't release Eva soon, you will not get to exist."

I scream at the top of a cliff.

My own cliff outside Bloodcreek, away from the river, and away from Leo and Alora's kissing.

Eva's no longer Eva, and Leo's . . . I can't believe . . . but he said the only girl for him has only ever been me.

How is it that the two people I love most in the world are both right here, and yet so very far away?

I feel so stupid for ever thinking I could get them back. I feel so stupid for thinking I could find Raylan. Or Maggie.

Alora's too powerful. Knows too much. Tess, Knox, and Lindy were infants compared to her. Dom was just a pre-show to the real thing.

I pull out my phone to text Maggie, but, *of course*, I don't have a signal up here. How have I gone this long without talking to her? I miss her. I need her hugs and her donuts and kolaches.

How is it that I could've worked so hard, for so long, and not have a single thing to show for it?

Nothing.

I killed my dad. I didn't protect my sister, and now she's gone. Poof! Not responding. The entire human existence probably hinges on Alora not finding that tree. And why did Eva and I want to look into the Blurred Ones in the beginning?

"I thought I'd find ya up here." Rocks scatter as Beau traipses up the slope, holding the seraph's flaming sword, of all things.

"Whew!" Dramatically, he wipes his brow with the back of his arm. "Now, *that* was a hike!"

I can't even . . .

"Uri's been givin' us pointers on how to secure the perimeter." He shakes the flaming sword like it's a dollar store toy. "We got *all sorts* o' tricks up our sleeve."

Beau must sense the lack of enthusiasm in my eyes, because he holds out the sword with the biggest smile on his face. "Uri finally managed to agree we're on the same side."

"Oh?"

"An' he let me borrow *this* 'cause it shields the location of the tree."

That's how Alora can't find it.

I'm sure he's waiting for a "congratulations" or a standing ovation, but I'm just so tired, and why would the seraph let Beau take it in the first place?

Seems like there would be a catch.

Seems like I'm missing a lot of things.

"She-devil don't know where it is." Beau refers to Alora under his breath, and I really do like that name.

But he shouldn't be waving the flaming sword around here, in broad, open daylight. One of Alora's cronies could see it.

"You should lock that up." I march past him as his eyebrows shoot up a mile high.

"No way." He pulls it toward his chest protectively. "Uri said, by luggin' this around, I can decipher my *true* callin'."

"So, he said you could bring it out here?"

"Well, no." Beau blanches before narrowing his eyes at me. "Say, what's got you all caddywhompus?"

I bite back a snarl, which is so uncharacteristic of me to have in the first place, but I'm just so tired of Alora winning at everything. I pick my way through the rocks to begin my descent. Maybe I'll feel more cheerful if I get my blood pumping. It's not like it's Beau's fault that Alora's made a mess of my life. Actually, the fact that he hasn't put a move on me since we got back from New Orleans makes me think his feelings might have changed.

Pausing by a partially smashed collection of cacti, I murmur, "I'm sorry. It's been a rough day."

"You saw 'er, huh."

The tenderness in his voice pricks tears in my eyes. I nod, but it's just all too much, and I can't bring myself to meet his gaze.

I can practically hear the wheels turning in his head as Beau fumbles with the right thing to say. His fingers graze his hunting knife, and he checks his flannel jacket to make sure all the buttons are done up right.

I pass even more boulders and cacti, wishing we were past winter and narrowly avoiding a slippery patch of ice.

"Say, I got a stellar idea," Beau says.

Without meaning to, I catch his eye.

"How 'bout I fix us up some razzleberry pie?"

The offer is so unexpected, so ordinary. The last time Beau and I ate something like that, we were in my kitchen. Before Tess came into our lives. And I actually let him kiss me.

How mortifying is it that I let that happen?

Not as mortifying as Leo kissing a Despairity.

I don't know how long it's been since I ate a decent meal, and Beau's a good friend to make the offer. It's not like things are going to get any worse anyway, so I might as well take a break. "Okay."

"Where were we?" Alora says aloud to me, pushing my hair back behind an ear. We watched Leo disappear, and Alora asked, pretty politely, considering, if I wouldn't mind "stepping into another room for a moment." She shoved me back into my mental box, but can't say I blame her. Leo's words were brutal, and I in no way like the girl.

Cloistered once again, I try to think through everything Leo just said, but I don't feel like I've learned anything new. Were there any hints? Maybe I missed something that could be useful.

Despite what Leo said, Alora hasn't actually tried to make me feel evil, just accept that I have influence. Raylan's the one who broke the news to me that I almost chose Team Blurred One. Maybe Dad, Knox, Tess, and I have had it right all along.

Eventually, Alora swung the door open on my box and allowed me back into the world. Real smooth system we've got going on these days.

"Eva," she postures, "we are going to win. There's no question. But I would like to do it in a way that allows you your consciousness. Do we still have a deal?" She must feel me calculating, because she adds, "Need I remind you that I could send you to your box, awake, for the next century, then have all of your friends possessed and do the same to them?"

Well, the hag has a point. But Christian did say there were "a couple" hunters here. If Raylan's free, maybe Leo got Mags, too. If they're free, I could just do my best to kill Alora and myself. If they're not? I think about the suffocating feeling of my discombobulated self—then the excruciating drowning—and I know I can't possibly let my loved ones get stuck in eternal torture. I'll play along for the time being.

Okay, I finally say. *You can't lay a finger on Raylan, Frost, Mags, Leo, or my mom. Or Beau,* I quickly add. Maybe I can talk Alora and crew into only possessing bad people? I fear I'm being terribly optimistic.

A reanimated corpse lumbers by, and we turn away from the river, back to the woods. I reckon we're not more than ten miles from Bloodcreek, although I don't recognize this area.

Just don't go destroying the entire human race, 'kay?

"Very well, Eva," she says without hesitation. Um-kay? And wow, she's sort of treating me like a person. "You're all yours." She smiles slightly and tangibly takes a backseat in my consciousness.

No. Freaking. Way. I'm completely in control?

I stretch my arms as high into the cool air as I can reach, brushing a damp leaf dangling from a nearby oak. Holy smokes, it feels *amazing* to be free to move. I rub my face, tie a knot in my hair for good measure, then push my shoulders back in a renewed dedication to have good posture. I shake my entire body out of sheer joy, promising to myself to never say mean things about my body again.

Zillah strolls by with a melancholy wave, interrupting my moment of revelry.

I guess it's time to see what's next. No time like the present.

"Where to, toots?" I murmur, not sure I'm supposed to let the other monsters in on our little deal, but also not able to resist the temptation to use my own voice on my own accord. An inward, light nudge of my chin tells me the direction to head in.

I can sense some smugness in her, undoubtedly wanting to tell me all the tragic ways the beasts nearby could vivisect my liver if I "try something funny," but my captor stays silent. Girl's got some restraint.

I practically sashay through camp and shove my hands in my pockets to keep from doing gun fingers, I feel so good. I know things are still probably about to go apocalypse wrong, but hey, tiny victories! Hopefully, my first task isn't to "influence" a group of serial killer vampires.

Ahead, I can just make out the outline of a tree the size of my house, limbs stretching as wide as a jumbo jet. Looks pretty ominous.

Sage with hints of iron waft through the area, and someone's throat is gurgling like they're taking their last breath. My hands twitch for the gun I know isn't there and feel my lack of actual power renewed.

Determined to soldier on, I brush back what must be the most disgusting mane of hair the world has ever seen and *holy crap, something just scuttled up my hand*. I squeal like a girl at the front row of her favorite boy band concert. If this keeps up, Alora and I are gonna have to have a chitty-chat about hygiene.

Something small moves on the massive tree trunk. Squinting, I make out the rope wrapped around the trunk. Someone's tied there, struggling against the ties.

"Raylan?" I gasp, worried I was wrong to believe he actually got free. Or is it Mags? Please be some escaped convict Alora wants to be a human guinea pig. I break into a run toward the tree but snag my foot on a root. I impress myself by not face-planting, but instead nimbly catching myself with my other foot and restoring my balance in half a breath.

Muffled sounds, like a voice around a gag, come from the far side of the tree, and my heart thumps in fear and anticipation. I round the tree and stare for a full five seconds.

Mags' arms, both muscular but also soft and warm, are snared in what must be fifty feet of rope. A classic red bandana is tied around her head and shoved into her mouth to gag her, and her hair is plastered to her forehead, slick with sweat.

"Mags," I gasp, then I kneel down and throw my arms around her.

She tenses beneath my touch, and I reel back. "Crap, did I hurt you?" I notice the purple and yellow bruises dotting her arms and a nasty gash on her right temple.

I scramble to remove the gag, Alora be darned, but the knot is so tight, I can't get a good grip. Who knows how long she's been struggling against it.

"Sorry," I murmur, "just a second." I try to meet her deep brown eyes to assure her I am here and will do my best to take care of her. Show her we're in this together now, but when she looks back at me, the lines around her eyes don't relax. Her eyes don't crinkle with happiness or tear with relief. Instead, there's a familiar glint there I haven't seen since . . . Dad.

"Mags, it's okay," I try to reassure her, "it's me." Squatting back onto a root, I suddenly feel winded. When is the last time we ate? Maybe the weird vibe I'm getting from Mags is just hunger.

Mags spits out what looks like a bit of bandana she must have bit off and takes a steadying breath.

"You're not fooling me, Alora," her alto voice drawls.

Alora twirls inside of me, and I feel an enormous pressure on my throat, but coming from the inside. My body tenses, my head is thrown back, and my mouth opens for a scream. But instead of a scream coming out, black smoke spews into the sky. It erupts like a volcano for a full five seconds, and as quickly as it started, it's over.

By golly, Alora is standing next to me in all her Despairity glory. Only she looks way better than she used to. Guess I really did charge her immortal batteries.

I'm . . . free?

"Now there can be no doubt," Alora purrs, gesturing to the space between us. "Margaret, here's your Eva."

CHAPTER 27 - FROST

I set my fork down on the counter, absorbing the transformation of Beau's diner from *Lindy's*. He calls it *Sasquatch n' Koi*. I think it's his way of proving he likes to try new things.

Of course, the Cadillac couch is still here, but the TV broke when Beau got a little too excited about his latest idea of cowboy sushi. The checkered tablecloths look freshly pressed, the lights are newly dusted, and a big, furry Sasquatch statue now stands in the center of the entire diner.

Beau flips over the "Mosey on in" sign and chases out the last of the customers with a promise of a free breakfast in the morning.

"You didn't have to do that," I say as he shoots me his trademark wink.

"I been wantin' to do that since I took over the place!"

When he wanders to the back of the kitchen, I follow, still a little lost as to what to say. He lifts himself onto the counter, and I join him. Just because I don't know what else to do. Still feels like old times. Alora may be out there, but

Beau's still got the flaming sword. It's just laying on the other counter.

Who knew that was what hid the location of the tree, and that it apparently works when it's in other places.

"Froster, I gotta tell ya somethin'." Beau hands me a meaty plate of razzleberry pie. "But I don't want you to take it the wrong way."

"Okay . . ."

He scratches the back of his head with a fork. "I, uh, no longer like you 'that way.' I mean, I *do*." He cringes. "But I don't. It's more of a puppy dog kinda thing."

All I can do is set my fork on the counter. My throat suddenly feels very dry.

"You 'n' Leo got somethin' real special, an', well, I know whatever's between us pales, comparatively speakin'."

I try to think of something poignant or clever to say, but he's telling me this *now*? Why?

"I mean, I'm still attracted to you, because who wouldn't be, but I gotta move onto bigger an' more spooktacular things."

I'm suddenly jumping down from the counter. Why is Beau bringing this up now? I begin to pace, looking for a broom or mop to keep my hands busy.

"You should give it another go with Leo, though." He smiles sympathetically. "You know the last few days that boy's been scarin' the devil out of people in town, so they boot scoot 'n' boogie?" Beau laughs like he made up the refrain. "Doesn't want 'em gettin' hurt by A-lora's army."

Wait, what?

I didn't know that. I don't remember the last time Leo even confided in me. Still, Beau seems to be waiting for me to respond, so I settle with something bland and straightforward. "I'm glad he's found a task to focus on."

"You mean, other than *you*." He playfully taps his boot against my thigh.

I press my palms into the metal counter, which is freezing. "I'm not so sure he feels that way anymore . . . about me."

"HA!" Beau holds his side. "You could be dumb if ya weren't so funny."

My ears burn in embarrassment, but that doesn't change the fact that I know I'm right. "He hid his relationship with *her* from me. He hasn't really touched me in ages, and he won't tell me what he's thinking."

Beau's eyes bunch together like I'm a puzzle he's *this* close to solving. "You know he checks on you every night when you're asleep, right?"

Not sure if that's sweet or creepy . . .

"Last time your mama had a panic attack, did ya know it was him who helped ease her pain?"

I didn't even know Mom was having panic attacks. How long has this been going on?

"And *then,* when A-lora decided to pull her whole 'boogeyman' scenario and bring you to the heart of her posse, did ya know that it was *Leonardo* who made sure you could escape?"

I remember the smoke and the weird sounds in the woods when I ran out, but I didn't know he was trailing me. I thought Alora was just saving me for later for some reason. Letting me stew with the memory she showed me.

"She-devil wouldn' have let you outta her web so easily."

I nod, stomach clenching. "But Leo . . . he won't talk to me . . . "

Beau tsks. "*That's* 'cause he's feelin' guilty!"

For choosing the wrong path. For being with Alora. For all the people he hurt before he reconnected with me.

"How do I get him to forgive himself?" I sag against the counter, feeling the impossibility of the question. I thought he had gotten over his past when he left to be born, but Tess trapped him in that basement. Ever since then, he's never really talked about being born. It's like he's given up on the idea.

Beau boosts a shoulder. "Maybe ya need to remind him he's worthy of savin'."

His words twist like a dagger in my heart. Beau is right. The mysterious silences. The pained look in Leo's eyes every time he looks at me. But how do I help him see that?

Beau slips his hand to my side and tickles my waist. "I'm sure you'll think of somethin'."

CHAPTER 28 - EVA

Oooh my gosh, this has to be too good to be true! Well, of course, it is. But, still!

I look at Alora, shock all over my face, then at Mags. Why doesn't she look happier?

"What's going on, Alora?" I ask cautiously, fully aware she can take me back over whenever she'd like.

"Get Margaret to tell me the location of the tree," she commands, placing a regal hand on her hip. Her ghostly face is still smeared, but instead of just smudges, I can differentiate real features. She's got the same intensity in her cheeks as when Frost plays Rachmaninoff. "Then, not only will I honor our agreement to let her live, but after we are finished, I will let you go."

Oh, crud. Telling an evil immortal where to find the Tree of Knowledge of Good and Evil definitely can't be a good thing, buuuut . . .

I shoot a grim look at Mags. She appears to be calculating.

"Heck no," I respond for Team Good People. "I don't know where it is, but we ain't telling you, 'cause no way we're gonna get on God's bad side like that." I don't know what the tree does, but I know enough about the Bible to know it's got some serious consequences attached to it.

Alora looks unconcerned with my answer, shooting her intense laser gaze at Mags.

"What do you want with the tree?" Mags asks. I'm a little miffed she's even asking that much. Maybe she has a plan up her sleeve.

"We want bodies," Alora answers.

"You can have all the bodies you want already," Mags scoffs. "The real answer. Now."

Alora is quiet, considering, but I've had enough with being a silent bystander to wait for her to do all the talking.

"Mags is not giving up the location," I say, pulling myself to my feet to feel a little more powerful. "You'll have my influence, so you'll let her go, like you promised. If you're that determined, you can find the tree on your own. Leave her out of this."

"What influence?" Mags asks.

I stretch my neck, uncomfortable with the subject. But I'd rather elaborate than have Alora do it, so I muster up some words on the subject.

"Apparently," I start to tie a knot in my hair, but remember the bugs and think better of it, "I'm good at persuading people to do things." Mags' face is a mask, so I continue. "*Apparently*, even in the premortal world, I was pretty good at it." I'm watching Mags carefully, but she looks at Alora, who nods in confirmation.

"So," Mags says, shifting against the ropes, "you're going to have her persuade people to what, join the dark side?"

"Just like she did before," Alora says with a wry grin. My cheeks burn with shame.

"Until I changed my mind," I say to the ground. "I changed my mind and chose to come to Earth." I steal a glance at Mags, hoping this isn't changing the way she feels about me. She finally looks at me, and that unsettling glint in her eyes is back. I feel about six inches tall.

"So he was right," she says, voice resigned. "Your dad. He warned me you had something dark in you."

"What?" I cry, my skin burning like it's on fire. Alora looks distantly pleased.

"He said there might come a time where I would need to protect Frost and your mom from you. That you might not be strong enough to resist it."

I want to curl up into a ball so small, I cease to exist. My own dad? I knew we weren't on the best terms, but this . . .

"I've always tried to do the right thing," I say, but I sound so weak, like a tiny little girl.

Alora puts a wispy hand on my arm. "There comes a time when one must give in to their true nature."

A pit opens in my gut. Deeper than the abandoned mine shaft. I want to sob in disagreement, but even Raylan said it —I was no stellar spirit. And Frost didn't look very hopeful when she was here tonight.

Tears race down my cheeks and fall onto my chest in hot splashes.

"I ain't giving up the tree," Mags says resolutely. "But you'll let me go anyway."

Alora runs her index finger down my arm and says, "Why is that?"

"Because you can keep her." She nods at me.

"Mags!" I yell, not believing what I just heard.

"And," she adds, not looking at me, "I'll see to gettin' Leo to scoot on over your way."

"What? No, I'm not bad!" I wipe my face free of tears and try not to sound hysterical. "Maybe I was wishy-washy back then, but I've been trying so hard. And Leo, too! You know this!"

"As much as I hate to have anything in common with this

creature here," Mags says, indicating Alora as she leans her head back against the tree, "I reckon she is right when it comes to true nature. I gotta protect the rest of us from bad influences. I'm sorry, Eva. I loved you, and I really hoped it would never happen."

The pit in my gut churns and widens, the rest of me desperately grasping for any reason to not believe I'm inherently evil. In this moment, I can't come up with anything. "Dad said I'd hurt Mom and Frost?"

Mags shifts again against the tree and hums in agreement. "He thought Leo never would've come and corrupted Frost if you weren't so much like your Aunt Eva. And look at us now. A Blurred One shouldn't have been able to possess you, even a Despairity, with all we'd taught you."

"But, the witch doctor . . ."

"Eva," she says, eyes angry. "Notice none of the rest of us got possessed."

I need . . . I need a second to think. It's too much. Have I really been fighting the inevitable all this time? Maybe it *is* my fault Knox latched onto me. Like Aunt Eva and I somehow signaled him. Maybe Tess' intuition about me was right all along. But Raylan still thought I had a chance, and Frost has always seen the best in me. And Leo? Are we both really destined to be bad, like some terrible Rosemary's Baby-type horror movie?

The evidence is overwhelming.

I crumple to the ground and hug Mags' feet. Maybe she's right. They'd all really be better off without me.

"Very well," Alora says above me, interrupting my thoughts. "I won't need you, Margaret. This is all I need."

She swirls around me, and as I take my next breath, she dives back into my body.

I don't fight it.

Sitting up, we look at Maggie. The woman I loved like a

second mom. Who taught me how to shoot a gun, start a fire, and mend a shirt. Who bought me my first art set, and now has finally gotten me to accept the truth about myself.

With Alora back in my body, I curl my consciousness into that little ball I longed for. In my mental box, door wide open, I watch with detachment as we wrap my hands around Mags' throat. I should stop this, but I really can't move.

We maintain eye contact with Mags while we squeeze. And squeeze. Harder and harder. I hardly know what we're doing.

Mags' eyes bulge, her face turns red, then a deep purple.

She throws herself hard against the ropes, so we dig my knee into her thigh.

I stay in my little ball, and we keep squeezing.

Tighter. Until I feel a lump of bone *crush*.

CHAPTER 29 - FROST

I need to find Leo. Make him explain. I'll explain. Somebody needs to explain!

We need to hash out exactly what happened between him and Alora in The Before. Then we move past it. We can do that, right?

Surprisingly, Beau's been silently reading the entire drive. He must have grabbed the paperback from my house—*The Girl Who Could Fly*. Eva bought it for me three years ago for my birthday.

Beau seems utterly intrigued.

What would it be like to be shut in a box for years and years, only to have your power siphoned from you by your own mother, to emerge, years later, with a hunger for knowledge? And, of all places, in Bloodcreek?

I've always thought of Beau as being kind of behind. But, for all I know, his brain is simply catching up; he'll be quizzing me on *Crime and Punishment* in a few weeks.

When we get to the park, the parking lot's a lot fuller than last time. A banged-up jeep missing half a door is parked sideways, and at least half a dozen motorcycles are parked near a horse trailer with claw marks and a minivan with a broken tail light.

Looks like the hunters arrived. That's what Maggie meant when she texted me.

A few paces from the gazebo, a burly hunter with a beard that looks fresh out of *Duck Dynasty* slides a pack of C-4 into a hole rimmed by a devil's trap. Seems to be a lot of those, spray painted on the grass. I'm glad I'm not the only one who knows how to handle explosives. I give the guy a nod as Beau and I pass by.

Another long-haired biker with several triquetra tattoos up and down his neck slips on a sash of ammunition as my phone dings.

Missed voicemail.

From a day ago.

My stomach lurches as I see it's from Maggie.

Ugh, how did I miss her call for so long? I guess reception has always been terrible in Bloodcreek.

As I listen to the choppy message, though, all I can make out is this faraway female voice, and the cruel raspiness tells me it might be Alora inside Eva speaking, but I can't actually make out any of the words, and *why* does it have to be so hard to get ahold of Maggie?

The hunters are here, though, so Maggie, Beau, or Leo must have passed on the location of the tree. I just wish Maggie were here. What I would give for that small hint of normalcy.

What I would give to hear Raylan rip that hunter with the neck tattoos a new one for starting a fire, which Alora will undoubtedly see.

"Put it out," I tell him as his weasel-y eyes meet mine. "The Blurred Ones don't know where we are yet. I say we keep it that way."

He kicks a pile of dirt into the fire as guilt flashes over his eyes. "Sorry."

Not that I can blame him. It's freezing. And then, seeing how red the tattoos are on his neck, and knowing he must be really green, I reach into my backpack and toss him a heat pouch. All he has to do is rip it open; air activates it.

"Sorry I don't have anything better," I say as Beau looks up from his novel.

"I got my campin' stove in the truck!" He snaps his book closed. "Whipped up a batch of 'coon stew just yesterday!"

The newbie hunter's eyes dart to mine, and I don't have time to debate the merits of Beau's cooking, so I pat the hunter on the shoulder. "It will change your life."

As Beau tears off for his truck, I survey the other hunters nearby. A woman about five years older than me cleans her rifle, all the while keeping her eyes trained on the rubble surrounding the hole in the gazebo, and a skinny guy with hair as tall as Mount Everest eyes the seraph with his massive, alabaster wings.

"Uri" looks to be teaching a group of hunters how to attack future enemies from higher vantage points in the field—random statues from town, a few cars that have seen better days, and a cannon from the Civil War era. A nimble-looking hunter sneak attacks a pretend Blurred One housing a vessel by jumping from a tree. I like how everyone's using the full scale of what we're offered in our setting—above *and* below ground.

Funny how it reminds me of the masked Blurred Ones leaping from the waterfall in The Before. Maybe that's where Uriel got the idea.

Leo's filling up a kiddie pool with a garden hose by the time I find him behind a copse of trees. It's a little laughable, since I never thought I'd see him bothering with a child's toy.

But, then again, when I was a kid, he did play tea set with

me. Helped me paint those Peeches, Q-cumbers, Zookeene, and Sqwash signs.

Leo shoots me a warm yet sorrowful look that shreds my insides. "Frost." He says my name with so much care that it reminds me of when he first bestowed that name on me. He touched that thin layer of ice and invited me to do the same. And it's still freezing, just like that day, so I blow on my hands, trying to find the strength to say what I have to say.

He stares at my hands, like he wants, more than ever, to say something, but he just stands there, water filling up the tub. How long is he going to keep me in the dark from what he's thinking? Has he always cared about Alora? Was I always his second choice?

Beau claps Leo on the shoulder as he moseys on by. "Thanks for fillin' that up, Le-o-nardo!" The water from the hose slows before coming to a stop.

Setting the hose on the grass, Leo glances up at me, a deep flush creeping across his cheeks. "I thought someone could bless it as holy water to have on standby . . ."

I take a step closer, unable to think about holy water or the sexy way he recites those Latin refrains. All I can think about is when Eva got him to eat a beignet, just before Dom called and lured them to the Metairie Cemetery. What if we had never gone? What if we never met Tess or Lindy? Alora wouldn't have been able to possess Eva.

But she would have possessed Eva another way. She predates everything I have with Leo. She predates *me*.

"There's something I need to tell you," Leo says, looking across the field at something.

"Well, that sounds ominous," I joke, praying there's not really anything to be nervous about.

"It's about Raylan and Maggie . . ." He scrubs his hand over his face. "I went to Alora's camp and freed Raylan, but Maggie . . ."

I spin to see what Leo keeps looking at, hoping it's Raylan, but it's just Uriel and all the other hunters practicing. "So where's Raylan? And what happened with Maggie?"

Leo gently takes my hand. "Raylan's actually here somewhere. He's fine."

My heart flips and jigs with relief. Little turd needs to show up so I can give him the biggest hug of his life.

"But Alora . . . she held onto Maggie."

Worry tugs at my heart, and I feel like there's more, but Leo's not talking. Tugging his hand, I pull him toward the woods. Maybe he'll communicate better if there's no one else who can hear us. And maybe Raylan will come around, and Leo will tell me the other pieces he's not saying. He has to know, *I am here*. He can talk to me. Even though he and Alora have a huge past, we are stronger than them. Especially now that Raylan is back with our team.

When we make it behind a throng of cedar trees, their heady scent filling me with hope and bravery, I release Leo's hand.

Please, God, help me know what to say.

"So, what happened to Maggie?"

Leo looks away. "Raylan said he tried to free her, but she was still tied to a tree."

If I cursed, now would be the time. "We'll go in again."

Leo blocks my arm. "I already told Alora, she had better turn Maggie free."

There's more to their conversation, but I can tell he's not going to expound from the pain riddling his eyes. "Alora showed you what we were in The Before," he says without blinking. He scans the bruises on my arms. "I . . . am so sorry."

I don't care what she did; I don't care if they have a past or if she thinks she can keep Maggie temporarily. We'll get her back. And we'll *get* Eva. Leo needs to keep holding onto hope with me.

Seizing his arm, I say, "You're not together anymore, Leo. *You chose me.*"

He doesn't push away my hand, but he doesn't accept it, either. His voice is toneless. "You deserve someone who will make you happy."

Why is he saying this? I squeeze his arm tighter. "*You* make me happy."

"You deserve someone who makes you laugh."

I don't know why, but I say, "Beau doesn't even like me!"

Leo's face grows so hard it's like flint, and . . . it's terrifying. "I am certain Beauregard will come around again with a little more time."

I cannot *believe* he's taking that turn. It's like I don't know him anymore. His eyes are vacant, and his Adam's apple is bobbing. Taking my other hand in his, he says in measured tones, "You are learning that a girl like you doesn't belong with a demon like me."

"You aren't a demon!" My voice rebounds from the sky.

"I am on the devil's side."

It's like he's forgotten everything we've gone through. Everything with Knox and Tess. And Dom. And Eva and Raylan. And the Despairity.

He's the one who decided to show up and uproot my life.

"You're the one who came to *me* in San Antonio," I say with bite.

"I shouldn't have." He nearly doesn't have a hitch in his voice.

My chest constricts. My throat has gone so sore, and my heart's racing so fast, I'm feeling dizzy.

Unable to believe Leo's being like this, I reach for the trump card I never thought I would play. Thinking of the time we climbed that tree at Maggie's place, and he showed me the stars, I say, "You are the one who said you loved me."

Leo abruptly turns away at that, and I imagine he doesn't want me to see the emotion in his face. But I can't do this without him; I can't. Reaching out to cup the side of his face, I say, "I need you." I hate that my voice sounds so wobbly.

Leo takes a shaky step away from me. "Forget about me. I'll stay through the end of the battle, but . . . once it's over, I'm leaving."

He didn't really say that.

He'll change his mind.

He'll backpedal. Feed me some cheesy line about how Beau dared him to freak me out before—I don't know—proposing to me.

Leo staggers farther and farther into the woods, the sunlight glinting off the metal clasp on his suspenders, warning me to stay away.

But I can't listen.

I can't.

"Leo!" It all feels so much better if I pretend this is a Hallmark movie, but he just walks faster and faster, and when I run to catch up, his body jerks like he's just been electrocuted, and he slumps to the ground.

Black smoke barrels from his lips.

Leo's essence shoots to the sky.

CHAPTER 30 - EVA

Eva doesn't know if she's home right now.

CHAPTER 31 - FROST

I don't even remember driving. One minute, I was in the park, the next, I'm standing outside the storage room at my place.

I should have tried to find Raylan, invite him or Beau to come along, but I had to get out of there.

Leo, he . . .

I should check on Mom. See if there's any way I can get ahold of Maggie. Ah, Raylan, Leo, and I were all *there!* We should have been able to free her. But we didn't and couldn't, and my movements have become so mechanical ever since Leo smoked out on me.

Drive to house.

Get more supplies.

As Beau was ladling up more soup, I couldn't even tell him where I was going.

Something . . . hiccups . . . or clicks down by the creek.

Possum?

Squirrel?

I don't want to go down there if there are snakes.

Besides, it's probably just the wind, so I unlock the

storage room where Leo and I made out on wheat buckets and were interrupted by Maggie.

The bricks of C-4 in my hands are light.

Extra throwing knives?

But it's more barrels of rock salt I'm sure we'll need.

I should really spend more time lifting weights . . .

Gurgle, gurgle, rattle.

There's definitely something down by the creek, but no one should be home besides Mom. And Mom doesn't go to that side of the yard since Dad died.

I'm just locking up the storage room when something stirs a pile of leaves. It could just be an animal, but I secure the first dagger from my boot, just in case.

Treading over the winterized grass, I squint past the woodpile and Dad's favorite redbud tree to see something floating in the water.

It's big.

Bloated.

Could be wrong, but I'm pretty sure it's human-shaped.

At first, I think it might be Maggie, but that's crazy.

Except she left me that voicemail days ago . . .

I tear across the yard, wiry tree limbs smacking my face. When I scamper a few more paces, my foot finds a hole in the grass, and my ankle twists painfully. Something is wrong. I can feel it in my gut, so I keep on running.

Whoever's facedown in the water is in a paisley shirt, but it can't be Maggie.

That fanny pack twisted around to her side isn't really a fanny pack.

Maggie!

My hand flies to my mouth. I wade knee-deep into the water, biting back a cry. The water's frigid; it cuts into my thighs, and that brown hair, those cropped curls *can't be Maggie's.*

I'm holding back a scream. Her heavy, bloated arms are like dead weights, and water sloshes as I pull her toward the bank.

Stupid log gets in the way. I shove it away with my foot and keep pulling.

Heat floods my ears.

Adrenaline's pumping.

"Maggie?"

CPR. I need to do CPR. Maggie's always teaching Eva and me. So I check her pulse, then place my hands on the center of her chest, which is firm, but also full of dead weight.

Chest compressions. I begin chest compressions.

Throw on all my weight.

In my head, I can hear Maggie's cheerful alto voice sing, "Stayin' Alive, Stayin' Alive!" Which tells me she's not really dead. She's here; I can wake her. She'll be okay.

Mouth-to-mouth time.

I plug her nose, seal my mouth over hers like I did on that dummy, and blow, but air does nothing.

This isn't how it's supposed to be.

She's supposed to cough up water. Tell me she's been tracking Alora for forever, but stupid Dom got in the way.

Stayin' Alive, Stayin' Alive.

Chest compressions will resuscitate Maggie.

Maggie swore it worked on the dummy—the one we dressed in a red shirt and hero hair to look like James Dean.

Come on, come on, come on, James Dean.

Blow.

Stayin' Alive, Stayin' Alive.

Come. On. Maggie!

Hands are starting to feel tired. Ears are ringing. Her mouth feels like Play-Doh as I lift her jaw for the thousandth time.

Saliva's dripping everywhere.

Should wipe it off.

There isn't time.

Two firm, masculine arms wrap around my sides. I faintly hear the groan of someone as they analyze Maggie's throat.

"It's crushed," a voice like Raylan's says, and he can't be here under these circumstances. This isn't right. He wasn't ever supposed to move his eyes from my sister. I don't care that Leo freed him. He's supposed to be protecting her.

With Maggie.

"Frost!" he yells. I have a feeling it isn't the first time.

I keep pressing Maggie's chest.

Stayin' Alive, Stayin' Alive.

He wraps his arms around me tighter, and I want to keep going, but my body gives out.

I sag against him, and he feels like a human tank.

This isn't happening.

And that, my friends, is how I found my answer to all my struggles. Everything I've been fighting for my entire life. Knox knew it. Tess knew it. I think even Mom and Dad do, or did. I certainly should have truly believed it by now. Who knew Alora would be the one to help me finally see the light?

Hadn't realized Mags felt the same way.

I am nothing. Less than nothing, actually. Just a blip on the eternal radar whose sole purpose is to help bad people be worse. Should come in handy for whatever it is we're getting ready to do tonight. Alora said she'll give me a minute to adjust before she fills me in on the details.

At least I don't need to fight it anymore.

I threw Mags' lifeless shell into the creek with my new surprising strength. When I didn't even blink as my new sisters each drowned a new victim so their score could be even tonight, I felt a small satisfaction for finally just accepting it.

Not only am I nothing, I am worse than nothing. Because I can cause *so much pain*.

Alora and I stand slightly apart from the rest of the camp, watching their debauchery with mild contempt. I know she'd rather go storm Bloodcreek now, but she's a good enough leader to know the value of pre-battle festivities. Who knows how many battles she fought in the Before? What must that have been like?

In most battles I've seen in movies, they take place at dawn, so the party is the night before . . . but I guess dusk is kinda the dawn for all supernatural creatures—slimy, ghostly, or furry. This gorgeous, crisp winter day doesn't deserve to see this kind of mayhem. It should be more of a sad, melancholic '70s movie, not Mad Max of Missouri.

A group of Blurred Ones in their new vessels stand around punching, stabbing, and kicking each other like paranormal frat boys taking their bodies for a joy ride. A large, ripped Polynesian woman shoves a scrawny kid I swear I've seen at the Bloodcreek gas station, and he flies onto a rural Mardi Gras groupie, impaling him on the beaked mask.

The masked groupie rips his beak out of the Blurred One, but quickly digs back in and rips out a chunk of flesh. How did he make the beak move like that? With a howl, the Blurred One launches himself back to his own kind, already starting to heal. How did we ever think we stood a chance against all these dark things?

The masked man reaches up with greedy fingers and yanks the flesh from his beak. A handful of other rural Mardi Gras followers fall on the first. It's a frenzy of displaced body parts, each person scratching and bumping at the first chance to get a piece of the meat. The first one screams, short and carnal, and shoves the flesh under his mask into his mouth.

The other rural Mardi Gras followers fall back, disappointed, but eye the group of Blurred Ones with their dead eyes—probably waiting for one to come too close. I imagine Mardi Gras groupies are human under those masks, or used to be, but who knows what toll their evil magic has taken on their souls?

I sigh internally and roll over to my other side in the corner of my mental box.

Something shifts outside my cage. A new presence?

"Raylan?" It better not be Raylan. That fool better be ten miles into safety by now.

Alora tenses. *Quiet,* she commands. I obey.

Your tent, the new presence says, but I can't make out who it is. Everything's fuzzy. Like I'm seeing and hearing everything through a really thick filter or screen.

We quickly head back to our tent. Dang, Alora obeying someone? Is it the devil himself?

We pass creature after creature, and I sense Alora now sees them more as annoyances than allies at the moment. She's impatient.

We get to the tent, and a black smoke essence hovers there.

A question enters my mind. Asking for permission, perhaps?

Alora has us give a curt nod, and a tendril of the essence reaches toward me. We don't react but wait as it lightly touches my temple.

In a blink, we're somewhere else. Still in my mind, but instead of the concrete walls of my box, it's a vast world of enchanting trees, mountains, and waterfalls. Nowhere on Earth is possibly this beautiful.

I stand at the edge of a cliff, and below me churns a river of sick brown that doesn't belong. While everything else—the beautiful, iridescent butterflies, the pearl gazelle—looks serene and tranquil, the river screams malice. Something about it is wrong.

Even though I'm wary of taking my eyes off the river, I have to see what's going on. I start to turn, but vines race up from the ground, binding me with their pokey fibers. They swirl around my legs and run up my arms as they pull me to the ground to a kneel. They keep growing, squeezing my chest tight, and cover my mouth. Mercifully, they stop there. I imagine if I had the willpower to fight, those thorns could really tear me up.

Lifting my eyes, I see Alora back in her spiky battle gear, statuesque in her sad glory. Next to her stands a young man with a red cape and a hesitant smile.

"Leonardo," Alora simpers. "Are you here to attempt to deliver on your promise? To end me?"

"I'll be leaving Bloodcreek after we defeat you." His eyes shift to me for just a second, then back to Alora. "Eva and Frost. There's no reason to target them. Let Eva go." He kicks a rock off the cliff, into the river below. "This is where it all started. Let it be the end."

"Eva has finally accepted her true nature, *amare*," Alora purrs smugly. The pearl gazelle leaps by, flying ten feet with each jump. Alora throws out an arm and grips a spiraled horn. Unused to predators in this place, the gazelle doesn't fight, and Alora forces it to the ground by the horn. With her sadistic intensity back in her face, she grips a horn in each hand and jerks, *hard*. The gazelle's neck twists and snaps. The beautiful creature explodes into dust, which is carried in a gust of wind, down into the ravenous river.

Leo's face tears with grief. "If that were true, you'd be down in that river instead. Will it ever be enough for you?"

"I've only ever wanted you," she says, deathly calm, wiping her hands together, as if shaking the dust off.

"I'll end you and then myself," he says, equally stoic.

"Eva doesn't even care about being saved anymore," she spits, facade of control gone. "Look at her!"

I meet Leo's eyes and try to come up with the fight to prove her otherwise, but really, what good would freeing me do? I'd probably be all selfish and go back home, only to get all my loved ones killed.

"Eva," Leo calls. "We need you."

I can't look at him anymore.

"There's no use giving her false hope, Leonardo," Alora says in a low voice.

The world rocks with a jolt. Something's happening outside this world in my head. Alora starts to reach her hand out to Leo, as if asking him to wait, but we're suddenly snapped back to the camp outside Bloodcreek. Me in my box, Alora in charge, and Leo's essence floating nearby in what looks like a kind of devil's trap. Next to the trap is a seriously pissed off-looking Dominick.

"You dare interrupt me?" Alora seethes at Dom, raising my hand to probably Darth Vader choke him.

"You take too long," he snarls, "playing your silly girl games. We finish dis now."

"We do what I say," she retorts, and we backhand him with the force of a renegade semi-truck, right out of the tent.

Dom lands with a thud ten feet away on the dusty ground. Snatching a small blade from inside his vest, he quickly slices his palm open, spits into the wound, and plants his wounded hand firmly in the dirt.

Nausea consumes my body, every inch of me instantly feeling like I've contracted some crazy illness, like the bubonic plague. My face breaks into a cold sweat, and I assume Alora's gonna have us throw the smackdown on Dom, but she turns to Leo instead.

"We're doing this *my* way," we say and throw ourselves onto the invisible barrier holding in Leo's essence. It's like we just jumped onto that old electric fence near home. Power invades my body, torturing every cell, but Alora makes us stay. She holds us there, gritting my teeth, holding back a scream, throwing all our power onto the barrier.

It weakens for a second, then it's back. Like it's shorting out. Between the nausea and electrocution, I just know we'll collapse any second. But the trap glitches again, and Leo bursts from inside and escapes into the darkening woods.

You've never seen a staredown until you've seen one between a Despairity and an old, cranky witch doctor. I'm pretty sure Alora is gonna make one of my arteries blow, but holding the stare, we, very casually, make our way to a chair, sit, and glare at Dominick, daring him to challenge us.

We glare, he glares, until eventually, with a flip of a hand, she closes the flap on the tent. Slumping back in the chair, we're still for a moment. I think we're both needing to collect ourselves.

It was nice having Leo around for a minute, but of course I'm glad he got away. I'm just kind of done with everything right now. I roll over in my box and try to think of nothing but the beating of my heart.

CHAPTER 33 - FROST

*B*ack and forth, back and forth, Raylan and I swing. It's a calming rhythm. I don't know why I haven't done this more regularly.

Shewww, groan. Shewww, *creak, creak.*

It's a soothing sound, the flex and release of the chains. They almost make me believe Maggie's still here. Any second, she's going to open that screen door with the biggest smile and a box of kolaches. She'll tell me of some gremlin she took down in Alora's posse, and how it was Dom's third cousin or something.

A little while ago, Raylan gave me a cup of hot cocoa, but I can't drink it. I just stare at it in my hands as it cools to sixty degrees. Mom went to bed hours ago, and I just couldn't find the nerve to tell her what happened to Maggie.

As I stare down at the liquid that's long lost its steam, I can't help thinking what I could have done differently. *I* should have been the one to infiltrate the camp. I shouldn't have put all that on Raylan and Maggie. Eva's *my* sister. It should have been me.

Raylan takes the cup from my hands, seeing as the cocoa's

very nearly spilled to the wooden porch beneath our feet. "There's something you need to know." He swallows uncomfortably. Ginormous red circles rim his eyes, and as he stares out at the lawn, it's like he can see what I see: Eva and me last year, chopping stumps. Grumbling about the fact that we had to pick morning glory. Maggie showing up with a newly constructed AR-15.

Taking a shaky breath, Raylan suddenly barks out, "Maggie isn't the person we thought she was."

Uh . . . what's he talking about? That doesn't sit right.

But Raylan's shoulders hunch in this rare, defeated way as he stares down at the wooden porch floor we rebuilt with Maggie. "This isn't easy for me to say, but . . . looks like Maggie was drinking some of your Dad's Kool-Aid."

"Huh?"

He shakes his head. "No, that's sugarcoating it."

Now that's an awful pun I don't even think he means.

"MAGGIE DIDN'T BELIEVE IN EVA, ALL RIGHT?"

"What?" I say. He probably just needs to lie down, get some rest.

"There were subtle comments at first." Raylan uses his hands to talk. "When we first started tracking Eva . . . everything Maggie said . . . I thought she was joking." He digs his hands into his hair before wiping a sheen of sweat from his forehead, even though it's only forty degrees. "But then she started saying these weird things about Eva and how, *'of course,'* she was the one who wasn't strong enough to prevent herself from being possessed by the Despairity."

"Wait . . ." Nothing he's saying is making sense. "Eva got possessed because Dom wore down her triquetra. And she doesn't have the barrier gift Leo gave me."

Raylan slowly shakes his head, stony faced. "Maggie . . . didn't see it that way. She said the reason why Eva was possessed was because" —his voice cracks— "she was weak."

A flash of anger boils in my eyes.

Maggie said what? But she would never say that. Why is Raylan lying? I thought he loved Eva. Why is he making this up? Eva is *not* weak. She got freaking possessed because Dom and Tess captured her. If it weren't for Leo, it could have so easily been me.

I think of all the times Maggie arrived at our house—our bona fide rescuer with a new season of *Blue Bloods* and fresh Bavarian creams. She even tried to save our aunt before we were born, when Knox led Aunt Eva away to Cadillac Ranch. "Raylan . . ." I don't know how to put it, but the pressure to get Eva back is too much. He must be cracking.

His gaze bounces from the lump on the grass—Maggie's body that Raylan covered with a blanket covered in grease—to the porch steps, to my lap. "I know, I know . . . it's crazy, but the closer we'd get to Alora's camp, the more Maggie would say stupid crap about Eva not even putting up a fight. She" —he pounds his fist in his lap— "said it was what your dad always said would happen. That Eva's childish." His voice cracks again. "And weak."

None of this is real. Raylan's come to me in some sort of sick dream. Maggie's the one friend who understands everything we went through with Dad—who was there when we needed to get out, when we needed rides.

She's the one who picked us up in San Antonio when Knox came after us.

She took a beating from Tess. Helped us beat her and Dominick.

Not to mention all the wisdom she imparted round the campfire and on our drives.

"You're lying." I grit my teeth. "This is your messed up way of helping me with my grief."

Raylan rubs the bristle on his face. "Trust me, I *wish* that were the case. She was like a surrogate sister. Took me in when I needed a place."

But what he's saying doesn't make sense. Eva would never give up! Why's he saying Maggie would think she ever would? Eva is the frickin' General of the East. She's strong. She, better than anyone, understands the necessity of fighting.

She wouldn't let some freaky Despairity witch ruin her life. I know it's hard. Harder than I could even imagine. But Eva would never give up.

How could Dad or Maggie ever call her weak?

"Eva's strong." When Raylan talks, it's like he knows what I'm thinking. "But . . . given everything she's going through, I'm not sure if *anyone* could survive."

I swallow the lump in my throat. Not sure I can handle any more details at this point.

Not sure I could handle the psychological warfare I *know* Alora must be dishing to Eva. Alora was in my head all of two minutes, and I tore off for the nearest cliff to scream.

Eva. Out of habit, I reach for her through my mind, but there's nothing there. Nothing there. Just like always.

"I know it's a lot to handle," Raylan says. "With every-thing going on with witch doctors, monsters, and now these bi—" He grabs my hand. "Eva *will* get through this. She *knows* we are coming."

Shewwww, groan. Creak, creak.

I don't know how it's happened, but Raylan and I can't string together a coherent sentence to save our lives. He lets go of my hand, and, despite everything he must be feeling, I can *feel* his unrelenting wave of concern and love for Eva and me.

He is my brother.

We will do *anything* to make sure Eva comes back to us safely.

Despite my initial thought when Eva told me that she and

leather jacket boy made out the first day they met on the street, I couldn't imagine a better guy for her.

He *really* loves her. He's gentle, intuitive, honest, and will *never* give up on Eves. And even if Eva's temporarily been beaten into submission by Alora, my sister's still in there. We *will* find a way to help her escape.

Digging into his pocket, Raylan pulls out a piece of paper, hands shaking. Doesn't take me long to notice Maggie's bulky handwriting.

I don't want to look at it, so I turn away.

"Mags tried to convince me to leave camp," Raylan says, paper crackling. "She wanted me to get back to you. Leo. Beau. Everybody."

I don't mean to look, but my eyes betray my inner desire. Darting to the third line, I read, *She's gone. Go home, Ray. We all knew Eva would never be strong enough to withstand possession by the Desp—*

My eyes break away.

Not *strong* enough?

Who's the girl who lured Knox into a hotel room in nothing but a black mini dress to save *our* butts when she learned he'd killed Jenny? Who's the freaking warrior who choked the bastard to death with nothing but her raw hands and this swing's chain?

But Maggie did everything in her power to make sure we would never be possessed . . . because she wanted us safe— not because she believed Eva was inherently bad or weak. Maggie's our cheerleader, our Hagrid of Hogwarts, our Annie Oakley.

The nutcracker and the perfectly vacuumed carpet of my living room flash into my mind . . .

For years and years, Dad and Maggie had always been as thick as thieves.

Cleaning their weapons together, cracking up about the same

jokes that may or may not have been funny. . . . But, both freaked out when Eva missed the bus and came home with the boys.

Both asked me to keep my eye on Eva even *before* we went to San Antonio, because they thought she couldn't be trusted to make the right choices . . .

No.

No, no, no . . . Maggie's supposed to love us—until the day we die.

I bat away the tears that have stubbornly leaked to my cheeks. Smooshing them out with my palms, I resolve not to let any kind of betrayal show on my face.

Completely lost and empty as to what to say, I settle with the most unoriginal question that comes to mind. "Why was she even nearby?"

Raylan lets out a weary laugh. "Leo showed up last night, freed me, and I tried to free Mags, but . . ."

Fresh, hot tears prick my eyes. "Please tell me Leo didn't buy into her crap."

Raylan shakes his head swiftly. "No, no. He has no idea."

I exhale the breath I didn't know I was holding. And I let my fingers graze my throat, wishing I could have been there to see *exactly* how Maggie died. Did Alora crush Maggie's throat entirely on her own?

I'm not sure I can deal with any more bad news today. "Please tell me you have an idea. We *have* to get Eva back. Use a banishing spell or something."

Raylan's fist pounds the swing, causing it to twist. "Eva is strong." He pounds again. "But, from what I hear, Alora enjoys her mind games." All over again, his shoulders sag. "They kept us separate the whole time."

I don't mean for it to happen, but even more tears slide from my eyes. *Wish we were there for you, Eves!*

I don't know what's worse—that Alora's physically and

mentally attacking my sister, or that Maggie, *of all people,* slung mud on Eva's name.

What's that saying? The people you're closest to can hurt you the most?

Yes, absolutely.

I twist my own fist in my lap. "Just because Eva's good at expressing her emotions doesn't make her weak. She has a real zest for life! She loves art and music, things Dad and Maggie never really related to."

Raylan's shoulders square as I find my stride.

"She's strong because she acts *despite* intensely feeling things. Alora knows this. Leo said she wants a general in her ranks. Something about swaying other people to her side. But we *can't* turn our backs on Eva just because she was targeted. She needs our hope and faith more than ever *because* of what she has been enduring."

Raylan balls his hands into fists, his entire body tensed to rip something apart. Cords ripple through his neck, and his thumb taps the .45 in his holster as he fights to keep control of his rage.

Taking two quick breaths, he suddenly spins, and I'm thinking maybe he's going to tackle and pin me to the ground when he wraps his strong arms around my back and gives me the fiercest hug I've ever gotten in my life.

I can feel his panicked, pounding heart as he holds me. Nothing but muscles and love fill Raylan's body.

It's a long time before either one of us pulls away.

We *won't* allow Maggie's weakness to set the course for what happens to Eva or her name.

"Have you seen her at all?" I wipe the other tears that spilled from my eyes, my shoulder a natural handkerchief.

Raylan stares down at a rust-colored stain on his jeans. Rips tear apart his shirt, and old grease stains darken the knuckles on his hands. "A couple of times. I even got possessed by one of the other Despairity."

I want to ask more questions about what all that entailed, but a muscle feathers along his jaw. I don't need to stoke the anger.

I could tell him about Alora and Leo's history, but I don't think we need to get into that at this point.

The horrible fact now is, we have to figure out what to do with Maggie's body.

"Do whatever you want with her." I scoot off the bench and bend down to pluck up my mug of cocoa. "I'm heading back to guard the tree."

Not long after our face-off with Dom, we're up and after Alora's sinister plans, thanks to her uber healing.

Trees fly by, mixed with the bright moonlight, black and white before my eyes can register, like a massive strobe light. It's me that's moving, though; I'm that fast. Turns out when I'm possessed by a really powerful, ancient Blurred One, and I'm not fighting her, we're pretty amazing.

As we quickly crest a hill, even I can appreciate the beauty of the blazing trail of fire lit throughout the hills. Most were lit by the torch-wielding nymph, called a lampad. She's some ancient Greek mythological being. Well, scratch the mythological part.

The flames dance in many warm colors against the darkening sky. I want to bathe my skin in its ashes. Just sounds right.

Instead, we keep running. I don't know where anyone is, and I'm really just along for the ride. A vague tickle somewhere in my head says my friends will stop us from doing anything *too* evil, so I'm good to go where my new destiny takes me.

We're quite the crew. Besides my new sisters and me, we've got twenty or so Blurred Ones, a ten-foot golem, some zombie-looking dudes, the super creepy rural Mardi Gras people, and a mess of vampires. Those are the ones I know about, but there are enough moving shadows around to see we've got an army.

My job, according to Alora, is to sit back, relax, and just take over whenever I feel the instinct to do so. She promises she won't even hesitate to back off. I arch an inner eyebrow at that, though, after her making me into a vine mummy before. Whatever. I'm just here.

A horse whinnies from a neighbor's barn, and I refuse to worry about it. There's no point, anyway. We're passing the Share The Road sign with the horse and buggy pictured on it. We're getting close to Bloodcreek. Cool. As long as my friends don't get hurt, let's light up the town.

I hold a butane lighter to the trunk of another tree. I'm so glad the Despairity have learned to lighten up and have a little fun. Ha. I give exactly one chuckle at my pun. Seems we want to turn Bloodcreek into a giant bonfire. Whatever. The place should be wiped clean. And if there's nothing left, maybe Frost will finally leave. Not much here for her anymore, anyway.

We flit around from place to place so fast, I wonder how much of me is human anymore. But while the blue flame licks at the new, green bark of a young redbud, I spy a rusted, orange truck parked in a gravel driveway next to an old, tiny green house.

"I know that truck," I say, too tired to try to place where I know it from. I'm running purely on Alora and instincts at this point, and soon, I find myself skipping over a broken, wooden porch step onto a mostly rotted porch. A faded, red sign with once-white letters hangs askew on a rusted nail, and I can barely make out what it says. "Pinkman."

"Alora," I call to my other inner me. "I'll take that control now."

CHAPTER 35 - FROST

*B*ack at the park, with Alora nowhere in sight, I try to find Leo for the hundredth time.

I'd rather weed-eat the entire front yard. Wash Dad's old Chrysler fifteen times. But I need to get Leo's attention. Before he smokes out again, I *need* to get him to talk to me.

After checking with the swordsmiths and a hunter group practicing throwing grenades, I find him, crouching alone on the grass, shaking out a salt line.

When he glances my way, I nervously avert my eyes. All I can do is stare at the rose bushes that won't bloom again for a few more weeks.

Pushing off his knees to stand, Leo's soothing voice comes out hesitant. "You have been gone the better part of a day."

I don't have to be a genius to read the worry and reproof in his eyes—but *he's* the one who smoked out the last time we talked.

His eyes glint and crinkle at the corners, like there's something else he wants to say, but something catches his attention in the distance. "I'm glad Raylan found you."

He drops the canister of salt; a few crystals sizzle onto his hands like he's come in contact with acid. "Any news on Maggie?"

Already, I feel the rush of anger and hot tears pricking my eyes. I grab his arm, then silently curse myself for touching him so immediately.

His arm feels so warm and good, but I let go, and an abundance of fear swarms in his cool, blue eyes.

But I can't tell him. Admitting that Maggie's dead . . . that she didn't believe . . . Eva . . . I can't tell him. I can't find the words. I don't know what to say.

Stopping amidst a pile of shotguns and newly squashed salt boxes, I shiver in the cool wind and hold my jacket tighter against me. Avoiding the topic altogether, I say, "I need you to forgive yourself and join me in this fight."

Leo flinches a little before looking down at me with soft eyes. The smell of smoke washes over the park, and nobody had better be lighting a fire. Alora doesn't need any more clues to find the tree.

Looking down to a half-buried salt grenade, Leo admits, "I don't know how."

"I'll show you." I reach up and pretend to pull the guilt, like a thread, from his mind. It's something we did when we were kids, and I was upset about something Dad said, or when I wasn't allowed to join the soccer team. "See?" Daintily, I hold the invisible thread between my fingers. "Took it out of your mind."

I mean for it to be a joke, but Leo doesn't so much as humor me with a partial smile.

"I told you, I made too many bad decisions," he says, backing up two steps away from me. He swallows, his borrowed vessel's Adam's apple bobbing. "But I was never honest about who convinced me to go to Our Brother's side."

The vision of Alora jumping up and wrapping her legs

around him flares through my mind, and I shake my head real fast to push it out.

The way Leo's jaw twitches, I can tell he saw what I tried to screen.

"Why didn't you fight back?" I don't understand how he could be *my* Leo and yet succumb so easily to her vixen ways. "Why didn't you ever tell me about her?"

Leo's troubled eyes lock onto mine; and in that one look, I can see the stark, naked truth lurking alongside the fear in his eyes. *Because . . . I never wanted you to look at me this way.*

I clamp my jaw.

I'm not looking at him any "way."

I'm just looking at him! Needing him. Wanting his calming presence back in my life.

Leo . . . he needs to tell me everything will be okay. I can't look at him with accusation or judgment. I know the water from The Before played with his mind, and, even though I don't completely understand all that happened, I *do* know that I'm not going to give up on him or Eva or our mission. I will *never* step aside.

So I parrot what may be Beau's greatest line. "We all make mistakes."

Leo's fingers twitch for a cigarette in his pocket, but he's long since ditched those things. "What happened to Maggie?"

I can't tell him Maggie stopped believing. That she was selfish and faithless and thought Eva would go bad the whole time.

How is it that this world has so quickly turned upside down? How is it that we're freaking spray painting devil's traps on the grass and getting hunting lessons from seraphs and guarding a mystical tree? Why in the heck is my sister still possessed, and we still have *no clue* how to break her free?

Blinking, Leo looks wan as his voice goes cold. "*What* happened to Maggie?"

He fears the worst; I don't know what's going through his head, but maybe he saw her in Alora's camp. Maybe he saw her true colors when she tossed the dice on whether she would screw Eva at that moment, or the very next day.

Staggering back a little, I trip on a hole in the ground. If Leo, Raylan, a few random hunters, and I are the only ones truly standing between Alora's army and the tree, the world's in deep.

"Frost." Leo's voice has a frightening edge. "Talk to me." Insects scuttle under his skin beneath his hairline.

I can't push back the tears.

Two drip from my eyelids, and crap, oh crap. I'm losing my grip. Must stay strong for everybody.

From the stockpile of shotguns, Leo closes the distance, seizing my arms and gripping them tightly. "What aren't you saying?"

"Maggie . . ." My throat constricts. "She never believed Eva was worthy of saving."

Complete and utter disbelief washes over Leo's face.

"She gave up, Leo. And now she's dead. Eva probably killed her—I have no idea if she or Alora was pulling the strings—but now there's *no way* Eva will forgive herself for killing Maggie. Leo." My voice chokes up. "Just like Dad, Maggie *never believed* Eva would stay on the good side."

Leo's face goes so pale that the insects skittering beneath the surface take even more control of his face. His hands weaken their grip around my forearms, and he shakes his head hard twice. "Frost, you're not making sense . . ."

I lean into his arms, hungry for his touch. For anything. And I hate to say these words, because they feel like Dad's. "Maggie believed Eva got possessed because she's inherently weak."

"No. No. No, no, no!" Leo releases my arms and trips over

the salt grenade as he staggers away from me. "She wouldn't believe that."

"That's what I thought, but Raylan had a letter from her and everything."

Gritting his teeth, Leo leans down, picks up the salt grenade, and chucks it to a vacant section of the field—past the abandoned car. The explosion's a little sparse but would slow down a Despairity. A few of the hunters who just made it shout some unsavory words, but I ignore them and grab Leo's arm.

"We'll figure it out."

The fear in his eyes tells me he's not so sure he can believe that.

<hr>

CHAPTER 36 - EVA

The muffled sound of a TV floats through the door's cracked window. I wave my freakish companions on with a slight wave of the hand, then I grab the screen door's handle with my middle finger and thumb—germs, ya know? I yank, and it opens with a screech.

I pause for just a second, listening for the house's residents, but all I hear is some reality show about body paint and the merits of airbrushing a buttocks. The TV is on really loud, and for a second, I'm glad it will mask any little sounds I make, but then I remember. One, I don't care. And two, just try and stop me.

Eyeing the splintering paint on the door framing the broken window, I place both hands on either side of the glass. I lean up real close, as if I wanted to make a face on the disgusting glass, and I spy a bag of groceries on the floor. Uncle Julio's chips taunt me, and I feel a spark of satisfaction, knowing that I can finally eat what I want again. Maybe without even getting super fat. I tap my fingers lightly on the wood, then I push. Moderately hard.

The door flies back and slams into the wall, smashing the

light-up beer sign, which crashes to the floor. The TV sings to my left, and a very blond mullet on a very pasty head darts up from a mauve couch. My boots crunch the broken glass on the floor as I stalk inside.

"Wade," I coo. His freckles seem to have multiplied, and his midriff-baring shirt reveals Cheeto streaks on his baby beer belly.

"Eva?" he chokes as he backs up toward the TV.

"You finally learned my name," I say, closing the gap between us in a couple of steps.

"Yes, ma'am," he stutters, feeling behind himself, I'm assuming for a weapon. "Why ya lookin' so mean all a sudden?"

"I figured out who I am."

Now I step back inside myself, just a half step. Definitely not a backseat. More like a co-pilot. Alora revels in the slow, long stretch I give my neck, then does her thing.

We inhale. At first, I brace myself, because Wade Pinkman cannot smell good, but I'm not smelling with my natural senses. I don't get his bathroom cologne or body odor. We're inhaling *him*. His spirit, life, humanity, whatever . . . whatever it is, it is better than Beaver Nuggets washed down with Diet Coke and followed up by Flaming Hot Cheeto Puffs.

His eyes do look a little sad, all turned down and muddy green. Like he didn't expect me to actually hurt him. Sorry, Wade, this is just life now. I half-heartedly think to Alora, "Try not to kill him," then focus on the exquisite force we're consuming.

I know I should be on the field, guarding that tree, but Leo suggested we take a breather for a couple of hours. I tried to find Mom, but I guess she's still at work.

Now *I'm* playing the piano. Who'd have thought "Baba Yaga" was such a perfect song for getting out your rage? Mozart's "Fantasia" isn't too terrible, either. Marching band songs work, too. Rachmaninoff would probably work wonders if I could remember how to play . . .

But something tells me someone's been trying to contact me.

Eva, is that you?

For all I know, my emotions are all screwed up, and I'm imagining things. But it's like a slight tickle at the edge of my brain.

I'm just finishing up and heading to the kitchen to get a drink of water when a knock sounds from the front door. Not really in the mood to think who it could be—Alora? Banshees?—I swing the door open wide.

White hair, spectacles, and a beige shirt, of all things, greet me from outside.

"Mr. Harris?" I do my best not to openly gape. I totally forgot I could reach out to him for help, but I'm not sure where he stands on all things Maggie.

Peering at me through his coke-bottle glasses, Mr. Harris shifts a weighty tome in his hands. It's brown and thick. My heart drops. That's Maggie's sigil and rune book.

"Mm—may I come in?" Mr. Harris asks nervously. "I . . . have been trying to locate you all day."

"Oh, so you're the one." I spin away from the door, trying not to show the disappointment in my voice. "I'm a barrier, so I imagine I'm kind of hard to find."

But Mr. Harris doesn't move. In fact, he glances over his shoulder, like he's wary of being followed. "I . . . know about Maggie."

That she's dead, or that she'd rather betray her friends than believe they can be rescued and saved?

Both?

Honestly, I'm losing patience nowadays.

Plucking his glasses off his face, Mr. Harris uses his shoulder to wipe his wet eyes. "She" —his voice cuts off for a second— "never told me of her . . . reservations regarding Eva's integrity."

Well, at least *he's* not a liar.

Raylan must have told him.

Hip, hip, hooray.

I know I should be on the field, training hunters—any newbies—but Mr. Harris practically lured me here. Why?

He glances once again over his shoulder. "I . . . need you to come with me."

That's not ominous at all.

Pretending to be totally fine with his doomsday greeting, I waggle my eyebrows. "Why, Mr. Harris, are you asking me on a date?"

Mr. Harris' cheeks flush with embarrassment, and I wish

so much that Eva was here to coach me. She'd tell him he looks so great in those velcro loafers and tweed.

Clearly oblivious to what I'm thinking, Mr. Harris tucks his tome into his chest and levels his librarian eyes on me. "I need to show you something."

"Sure. All right." I reach for the house key around my neck to start locking up, but he seizes my hand, and I didn't notice he was shaking. Or how pale he is. Or the sweat now beading on his brow and lip line.

Wheezing, Mr. Harris tugs me through the door. "There isn't time."

I emerge from the house onto Wade's rickety porch and find increased apocalyptic chaos. Shadows dart between burning trees and smoking buildings. Dark smears stain the ground like a giant is walking around with a dripping baby doll, but the dolly is dripping blood. I'd be lying if I said it wasn't a little tantalizing.

Christian's lithe figure lingers by a torched honeysuckle tree, watching for me, looking deep in thought, as always. I really don't care to know what it is he's thinking so deeply about.

"Seriously, what is your deal?" I hiss at him, so perturbed he hangs out with this group of his own volition. When he hesitates, I snap in his face. "Hey. That's right, Eva speaking. Not Alora. Why. Are. You. Here?" I don't think I've ever been so rude to someone, but I don't much care.

"I always knew there was more," he blurts, and he yanks a honeysuckle branch too hard. It's brittle from the fire and collapses in his fingers. "My mom taught me there was more. To this life that I didn't understand." He goes to shove his hand in his pocket, but his hand is too big, so the pocket only fits his fingers. He looks down so I can see the top of his dark hair, like he's slightly embarrassed.

"Well, duh," is my eloquent response.

He settles his weight on his left leg and, to his credit, seems to gather his nerve. "She always had a feeling I would be part of something big. I did, too." He looks at me, green eyes intense even without the flames dancing in them. "When you all showed up at that canoe shop, I felt this crazy pull to you. Like you were what I've been waiting for. Mom felt it, too. That's why she told me to go, then joined us later."

"You thought it was your life's destiny to hang out with a bunch of freaky murderers." I don't say it like a question.

"I'll admit it hasn't exactly been what I thought it'd be," he says back to the ground, but then he squares his shoulders. "But I still feel like I'm supposed to be here, so I'm here."

His voice is so confident, I want to flat-out punch him in his GQ face. Heaven and Hell are basically at war here, right here in the Ozarks, and this guy doesn't seem to belong on either side.

So I take off. He must have Shorty hitchin' a ride in his body, because he keeps up quite nicely for a while. What's *that* dynamic like? But I'm motivated, so I lose him when he's distracted by some furry monster climbing a statue of an elephant. I don't need him around, making me think. I just want to keep living on primal instinct alone.

Alora and I soar over the twisty roads the rest of the way into town, running so fast that the wind throws back my hair. It clears my mind enough to ask the only pertinent question.

What's the plan? I think to Alora. She smirks her approval, using my lips, and I don't even mind.

We're finding the Tree of Knowledge of Good and Evil.

Mmmhmm. And we're gonna burn it?

It won't burn. Since your friends have been so stubborn about its location, burning all the others is one way we're narrowing it down. It's here somewhere.

Why do you want it? I ask, but I'm quickly losing the energy to care since the dark, black hole that is my chest is trying to demand my attention.

To right the world.

Whatever, Alora. I don't direct the thought at her. Instead, I just let it be.

I spy Bloodcreek Dollar up a stretch and secretly hope we're stopping for snacks.

You're being such a good little darling, Alora says. *A snack is warranted.*

K, but if you're gonna stick around in my head, you should really start letting me have some of my own thoughts.

I'll think about it.

I scoff aloud. Alora just used a pun.

We slip into the dollar store, the bell ringing on the door sounding way too cheery for this end-of-times type of night. The smell of lavender-infused ammonia is so strong, it stings my eyes right before it makes the black pit in my chest swirl like a black hole. Mags would use that cleaner because of its ridiculously strong scent. She'd say, "If it smells clean, chances are, it is clean." Ha. Not real big into being a neat freak, that one. Besides her weapons.

I didn't even use a weapon . . .

"Powdered donuts." Alora interrupts my thought. I give her a little nod.

"Most excellent suggestion," I say while grabbing a little tube of them. I go ahead and rip the plastic open and pop the first one in my mouth. Perfectly fresh. The powdered sugar is so dense, it almost feels wet.

"Those cost money, honey," a nasally voice says from behind the counter. The clerk rightfully looks at me like I'm a little off my rocker. "And don't you want to go for a nice little salad?"

I turn and take in the man in the green vest, deeply wrinkled skin, and black and gray comb over. It's hard to fathom anyone worrying about anything as normal as my body size, let alone money, right now. I guess the apocalypse hasn't hit inside Bloodcreek Dollar yet.

I'm about to mumble some sort of excuse when Alora does something, and our vision changes. Like a dark photo filter just got put on my eyes, everything is the same, but looks so different. The cashier's vest is a deep, dark green, but my donuts are blood red. I look back up at the man and suddenly notice his skin is covered in scales, and he licks his lips like an overgrown, disgusting komodo dragon.

"Take what you want," he grunts. He grabs his phone off the counter, plopping down on a stool.

If Alora had a face besides my own, I'd give her a significant look right now. Apparently, he's supernatural. I lean back in my own head and ready myself for the upcoming rush. Alora says out loud, "It's okay, Eva. Stay with me."

I cringe at the ease with which she reads me. But killing bad creatures is what I've been training to do all this time anyway, right?

The man's head is bent over his phone, so I see the freckled top of his head. I hover a couple of feet away until he feels me watching and looks up. I must have a slightly murderous look on my face, because his twists with confusion.

"We're on the same side, ma'am," he cries softly.

"We are on our own side," Alora says to him and, I think, to me. In one step, we leap over the counter and inhale. His essence is delectable, although it's a completely different flavor than Wade's. More . . . citrusy. I bask in it, letting it fill up the blackness in my chest. I wonder why I ever fought this. Why I fought so hard to believe I was good. This is what I was made for. Even God knows that.

Alora and I giggle, then breathe some more. I'm so disconnected, but also elated, and find it hilarious that Alora is giggling. She and her sisters used to be so depressed that they were named the Despairity. Times sure are a-changin'.

Alora licks our bottom lip. *You do bring a missing element of fun to the table.*

I laugh so hard, I snort and lean back against the counter, holding—name tag says "Mitch"—up by what's left of his hair. There's not much left of his soul, either. He's looking pretty bleak. I wonder how many people this disgusting creature has hurt.

We breathe him in one more time, then his essence is gone. He looks at us like he's never seen us before. We let go of his hair, and as he slumps to the ground, the doorbell jingles again.

We turn around to see who the next friend or foe, or friend-turned-foe, is. Perfectly coiffed, super blonde hair appears over the displayed donuts.

"Mom?"

My mama's head turns as she looks for the source of my voice. She must stand on her tippy toes, because she grows a couple of inches and looks over the display at me. Her eyes widen with delight before tightening with concern.

My heart constricts, and I'm in real danger of breaking down into a flood of tears right now.

"Eva, honey." She rushes toward me, concern etched on every inch of her face. "Are you okay? Frost said you were in some trouble. Are you safe now?"

I'm dying to run to her and wrap myself up in one of her perfect hugs, but Alora's gone completely silent in my head, and my instinct is to freeze to protect Mom. Thank goodness the counter is between her and us, and it's blocking Mitch.

"I'm okay," I say, trying to buy time to figure out what to really say. I slowly and deliberately start to walk around the counter, because really, hugging her would be the most normal thing for me to do in this circumstance. But the last person I hugged was Mags. I cannot go near Mom.

I throw the stool in front of myself, like that will somehow block me from getting to my mother.

She gives me the most perfectly Mom expression, eyebrows to the sky, lips to the floor. I could almost laugh again, except now I'm worried about peeing my pants.

Alora? I plead inwardly.

Silence.

"Sorry, Mom. Weird times."

She's stopped moving toward me, though, the distance we've had since Dad died resurfacing. I wish I could bask in any bit of comfort she can give me, but this is safer for both of us. I settle like a marble pillar by the cash register.

"What are you doing here, Mom?" I ask. "You hate the dollar store."

"I just came for a few things." She fiddles with the zipper on her navy blue purse. "Frost said you'd be coming home soon, and I didn't want you to come home to an empty pantry."

"Uh, she did? When?"

"She called a couple of hours ago." She starts fidgeting more, becoming agitated. Part of me thinks she'll just bolt. I hope that part is true. "She mentioned you might want some snacks."

ALORA? The black hole in my chest is growing exponentially.

I suppose it is time to finish this. A door like industrialized steel slams inside my head. Immediately, everything that is me is back in my concrete and steel box, and I don't think I'll ever see the light of day again.

Mr. Harris leads me past frost-covered ferns and weeping willows to a tiny hut at the back of a lake.

While I know he doesn't make much money as a librarian, this is a little crazy. The left side of his place looks like it's been run into by a truck, and the right side of the roof droops like it's about to fall clean off—a too-hot birthday cake that won't keep its icing.

Little screws and wingnuts hang from trees—just like at Maggie's and my place—and they clink and sway in arias, duets; even a symphony.

Pulling open a creaky, mildew-covered door, Mr. Harris stutters, "S-sorry."

Why? 'Cause his house is falling? But inside . . . inside, *holy cow,* rows and rows of books line each and every wall. I'm in the freaking Yale library.

Arches and pillars embellish every bookcase, and a fancy banister fronts a second story.

I turn to Mr. Harris. "If I'd known you had a place like this, I would've scheduled a study date."

Mr. Harris' cheeks flush bright pink as something rustles at the back of the library.

Maybe a dog or cat? A watery figure with long, dark hair and black circles under her eyes glides out from behind a bookcase. Instantly, the foul stench of sulfur settles over the room that formerly had a nice smell of old books and stained mahogany.

"Nice work, Rupert." Alora's echoey voice fills the library; she twists my sister's lips into a smile that's not Eva's in any way. Two men in those terrifying bone and teeth masks flank the demon on either side, and Mr. Harris sinks into a leather chair, which gives off an abrupt squeak.

He set me up?

He *was* working with Maggie.

"My sister thought we needed a little more insurance. Our fire's only getting us so far." Alora taps the leather spines of several books in a bookcase. "So . . . we used the warlock to get to *you*."

Way, way high up on the balcony, two black-blue spirits lift a feminine figure from the second story flooring. Chin-length hair and black, slimming clothes? *Mom*. Mom's being held by the other two Despairity.

They lay her on the high-up banister, and she teeters dangerously.

They'll make her fall.

Break her neck.

It's got to be at least twenty feet high.

Alora laughs at what must be a horrific look on my face. "All you need to do is lead us to the tree, *Frosty*."

Mom weeble-wobbles on the thin, wooden railing, and my voice stretches with a shriek. "Pull her back!"

"Please, please, please," Mom pleads, whimpering.

Alora taps the side of my sister's head. "In this arrangement, you listen to *me*."

Closing my sister's eyes, Alora breathes in deeply, arms stretched wide. "I can smell your fear from here. It really is succulent. Reminds me of those snickerdoodle cookies you used to make. Wouldn't you say so, Eves?"

Opening her eyes again, Alora causes a black photo lens to flit over my sister's eyes. This brief vulnerability erodes Eva's face. I think it's only a trick when Eva's true, panicked voice cries out, "Frost?"

Alora shuts her eyes. And when she reopens them, they shift to a darker shade of black. "Want to splash me again with that holy water, Frosty?"

I spin to yank Mr. Harris' spell book from his hands. If that's my family's ancestral book with all the sigils and runes, there has to be something in it that can help us.

Luckily, the book slips from Mr. Harris' hands easily, and I flip it open so fast, the power of the book's magic cuts through the room in a breeze.

I'll find the sigils and runes Maggie used to protect our house. Carve them somehow into Eva's skin with a pencil. My knife . . .

Out of nowhere, an unseen force grips my throat and lifts me to my toes. Threatens to lift me higher so I'm suspended in the air and can't breathe.

I reach for my throat, dropping the book to the bare wood ground.

It lands with a loud thump as Mr. Harris dives to retrieve it.

I don't know whether he's going to help me or give it to Alora. I hate that I don't know who's my friend or enemy.

Alora lifts my hand and swiftly swings it out so that my elbow joint pops out of place.

I shriek.

And while Alora's blue-black sisters pop and crackle in applause, I feel like we're all just part of a circus act.

Mom teeters even farther on the edge of the banister, so I throw a Hail Mary. "*Ad quos eieci te ad inferos*." *I banish you to hell*. It's been eons since I've said it. I don't think it will work—Alora's rural Mardi gras witch doctors mumble chants I don't recognize.

Mr. Harris reaches for the cuff of my pants, jerks me back so that my foot connects with the book, and this wave of reassurance and warmth washes over me. It's a wave of wind, but good. . . . Peace. Happiness. Godly.

Alora's sisters explode into poofs of dust; Alora herself shoots from my sister's lips in an incorporeal, charcoal stream.

Mom teeters off the edge of the banister, and *I forgot* she'd fall, so I sprint to catch her, arm throbbing.

Lifting his hands, Mr. Harris slows Mom's progress, and as she hits my one good arm and chest, I hug her so tightly, I don't have time for pain.

Mr. Harris must have known that could happen if I touched a certain page. Thankfully, he has faster reflexes than any old guy I've ever seen.

"Thank you," I say, helping a frazzled Mom to her feet.

"Th-they were going to murder Donna," Mr. Harris apologizes. He pushes his glasses up the bridge of his nose. He wasn't turning on us like Maggie.

I imagine the other things he could explain—how Alora somehow kidnapped Mom. How they found his house and sent him to find me. But the fact is, Alora *has* been banished. For a time.

I look to my sister's crumpled form on the floor, the heavy knot in my throat growing. She's still unconscious. Is that good or bad? "Eva!" I crouch down and try to shake her awake. "Eva!" Here she is, but her body just sags, lifeless. "Wake up, Eves!"

Mr. Harris rests a firm hand on my shoulder. "You must enter her consciousness. She's . . . a little lost, I'm afraid."

Mr. Harris grips my shoulder harder, and in that gesture, I can tell something is really wrong. Something deep.

"She will not wake on her own," he explains. "Alora . . . and others . . . have inflicted a great deal of damage. You *must* go in to retrieve her, but you must hurry."

Tears threaten to pool in my eyes, but I push them back. Stare down at my little sister, who doesn't move, her arms slumped over her face. How is it that she's finally here, free of Alora, but not awake?

Glancing around, I find Mom, who, with her smeared makeup and chaotic hair, looks dazed.

Mr. Harris, surrounded by all his books, waits.

"But should we do this somewhere else? Alora knows where we are. She could come back any second."

Mr. Harris shakes his head, causing his stick-straight hair to flutter. "We do not have the time."

I glance from the spell book to my sister and back to Mr. Harris. I don't know what to do, or even what to say. What if I can't get her? What if whatever we do isn't good enough?

What if she stays trapped in her mind? I can't even imagine what our lives would be like—Raylan and me taking turns spoon-feeding her. Reading lame comics and lyrics from bands we think she liked.

Mom must see the fears bubbling up in my mind, because she wraps her cool arms around me. I yelp from the pain, because Alora just freaking dislocated my shoulder.

"We should get you to a hospital." Mom frowns, her sweet pea lotion the most reassuring scent I've smelled in a very long time.

With my good arm, I reach up and squeeze Mom's soft, strong back. "I'm sure Mr. Harris will patch me up after I get Eves."

Mr. Harris nods, glasses wobbling. "I'll send your mother to my sister's house to keep her safe." His mouth trembles a little as he adds, "But I must warn you. The damage is . . . extensive. Your sister may not be as . . . compliant as you expect her to be."

"When has Eva been compliant a day in her life?" I cry.

Even so, I touch Mr. Harris' soft arm, grateful that he's really on our side. I haven't ever entered my sister's mind before, but I can handle it.

"I can do this," I say.

CHAPTER 40 - EVA

lora, I plead, and if my thoughts could get hoarse, they would be. I'm so sick of begging. It's pathetic. I plop myself down on my imaginary tush. That's not enough relief, so I lay back and stare into the nothing. It's gotten real quiet in here, and it seems Alora doesn't feel the need to even supply me with scenery anymore.

I lay there and contemplate my latest not-so-great state of affairs until Wade's wide eyes appear before my face. Impossible, but true. So, not scenery, but instead we're focused on our greatest hits?

Wade's eyes shine, despite their dull redness, but quickly fade until they're completely empty. My stomach clenches, not unpleasantly.

I sort of killed the guy. My reaction to the memory should be nothing short of pure horror and disgust.

I flop onto my stomach and cradle my face in my arms, fingers clawing in my hair. I miss Raylan's fingers in my hair, gently getting tangled until he tugged just enough that I'd have to fight to keep kissing him. Then I'd feel his lips turn up in a slight smile and he'd release me so I could dive in as deep as I could.

I coil my fingers around clumps of hair and pull until it stings. I relish the pain, but I realize I'll need to do much, much worse to ever feel better for what I've done. I dig into the tender skin on my scalp but feel a different flesh. Startled, I start to pull my hands off my head, but another hand snatches at me . . . it's calloused. Strong. Muscular fingers snatch my palms and hair. The smell of Dawn soap and engine oil makes me twist my head painfully to see my friend.

"Mags?" I cry. "How are you here?"

Her face is red, but it is often. The pressure pulling my hair stops, but my hands are around her throat. She's clawing at my hands, trying to pry even a finger from her neck. Her body twitches beneath me, trying to get any leverage to push me off. Why do I have to be so incredibly strong all of a sudden?

Her face gets redder. Purple. Popping sounds escape her mouth, then a gurgle, like I washed too much hair down her sink. Then her eyes are empty, like Wade's, but so much sadder.

I stare into them, unable to look away. I can't leave her.

"Mags," I groan. I thought she believed in me. Loved me. Was she just giving me a chance, against her better judgment?

Who knows what my real body is doing now? Could I be hurting Mom? Would she even know it's not really me? Or is it?

Does she believe I'm worth saving?

Mags' eyes blink, and her limp head straightens.

I blink back. "But . . ." I sputter and scramble onto my knees.

Her eyes still don't look quite right. Her irises are too small. Too much white. The beady eyes glance into her lap, and I follow her gaze. Rusty, black-handled scissors lay in her lap. She traces her index finger along the rusted edge, and I grimace, imagining the splinters lodging into her skin.

"You shoulda been a better girl," she scolds, looking at me with her now super-creepy eyes.

She grips the blades and twists her wrist, so the handles are pointed at me like in a perfect kindergarten safety video.

"You shoulda been a better girl!" she says, shoving the nasty, giant scissors at me.

"I *seriously* always tried," I say. "What do you want me to do with these?" I should just take the handles, but something tells me that's a really bad idea.

She coughs, and her voice is like she's still being strangled, all garbled like a leaky pipe. "You were always gonna be the death of me."

I watch my hand like it's not my own. I grab the scissors, and not two seconds later, plunge them into her stomach. Her beady eyes watch me without surprise. Blood trickles out of her mouth while a warmth seeps onto my hand. It's covered in my friend's almost black blood, my knuckles still pressed against her gut.

Stunned, I pull the scissors out as fast as I can and go to cover the wound with my other hand, but before the empty hand moves more than a few inches, I'm plunging the scissors in again with my left.

"No," I sob. "Maggie, no." Can I just restart? Die and be reborn and do this whole life over? I've done so much damage. Caused so much pain. I really didn't want to---was forced to---but what does that matter? It still happened.

I pull the blades out again, but I can't drop them. I wrench my right hand to cover the two wounds as best as I can, splaying my fingers wide. My left hand still grips the handles tightly. I put as much pressure on the wounds as I can, but it's useless. Blood is pouring out like a kitchen faucet on full blast.

My left hand plunges the blade through my other hand on Mags' stomach, thrusting so deep, the blades catch on what must be her spine.

"This has to stop!" I bellow as loudly as I can. "Alora!" What if I'm doing this to my mom? "THIS HAS TO STOP!" What have I not tried? I've tried everything. If I could go back in time, what would I do differently? Or was this always destined to happen? But I don't believe in destiny. I believe in choices, and I don't remember ever *choosing* to do any of this crap. In fact, I have fought it every single way I knew how.

Unless deep down, I wanted it this way. I thought I was trying my best, but a fat lot of good that did me.

My box goes black. My hands are suddenly empty. I heave a sigh of relief. But then, blinding light explodes in the room. I close my eyes as fast as I can to protect them, but even before they can close, I catch a glimpse of Mags' limp hand on the ground.

I throw my hands up to my face, digging my palms around my eyes. If I can just block out the light. If I can just block out Maggie. Wade. The people in the swamp. Everyone.

Something is in my hands. I can't cover my eyes anymore —the object is in the way. Squinting hard, I open my eyes slowly so they can adjust to the bright white light. My hands are curiously different. Smaller, smoother. Like I'm younger.

I look down at my body. I'm dressed in my favorite orange, pink, and black floral dress I had when I was ten. In my hands is a dull, golden wire hanger, smooth and cold. I run my fingers along the edge, avoiding the sharp hook.

Mags' hand twitches and her body stirs. She moans like she's waking from a beating.

A mad frenzy takes over me, and I crawl to her, snagging and tearing my white tights on the ground. Dad will be mad.

I scoot as fast as I can to her head. I bend the hanger, changing the triangle into a circle. I slip it over her head. She struggles, the wire digging into her throat. But she said I'm weak. I'll show her I'm strong.

CHAPTER 41 - FROST

Cobwebs eclipse the door where Eva is hiding. Were there cobwebs before? I feel like there weren't any.

I sneak my hands through the tiny threads, casting them aside. Thunder crackles in the distance; lightning cuts a myriad of odd angles into the stone black sky.

The sound of a bouncing ball echoes from somewhere in the dark, somewhere behind me.

Boing. Boing.

It grows heavier, shakier. The octagonal tiles rumble beneath my feet.

Another sound shoots toward me—an eerie, metallic clatter—and my hair floats from static electricity.

When I twist the cool doorknob, an electric shock splinters down my spine. Grabbing it again, I rattle it, praying the door will open.

But it doesn't budge. So I pound on it. "Eva!" I slap my palms on the metal twenty times.

I thought Mr. Harris said he would get me *inside* Eva's mind.

The bouncing ball hits the ground harder. Somewhere in the darkness, it *thwacks* like someone's pounding on a locker until the unmistakable sound of heavy footsteps takes over the noise.

Looking to my boot, I slide my fingers inside. Maybe if I imagine there's a dagger, it will still be there.

A sleek, metal one materializes before my eyes.

Something between an alligator and a dinosaur suddenly growls from right behind me, and as I begin to turn, all I can make out is the faint outline of something ten or so feet tall with a name tag that says Bloodcreek Dollar . . .

It bellows its guttural noise, so I slap the metal door even harder. "Eva, let me in!"

Through the door, childlike footsteps scamper toward me, and a voice I haven't heard in ages pitches, "Frosty?"

It sounds like Eva, but it's her kindergarten voice. Does being in here make her regress like that?

The footsteps come to a halt right behind me.

Warm, wet breath curls up my neck, and I'm just about to reel around and plunge the dagger into its face when the door swings wide open.

I dive inside.

Sharp, icy fingers graze my back as I spin around and kick the door closed, cutting off one of the creature's spindly fingers.

It severs and falls with a pathetic *clink*.

I have absolutely no idea what that was, but when it cries, it's the sound of eagles screeching.

Child-sized Eva curls up into a ball, ducks her head, and covers her ears with her hands. Rocking back and forth, she comforts herself, two beautiful ponytails waggling.

It hurts my heart to see her in this old black, orange, and pink dress, so unprotected and lonely, so I wrap her into the warmest hug I have.

She sinks into my arms, so skinny. Clammy. I'm afraid she's sick. Her smooth forehead's so hot.

When her big, terrified eyes look up at me, my heart teeters to the edge of a cliff. Her lower lip quivers. She's paler than I've ever seen her.

Combing a few of her sweaty strands of hair out of her face, I try to think of the other times she's sweated from fright. Once, her nightmares were so bad, she fell out of the top bunk bed and hit the bedside table with her teeth.

I don't want anything else like that to happen. I keep combing her sweaty hair out of her face, like that's how I'll ensure she'll be okay. "Want to get out of here?" I am careful to keep the fear from my voice.

Little Eva nods, ponytails bouncing. A chainsaw revs in the distance, sounding angry.

The room's as dark as the hallway, and somewhere in the black, a handful of people are crying.

Eva's entire frame shivers, and all I can do is hold her; protect her from whatever's here.

Pressing my hand into the tiled floor to push off, I look for the door, but it's gone. Through the thick, black mist . . . it's missing.

"Where are we, Eves?"

Little Eva shakes her head, far too afraid. She buries her head in my neck, her cheek sticky from sweat. "He's *so* angry."

I don't know who she means until I make out our parents' sage green recliners a little ways off. Dad's black wool slippers rest on the floor, indicating, at any moment, he'll be back.

He isn't here now, though, so I run my fingers down the small of my sister's back. "I'll keep you safe."

Her breath comes out so hot and rushed. "*Not* just Daddy."

The sound of rusty hinges groan; we're hit with too much

air—revolving fans—and in the splotchy, red mist, I absorb what my baby sister's trying to say.

We are not alone.

How many enemies?

When Eva's terrified eyes lock on an object right behind me, I don't even want to see it.

I turn around.

A semi-circle of skinny, super-short, nearly-naked zombies feast on a wad of pink flesh—an arm, child-sized. So much blood shines on their pale, gray faces, and blood dribbles down their necks from their teeth.

I try not to register the croaking, wheezing noises, which sound like Mr. Harris, but deranged.

Somehow, I manage to cover my sister's ears. A little behind us and to our right comes a teen Wade—replete with a belly shirt and stomach with orange stains. He approaches an apparition of a teen Eva and cups her butt. I lift my baby sister and turn her around so she faces away.

In front of us, the blackness dissipates. A strobe light flickers and pops, and I'm just squinting through the darkness when another projection of my sister in her black mini dress comes into view—dancing with Knox.

He's in his debonair suit in the Gunter hotel lobby.

It's just the two of them, dancing as a trumpeter blares and bleats.

The music croons on and on as a figure in a black leather jacket stalks past.

Raylan . . . ?

Please don't let there be something that casts him as the bad guy.

But Raylan's fleeing another scene.

Seagulls flap in the distance. My teen sister's falling to the sand, crashing to her knees, when another body emerges in front of her on the ground.

As if blind, the Eva in front of me, not the one on my lap, reaches out and chokes that person.

That person's in a paisley shirt.

My heart hiccups.

Eva's choking Maggie.

There's this terrible, satisfied smile on my sister's face, and I can imagine what she's feeling. Maggie betrayed her; didn't believe in her, but those hands aren't her hands. How much of this is Alora and how much is Eves?

A pit revolves in my stomach, helicopters too terrified for landing.

Because I know these are the absolute worst moments in Eva's life.

Wade, Dad; Raylan breaking up with her; Knox, Maggie.

Even her nightmares with the zombies. They make a low, wide groan, casting a spell on the dream.

But Eva *didn't* murder Maggie. She couldn't have.

That was Alora.

I wish I could shield childhood Eves.

Other images flash faster in a strobe light.

Knox has my sister chained to a hotel bed.

Knox has her chained to another bed—the guest room at Maggie's.

Knox throws her out the window like she's a rotten piece of produce, and I want to take this from childhood Eva's eyes.

Rubbing her back, I whisper, "I won't let them hurt you, Eves."

She shudders in my arms; she's so small. So broken and tiny.

I wish I didn't have to ask her this, but I press her a little bit. "Why do you think you're locked away like this?"

Dad-Knox slaps a teen Eva on my left.

So sharp.

Again and again, he slaps her repeatedly.

My sister on my lap grows still. She's fixated on the scene.

Dad lifts his hand like he's going to strike teen Eva again, and his eyes go black, just like when Knox inhabited his body.

I can't let little Eva see any more, so I lean in real close to her. "Close your eyes."

With my fingers, I comb the back of her hair.

She whimpers.

"Shh, Eva. Shh."

She sags in my arms.

I trail my fingers down her super soft hair and try to think of the *best* possible way I can help her escape.

It's psychological. Always psychological. So I hold her in my arms and say, "Think of a time when you felt brave."

A shadow of disbelief flickers in her eyes.

I try again. "Think of a time when you felt strong, Eves."

It takes a few seconds, but eventually an echo of a smile flickers across Eva's face. But that's only a hint of the true emotion we're going for. We need her to experience *true* joy.

Other hurried footsteps emerge from the dark mist—it could be any number of creatures or people—but I will not allow her to be distracted. "Think of that time, Eva. Do it for me."

Trusting me—she's trusting me—Eva closes her eyes. Behind her appears a projection of us holding onto a donut-shaped floating tube. We're boating.

It's not when we floated the Comal, but a year or two earlier. A friend from church took us one time. The driver's going maybe thirty miles per hour, and while I'm holding on for dear life, Eva's joking that it's so relaxing, she could take a nap. She leans into the wind, closes her eyes, and gets the biggest smile on her face.

In the memory, I'm leaning back, too. Mimicking her, I learn to enjoy the ride. Even though the bumps and jolts from the boat pulling us don't slow. Even though I'm terrified we'll get thrown. But, for her, I learn to live in the moment.

All at once, the room around us morphs into this purple-ish, motionless shade. Not evil or sinister. Just . . . different. At first, I think we're in Eva's bedroom, but, no, we're . . . on the front deck.

By the porch swing.

Eva's grabbing the chain and choking Knox.

She's showing him *she's* not the one who's chained.

To our left, Eva and Raylan are holding hands and jumping, in just their underwear, into a lake.

Eva!

The entire room echoes with her contagious laughter, and I can *feel* her goodness, her bravery.

When a tall, marble mausoleum like we found at the Metairie Cemetery appears a few feet before us, I watch, horrified, as a teen Eva falls to the ground.

Bubbles curl from her mouth. She's convulsing.

She's surrounded by the masked witch doctors and Dominick.

She's having a seizure as Alora's bluish-black spirit needles into her mind.

Eva tries and tries to push her out, but it's not working.

You are not strong enough, Alora lies.

I don't know whether it's because Eva just learned Leo's responsible for Raylan's parents' death, or if she's as tired as Alora is fresh and awake. But Eva can't stop her intruder.

Even now, I can feel her overwhelming fatigue.

Panting, childhood Eva sags even farther into my lap. "I wasn't strong enough," she whispers. "I was weak."

I kiss her forehead; this *can't* be my little sister's farfetched belief.

She's my big, tall, *beautiful* little sister who freaking led God's army.

Wiping her matted hair back from her face, I shush and tell her the crux of what I know. "You are *much* stronger than you think."

CHAPTER 42 - EVA

ould I be? Really? Doubtful. But I am so happy to see my sister. And to have her talking to me instead of Alora. I sag with relief into her arms but immediately stiffen when I realize she doesn't truly know the terrible things I've done.

She would push me away like a monstrous snake if she knew. Would she have to fight the dilemma that she might have to dispatch me like the other monsters she's faced?

"Frost?" a woman's childlike voice questions from somewhere far away. "Can you do something for her?" The voice drips too sweetly to hold accountability or conviction. Encourage others to do the right thing, but stay out of the spotlight, and you won't get burned.

"Her breathing is calming." Frost's voice is strong. Assertive. And . . . not coming from the Frost currently holding me, trying to protect me from my nightmare. Somewhere else.

My eyes dart around, straining to see the boundaries of my cage. I shove outward with my brain to see if there are any weak spots.

"Lil' firecracker just needed her friend Beauregard, eh?" This voice comes from the same general area of *outside*. Where the heck are we, and why is Alora letting me hear but not see?

"Back off, Beau, it's not you," Frost snaps. Dude, is Beau here? So, Frost, Beau, and . . .

"*Mom?*" I cry with my own voice. I sit up, sweaty and half-crazed, like I'm waking from a fever dream. "I'm *me?!*"

I scan the room, an absolutely stunning, multi-floored library, and I spy my mother's wispy blonde hair and brow creased with way too many worry lines. "And you're not dead?"

I scramble to get up, yearning to throw my arms around her. But then I remember the last time I had control over my faculties. *Mags.*

"Quick, tie me up or drill me," I say to Frost. I shoot her with the sharpest laser beam eyes ever so she'll listen. "Whatever you need to do so Alora can't control me again."

Instead of springing into action, though, Frost's intense eyes soften. "Eva, she *can't* control you. Oh my gosh, not ever, ever again! Eva, I have *so* much to tell you!" What's she talking about? All I know is she can't know how bad I really am.

"Beau!" I call, even more desperate. He'll do what needs to be done. But his ever-present goofy grin just lazily rolls over his face. "It's a trap."

"Eva," Frost soothes, placing her pretty, freckled hand on my forearm. "Alora's gone."

"For now," Mr. Harris croaks.

"Her sisters are fightin' like the dickens to get her back, though," Beau says, cringing. "Glad I found y'all. It's been one de-ram-atic day."

"What?" I say, in no way believing we've gotten to this

point. "No, Alora just had me locked away. She made me—she made me ki—" I choke down the word.

"Mr. Harris and I did a spell," Frost says. "She'll definitely try to come back, but she's gone for now. It's just you in there."

I look at her like I'm penniless and she's the best warm, gooey brownie in the shop. But Mr. Harris, Beau, and Mom's calm demeanors all seem to confirm it's true. "She's out?" I ask.

Frost's head dips a fraction of an inch in the beginnings of a nod. It's all I need to believe. I throw my arms around her and tackle her to the floor.

"Baaah!" she giggles as she falls. But her giggle falls short at the end, and I know something's wrong. My stomach drops.

Do they know?

They're not looking at me with daggers for eyes. I give Frost's shoulders a tight squeeze and struggle to my feet. My body feels like it's had a few real rough miles, and my favorite Depeche Mode shirt has more than five layers of crust on it. Frost leaps to her feet like a gazelle while clutching her arm.

"What's going on?" I ask. Then I remember that Mags is the one who introduced me to Depeche Mode, and I get a weird tight feeling just under my collarbone.

"Just maybe the end of the world," Beau drawls.

"Well, perhaps not." Mr. Harris shuffles over to a desk brimming with a mountain of books in all sorts of disarray.

I still can't get over that this beige cardigan of a man is a powerful warlock.

Do they know about Mags? Is that why Raylan isn't here? Or Leo? They're going to regret wasting precious time trying to save me.

"Y'all," I mutter, trying to gather the courage to say it. They absolutely cannot go any longer not knowing. "Mags is

—" My voice refuses to work, and a primal groan of excruciating pain wrenches from my lungs.

Frost scoops me up in one arm, and Mom rushes over and hugs us both.

"We know, Eves," Frost says, trying to soothe me through her own tears.

"I am *so, so* sorry," I sob.

Frost pulls back from me, causing Mom to do the same, and for a second, I think Frost's going to bring her full wrath down on me.

Instead, she puts her hand on my shoulder and gives me a little shake. "Look at me," she scolds.

I try, but I can't keep looking in her eyes. She doesn't understand how terrible I really am. She wouldn't allow herself to believe—a quality that comes in handy for Leo, but he deserves it, not me.

"It wasn't you," she says bluntly, but do I sense a lack of conviction?

"Ladies," Mr. Harris coughs. "It is a tragedy, yes, but time is of the essence."

He's right, so I give Frost a little nod and my mom a tiny smile to let them think I believe. Time to hand out my sentence later.

"What's the plan?" I ask for the second time today, grateful this time I get to fight for the good team.

Regardless of the circumstances, my chest swells with love for these people. They've fought and risked so much. They deserve a world free from evil. And after seeing so much of that evil, to be in the presence of goodness again makes me want to crumble to dust. So, while I know I'm not worthy of them, I will fight like a dragon so they will *never* have to become like me.

CHAPTER 43 - FROST

Mr. Harris' wingnut wind chimes clink as we head out, marching through his woods like infantry. Good thing he already healed my arm just now. I love having a warlock as an ally.

My nose twitches at a funny scent. Is that smoke? Something's burning.

My phone rings with "Goin' to the chapel," a ringtone Eva put on my phone way before we went to New Orleans.

Our eyes lock.

Raylan's calling?

All of this feels so weird, yet so normal. *I have my sister back!* My hands, my heart—everything's giddy. With shaking hands, I accept the call and, glancing at Eva, put it on speakerphone so she can hear Raylan's manly voice.

"Raylan?" I say.

I sort of expect Eva to jump in and start talking, but she looks a little pale and starts tying knots in her hair, double time. Everything's still so raw for her; maybe I shouldn't have put him on speakerphone.

"Frost," Raylan's no-nonsense voice says. "I'm sorry to tell you this, but Alora found the tree."

Beau, Mr. Harris, Mom, and Eva stop walking.

A squirrel freezes midway up a tree like it, too, knows something terrible is happening.

"We'll be right over," I say, and nearly hang up before I spot the four knots my sister's tied in her hair. I want to whoop and yell to Raylan that *finally,* we've got Eva back—victory!—but I drop my voice to a low whisper. "We got her."

"Hm?" Raylan sounds equal parts hopeful and out of breath. A few thwaps echo in the background, confirming he's fighting somebody on the front lines.

"Eva," I explain.

I let that sink in before Raylan yells, "EVA, GET YOUR BUTT DOWN HERE. I LOVE YOU, BABE!"

I hold my phone out to my sister, but she just smiles this lost, goofy smile, and I can tell she's not up to talking.

"She can't wait to see you," I reassure Raylan.

Thwap, thwap; scrrrape, supernatural scream. "OOH, BABY, NEITHER CAN I!"

I smile, knowing the last thing I need is to distract Raylan from finishing off whatever that was, so I end the call and let out a shaky breath.

I catch Eva's eye. "You okay?"

Both of us know she's not; she still has a lot more ground to cover, but she nods. She's doing her best at the moment to be okay. Knowing Mr. Harris is waiting to lead us out of here, I look in his direction.

"Can we ride with you?"

Like a bad omen, a venue of vultures soars through the sky.

Without even a hint of hesitation, Mr. Harris hands me a mess of rusty old keys. "You drive."

I don't know what I expected, but it definitely wasn't apocalyptic Bloodcreek.

Everything smells of sulfur. Smoke and ash coat everything.

Eva says Alora's army was burning down the town to find the tree. I can't believe how fast they got it all. I'm glad Mom doesn't have to see all this, since Mr. Harris' sister's house was just down the road from his place. But even our school, which has never received *any* positive feelings from me, has fallen into a charred, sunken structure that will cost the town millions to revive.

Miss B's Anteeks, Hair Cuts 4 U . . . everything looks like it's been through a bombing, and *Lindy's* . . . er, Beau's *Sasquatch n' Koi* . . .

Beau gasps as we drive by.

The entire business is covered in ash, except for his "Mosey on In" sign. Honestly, I didn't know fire could consume a town so quickly. That nasty rotten egg smell makes me feel like I'll never smell anything clean again.

Beau whips his car door open, I'm sure to find his siblings, even though we're going like forty miles per hour. Mr. Harris telekinetically slams the door shut before Beau can hop outside.

Mr. Harris also uses his witchery powers to cause my foot to press down harder on the accelerator. Always underestimated this guy.

"Leonardo already whisked your brothers and sisters to safety," Mr. Harris explains curtly to Beau.

Eva gazes out the window, looking as lost as the mother of all PTSD.

Her eyes see through Bloodcreek's newest tractor supply

and Brookshire's . . . though there's no telling what's going on in her mind.

Beau's hand trembles on the door handle, even when the park's like half a mile away. To him, the safety of his siblings is more important than anything.

"Leonardo brought your siblings to the safety of the wading pool," Mr. Harris says. "And we relocated that pool to a safer place."

Beau's chest inflates, then deflates as he processes what Mr. Harris is saying. He pulls *The Girl Who Could Fly* out of his back pocket and nervously bends the entire book's pages. "Yer sure they're okay?"

"I understand you are worried, Bogard, but I need you to listen to me."

That's unlike Mr. Harris to mispronounce Beau's name. But Beau doesn't correct him, either. Am I missing something?

On top of everything else, Mr. Harris seems to read my thoughts. "Yes, Bogard is his proper name, but that takes us back to another time."

I click the turn signal to turn right, then turn it off when I realize there aren't any cars on the road—in front *or* behind us. By the time I round the turn, Mr. Harris eases my foot down even further so that we're going seventy.

Eighty.

It's easier to stomach a burned-up town when you're going faster, maybe.

"What happened to all the people?" I ask as Mr. Harris flips through one of his tomes from his seat next to me.

"I had my people move them." He pushes his glasses up the bridge of his nose. "They are safe."

So that means Bloodcreek is only full of hunters . . . and Alora's army.

Good, I'm glad. There's no need for innocent people to die.

Looking at my sister in the rearview mirror, though, all I find is her stoic, emotionless face. What did she have to endure in there? Oh, what I would give to see her brightness and joy.

Mr. Harris does this nasally thing when he clears his throat, but not even a tinge of amusement flares over Eva's eyes. "Ah, there it is." He animatedly taps the page. "Bogard, would you read this passage for us, please?"

Mr. Harris turns around to hand Beau the weighty tome.

Beau puts on his adorable scholarly voice. "And the sires shall return home an' make right that which shall be made right . . ." Beau pauses. "That all, Mr. H?"

Mr. Harris nods before taking his book back and looking straight ahead. "Do you know what that means?"

I veer around a charred dead possum in the road—uh, no, that would be a charred gremlin. The arms are sticking up, almost like whoever burnt it displayed it that way.

Slowly and deliberately, Mr. Harris says, "Throughout the years, your mother, the Whore of Babylon, leeched your power, did she not? When she tucked your brothers and sisters and you into your respective boxes, she used dark magic to siphon your power."

"Well, yeah . . ." Beau scratches the back of his head sophisticatedly.

"When doing so, she created all the fantastical creatures we have today. The witches, the vampires, the chupacabras, everything—making you and your siblings the lowest creatures on the theoretical totem pole."

Beau lowers his paperback to his lap. "Hey!"

"And then," Mr. Harris continues, "your mother died. Since her power had become so ingrained and interconnected with you, the power she'd been leeching slipped right out of you and your siblings—like a slippery wick in a melted candle."

In the rearview mirror, I can see Beau glancing, dumbfounded and aghast, at Eva. He's moving his lips, silently sorting through all the new information before his eyes go wide. "*That's* why I don' have my power anymore!"

"However." Mr. Harris taps the book with authority. "Your mother only stole *one* part of who you've come to be. Whilst you lost your power, somehow you still retained your life force. Since the creatures your mother created were connected to *you* and *your* siblings' life forces, they're still alive."

Beau's voice rises a full three notches as this thought clicks into place. "So, I need to die . . ."

Mr. Harris stares straight ahead, which frightens me more than if he said we needed to do some elaborate spell with the hair of a unicorn and phoenix wings.

A burning windmill revolves and revolves in the wind, and I can practically *feel* Beau watching it when he says, "To save the world, me n' my brothers and sisters need to die."

Mr. Harris pulls off his coke bottle glasses and polishes them on his shirt. "I wouldn't say 'save,' since the Blurred Ones are still very much at large, but you could make a difference, yes. If you chose to do your part to protect humanity."

Tires screeching, I pull up to the parking lot and throw the car in park. "*Nobody's* dying." Last thing we need is to lose the actual allies we have. Beau and his siblings are good and innocent. No way am I letting them sacrifice themselves so easily.

Out of nowhere, a body flies and lands on the windshield, splintering a nasty web of cracks about four feet long.

Vile, pointy teeth snap at us, and with the bloodshot eyes

and blood dripping down her chin, the vampire seems to be saying, "Hey."

She's pretty gross, so I offer a compromise. "Except her. You can kill her." I snatch my daggers from my boots. "And anybody else who threatens my friends, this town, *or* my family."

CHAPTER 44 - EVA

"Mine!" I holler to all the car's occupants, jumping out as Frost unlocks the doors. My anger feels slightly more righteous than it did just hours ago, and I aim to make somethin' bleed.

The vampire hops to her feet, agile for just getting chucked into a windshield. Her face drips with the blood of some poor, unknown hunter, but I spy my dear friend Leo, not too far off, with his hands outstretched. Doing all kinds of damage to his own kind, no doubt. He beams when he sees me, but I don't know why. He saw how weak I am. Not to be a downer, I wink at him while I grab the machete I'm borrowing from Mr. H.

"Hello, darlin'," I say to the vampire with long, braided, red hair. "You mad 'cause you used to be pretty?"

She growls and lunges at me, all nails and teeth. I twist and take a half step away from the car, letting her sail into the door Mr. Harris just opened. I'm a little slower than I'd like, now that I'm without my ancient demon power source and all, but my anger does right by me.

I spin a full circle, and right before the ginger tries to

crawl over the door to attack our favorite librarian, I lob her head off. Her head flies over the car, braid and all, where Beau catches it with a grin.

"Aw, Evalou," he says, spinning the head by the braid. "You shouldn't have." I grunt a laugh, check that Frost is good to fight, and take off looking for more creatures to kill and a certain man I'd like to maul. Romantically. Whether that's right or wrong, or if he'll even have me, we'll determine later.

"Raylan's by the gazebo," Leo calls.

Always got my back, that one. I jog toward where I know the gazebo once was, but all I see is chaos. Charred trees, fallen bodies, a car on fire, and trampled vegetation.

I slide my machete back into its ring on my belt and snag both my guns. Two matching Beretta M9s that were Mags' daddy's back in the day.

You know, I'd be lying if I said that at this point in things, I wasn't feeling a little unhinged, but I pretend I'm listening to some kind of gorgeous classical waltz and dance through the field, shooting a banshee here, a currently shifting shapeshifter there. Half cat, half bird. Fancy. Overall, I'm just trying to stay alive and keep my loved ones the same. And get to Raylan.

A little bit of gore splashes on me from a slimy slug thing I dispatch, but add it to the filth that is me. Within a now-pillarless gazebo, I spy a handsome guy with dusty blond hair atop a mound of bodies. My heart pulses with joy, like he is my oasis in the desert.

I drop my empty clips and slide in two new ones, half skipping the rest of the way to my man.

A giant—a real giant—steps between Raylan and me, his head the size of an extra-large pizza. He's as tall as this here gazebo used to be. I cock both my guns and aim for his forehead.

Half a moment after I pull the triggers, the giant's head

explodes, sending his carnage in every direction. I don't reckon my two bullets were enough to do that, but the giant falls to the ground, and I see Raylan's .45 is aimed right where the giant's head used to be, too. He shot him at the same time. Now that is true love.

I holster my weapons and clamber over the giant's body. There are still plenty of monsters around trying to do us harm, so I throw my arms around Raylan while he shoots them down. I don't honestly know how he'll react to me, but he did just say he loves me, so I kiss him good and hard.

He fires another couple of shots, his muscular arms absorbing the shock from the guns with ease, and he's steady as the Rock of Gibraltar as he kisses me right back.

CHAPTER 45 - FROST

It's so good to see Eva fight, her dark hair rippling chaotically behind her as her face fills with light. Her eyes are a little wild, but that's to be expected after dealing with Alora. It's *so* rewarding to watch her and Raylan shoot up a trio of slug things on a rather gruesome pile of bodies.

Eva screams this war cry once all that's taken care of, and maybe I should have brought the *Braveheart* soundtrack and blue face paint. This is my sister—she's smiling and snarling at anything that would threaten Mom or me.

Even that half-starved zombie missing half its face.

The confidence with which she moves, the comfortable set to her shoulders tells me the battlefield is her home. It's an *exact*—or at least, very near—replica of when she was the General of the East.

When she catches me staring, Eva winks, and I give her the biggest smile I can. I can't wait to tell her about what Leo showed me in The Before. I'll show her how she convinced souls to come to earth. We'll wash away all that nonsense from Dad and Maggie.

A pair of gremlins scramble up my back, their slippery hands and enormous, bat-like ears making me secretly thankful Beau wasn't one of these, 'cause they smell like B.O. and raw meat.

As one nibbles on my ear, saliva dripping like fresh syrup down my face, I try to knock it off. It clings on like a leech.

I swat harder while the hunter with the Duck Dynasty beard holds the line. He's working with the hunter sporting Mount Everest hair. They contend with a bunch of wily humans with pitchforks and knives, and, uh, I recognize one of them—Bic, the neo-Nazi, loyal friend of Wade's. Those two personally supplied all the beer on our Comal River float trip, and Bic's wearing enough camo to outfit the entire army.

Bic ducks between Duck Dynasty's legs and, of all things, scrambles toward the giant crater by Uri. Guess Bic's one of the guys who actually wants to become a monster by eating the fruit of the tree.

Spotting Bic, with his combat boots and pale face, Uri seamlessly seizes him by the scruff of his shirt and throws him across the field, like he did to Beau when we were in the cave.

Bic slams into the torn apart car in the middle of the field that the hunters brought in to create higher fighting vantage points. The new hunter with all the neck tattoos scrambles down, rope in hand, and begins tying up Bic before he can do anything else stupid.

All of this happens in like fifteen seconds. Beau waves Uri's sword to fend off anyone approaching the other side of the hole to the tree, and I've got to say, my hunters are making me proud. Not to mention all the devil's traps, booby-traps, and the holding cell someone's made out of the park's old office building.

One of the gremlins sinks his nasty fangs into my gut.

Bleh! I stab him in the neck before he can go for one of

my kidneys. Everything's coming full circle, with me fighting with knives in The Before *and* now. I'm just missing the more ruined earth and purple sky. Random, supposedly unreal creatures are still trying to destroy humanity. But the rest of us? We believe in the good. We *can* win this fight.

As another long-eared gremlin scrambles to slip past me, I tug a vial of holy water out of my back pocket and douse the sucker. Aha! Look at that. Skin sizzles like bacon grease.

A tall, handsome hunter with short-cropped hair and olive-toned skin skips between the squirming gremlin and me. "Ms. Frost?" He holds out his hand for me to shake. "I don't believe we've met. My name's Christian Bordelon."

A C-4 mine shakes the entire field as someone—a human or a monster—screams. I don't see any triquetras on this guy's body, so I give "Christian" a swift nod. Just to be safe, I'd rather not shake.

Christian drops his hand, seemingly unoffended. "Ms. Alora sent me here to request your company."

A shoe—attached to a partial leg—flies straight at me, so I duck. And I give Christian a once-over. "You can tell your 'Ms. Alora' I'm busy."

The newly blown-up vampires hobble toward the crater—guess they also think they need the fruit of the tree—and they're holding a scared woman about Mom's age with thinning hair. The lady looks so terrified, so green, all I can see is Mom being forced to eat that fruit, so I dislocate both the vamps' heads with my knives. Their heads, with yellowing fangs, thump to the ground. I guess they thought teeth brushing was optional.

The lady flails, hair streaking as she runs in the other direction, and I'm just glad she'll be okay.

Christian holds up his hands as if he's only come to extend a peace offering. "I'm sorry, miss, but Ms. Alora *really* wants to be obeyed." He shoots me this charming, almost apologetic smile.

Who is this guy?

A hulking, dog-like creature trots up to us, and I'm so thrown by his lithe movements that I forget to react in any way. It's walking on its hind legs, and between its elongated claws, reptilian skin, and glowing eyes, I *know what it is*.

A chupacabra.

A chupacabra! They're supposed to be extinct.

The freaky, stunning anomaly raises its fist. I'm in such awe of its self-healing skin and the quills on its back that are said to be instantly deadly that I forget to move as it slugs me in the face, sending me to the ground.

"*Sororibus*," the chupacabra purrs, sounding like Alora or one of her sisters, all throaty. I do believe 'sororibus' is Latin for 'sisters.' The Depairity used to say it when Eva and I were little and would ride on our swings.

Christian shoots the creature an unhappy look. "Hey, I thought we said we wouldn't hurt her!"

The creature growls with pleasure, digging its sharp, calloused toes into my windpipe. Her voice bounces in her throat, sounding like she's grinding nails. "I fail to see the reason why she's caught the attention of Leo, Who Gleans."

"Hey, come on, now!" Christian tugs on the chupacabra's elbow. "Ms. Alora won't like it if we don't bring her back in one piece!"

The chupacabra smiles, revealing a slew of maggots under her skin and lip above her teeth. "I suppose there is comfort to be had, knowing there are only two sisters when we Despairity have three."

Alora's sister inside the chupacabra waits and waits until the last bits of breath leave my windpipe before she releases the pressure on my neck. Toe by toe, she lifts her foot, clearly enjoying her ability to inflict the most amount of pain.

Another mound of C-4 goes off as I gasp for breath.

The explosion masks my scream.

The church is a grave.

Between the missing shingles and vines choking the narrow, rectangle steeple, it's a wonder the building hasn't been torn down already. Mildew drips in heavy ropes from the wooden, chipped frame, and most of the pointed, stained glass windows have been knocked out by looters, or possibly the rain.

So, this is Alora's trump card. Her showdown now that Eva's free. Why isn't she down in the field, fighting her way to get to the tree?

The chupacabra's possessed by one of Alora's sisters, obviously, and, unfortunately for me, carrying me. Christian's eyes occasionally flit to black, bugs scuttling beneath his skin. So, if I were to guess, I'd say he's got the third prong of the Despairity team.

Almost makes me nostalgic for their water-heater-mimicking *buhhhr-tung* days.

But something about Christian's unsure gait and this sister's relationship with him tells me they're not quite as sadistic as the other two Despairity. Maybe I could find something to leverage to make Christian and his Despairity an ally.

Mostly, I'm glad I still have my vial of holy water, drill, and knives. It's weird that Christian and the chupacabra didn't pat me down. Maybe Alora told them to leave me armed. Maybe she's getting cocky. Even though I still don't have a way to kill Alora permanently—now that Zombi's dead —I can still slow her and her soldiers down with my silver, holy water, and drill.

With the tombstones pitching at odd angles and tree branches scratching at the sky, I have to say, *of course*, this is where Alora wants to meet. It almost reminds me of the Metairie Cemetery, with its massive mausoleums and crypts, so big and beautiful, you don't know whether to gasp in astonishment or cry. It also reminds me of my home growing up—Dad's moods were so black, he practically rolled out the red carpet for the Despairity.

Now?

All of this ends today.

For now, the chupacabra's pinning me in her arms, threatening to poison me with one of the quills on her spine, though Christian does keep glancing at her, as if saying, *Is that really necessary?*

The chupacabra skulks up the rickety steps of the church before pulling the heavy door open wide. Prayer candles greet us on a tiny table at the door, and it's so strange to lie in this creature's arms as it moves with this eerie grace. Maybe I could offer to do science experiments on her self-healing skin? Promise to make her an "I'm Not An Extinct Species" sign? If I could just reach my daggers . . .

Clutching me to her scaly chest, she glides across the floor, her feet lightly sticking to the tile. *Ka-cheem, ka-cheem.* Her claws scratch against the hard surface, and as her short tail grazes a statue of Jesus's mother, Mary, it seems the creature's glowing eyes aren't all that great at working in the somber light. The little slits in her nose flare—almost like a cat's. Observing. Searching.

Christian's footfalls echo the chupacabra's from just behind as we enter the chapel of pews, and I spot a lone boy with suspenders dangling over his pants.

His broad back faces me.

Leo?

Why isn't he turning around to look at me?

Statuesque figures lightly perch on the pews on my left and right. I look closer and would definitely say that Alora's got her ace of spades.

The figures aren't just people—they're covered in pale, white sheets; they don't flex or move a muscle. They're either dead, or they've been spelled not to move a muscle.

That dark feeling I mentioned we always had in our house while growing up? It settles over the pews. Churns in my stomach. Makes me feel like insects are devouring the insides of my body.

Behind Leo hangs a replica of Michelangelo's *The Creation of Adam,* one of my favorite paintings. Leo knows this—it shows God holding, under his arm, a premortal Eve. Her eyes are fixed on Adam, almost like she's thinking, *Be patient. Wait for me.*

I know it makes me crazy, but it always reminds me of Leo and me.

Leo . . . ? Mentally, I try to reach him, but he's as still as the pew people. Something's wrong. Maybe I need to do what I did to Eva and get him back by entering his mind.

But a translucent figure with black, slicked-back hair sidles up to Leo with her quiet, melancholy grace. Taking in her tall, confident stature and black, soulless eyes, I end up gulping. Alora's decided to return to her premortal form— down to her armor's thick Kevlar spikes.

All she needs is a bow and an arrow to shoot me dead for real this time.

I push back any twinges of inferiority, choosing to focus on the fact that she still smells like sulfur, which is like a fart, actually.

Leo . . . look at me!

As the wind shrills through a nearby stained glass window, I recognize the cool, spark-laden air from the Metairie Cemetery. It's the type of spell cast by a witch doctor. Alora's gotten someone to spell the church. Maybe even two or three witch doctors.

Beside Leo, in a small wicker basket on the podium, rests a collection of round, white fruit I never hoped to see outside the cave.

The fruit.

How has Alora already sent somebody down to get it?

Something rattles at the back of the chapel, and I turn to see Christian opening his mouth. Black smoke twists and curls from his teeth.

The Despairity that was in him becomes a thick, black scarf, whipping up to the mold-ridden, decorative ceiling.

The chupacabra flinches like it's being electrocuted as it does the same. Tar-like smoke barrels from its mouth in sharp rivulets. Feels dirty.

I'm able to slink to the floor as the newly vacated chupacabra grabs the edge of a pew like it's trying to stay awake. Luckily, it leaves me alone. Actually, it's as still and silent as the people on the pews.

Maybe the witch doctors are spelling everybody to be half awake.

Christian grabs one of the sconces on the wall, clearly fighting to be in charge of his own body as the newly freed Despairity float up, up, up to the cobwebbed ceiling. They circle round a terrifying statue with magnificent amber-colored wings like Uriel's, only darker. The being itself is black, unclothed, and possesses a gaunt, sunken-eyed face. Lucifer? A representation of him, anyway.

The Despairity whir about him like demented, drunken bees; they flit to Alora, their queen.

A new wave of sulfur wafts through the chapel like newly fallen pollen, and it's a good thing Leo's more of a *COCO by Chanel* guy.

Training her black eyes on her sisters, Alora reaches out

and rests her hand on Leo's shoulder. "I am *so* glad you decided to join us, Frosty."

So she wants me to watch her eat the fruit, along with all her new pals. If I were to guess, I'd say there are just enough pieces in that basket to feed everybody.

I clamp my jaw as I nod at the Lucifer statue, searching for any and all strategies. "Too bad your master's so short-sighted, he forgot to put on his undies."

Alora traipses her grubby fingers from Leo's arms to the massive statue to pet "Our Brother's" marble frame. She caresses the smooth small of his back, his stomach, his chest —all the way up, up, up to the tear-dropped edge of one of his eyes. "What you fail to know is, I am doing what *Our Brother* requested of me."

"What, throwing sheets over people? Your nobility is astonishing."

Alora's eyes flash, obsidian rocks newly washed clean by a lake. "*You* know nothing of nobility!"

"Oh, right." I do my best to ignore my pounding heart, which is fluttering like a bird in a cage. "Your idea of greatness is sucking up people's happiness and being Albert Knox's little B."

Think she'd wait while I text Eves?

Alora purposely ignores me, extending her greasy fingers along Lucifer's twelve-foot-long wings. She feels each and every crevice before dropping to his stomach and caressing it *way* too intimately.

Casually, she turns and runs her fingers along Leo's chest.

Leo . . . *LEO! Please, turn around and look at me!*

"Perhaps your naiveté is what Leonardo here finds so appealing." Alora raises her grubby paw to run alongside Leo's face. "While you and your sister have been shooting up vampires and gremlins I couldn't care less about, I have been here, securing everything I need."

One of her sister's auras pulses hungrily as the other floats to the back of the chapel as if securing the perimeter of the property.

Taking Leo by the shoulders, Alora shoots me a dark smile before turning him around to look at me.

His eyes are sewn shut with thick, black thread, the kind you use for stitches, and the fat head of a rusty screw secures his upper lip in place.

They've taken away his powers and stitched his eyes. He's like one of the voodoo dolls from New Orleans.

I'm sure Dom was more than happy to spell Leo this way.

Leo, can you hear me?

As I take a step toward the love of my life, Alora gives a flick to her hand, and my ankle twists.

I grab hold of one of the pews to prevent myself from falling, but, aah! *Hurts*. I bite back a cry.

"What you do not understand is," Alora explains, "I have invited you all here to view Leonardo's and my wedding."

My heart twists and catapults from my chest; sprints double time.

I'll find a way to get Leo out of the spell.

Fight the chupacabra.

Take down Alora *and* the other Despairity.

I don't know how, but Eva and Raylan *will* figure out where I am. Beau will bring his lasso, and Mr. Harris will do his fancy bubble-shield warlock thing. Maggie won't come, 'cause we no longer talk about Maggie, and Mom will be so grateful when all this is done and finished that she'll take us to CiCi's to celebrate.

I try to move toward Leo, but it's like moving through a mattress. Alora's holding me back.

Meanwhile, Christian paces behind me; he seems so uncomfortable with everything. *Tell me* this is driving him crazy. But the other Despairity? It floats over the crowd to suck away someone's essence from the pew, making this awful lapping, guzzling noise.

"*Manere*," Alora hisses from the front of the church. "Wait!"

Behind me, the feeding Despairity crackles and hisses before launching itself right at Alora's face.

Alora's eyes flash to silver, and the retaliating sister crackles a little more before slumping back to the chupacabra and resettling into the creature's dormant body.

Leo. I refuse to be distracted too long by the sisters spatting. *Can you hear me?*

Not even a hint of a muscle twinges beneath those marble cheeks. I get this weird impression of an Edward Scissorhands who's forced to live a completely solitary life.

An unearthly smile transforms Alora's way too happy face. "*Et pugnate!*" She raises her arms to speak with authority.

The chapel walls rumble as *The Creation of Adam* waffles from its hook and crashes to the ground, glass shattering.

The sheeted people rise.

Benches groan, and I think, *Leo, Leo*—look *at me!* I mentally try to prop open his mind, but the thick, black cloud cloaking his cerebral cortex is as wet and smooth as solid granite coated with grease.

And the people on the pews . . . their sheets are similar to the masks Our Brother's soldiers wore in The Before. They stand there, immune to wrong or right. They're unable to hear the truth—that by eating the fruit, they'll become monsters that shouldn't even be alive.

"Our witnesses." Alora holds out her hand like she's an ancient queen. "And do not fear, for Leonardo will accept our union, eventually."

If I could shove the wench in a devil's trap, I'd do it this very second. But I'm so unprepared. I didn't think she'd come at us from so far away from the tree. I didn't even think she'd make this so personal—attempt to enact what I've always wanted: the perfect, simple church wedding.

I look around for Christian, but before I can find him, Alora lifts her chin and takes two dominant steps toward me.

"It is time for you to accept what we are. *I* shall have Leonardo, and, together, we shall reign."

Her breath is like bile.

A disgusting siren's call I *hope* Leo isn't buying.

If I had a bow and arrow like she had in The Before, I'd shoot that smug expression right off her face.

"He'll never have you." I pry apart my gritted teeth.

"Oh, he's already had me many times," she slurs.

Is this the moment where I give up? Where I accept the fear and loss and bloody well admit that they are what they are, and she will always be stronger, more persuasive, and better than me?

She's going to laugh, she's going to call me weak, but I square my shoulders and look her straight in the face. "What you don't know is, Leo and I have dreams. We're going to travel the world. Go to college. Raise a family."

Alora scoffs so hard that I almost feel embarrassed for admitting the truth out loud. But she's not going to take what I believe is possible. Leo and I could live *good* lives. We could raise good children. He has atoned for his sins. Ever since joining Raylan as a hunter, he has endeavored to fight for the right side.

Alora's black hole smile widens; her eyes flicker. She's a plugged-in toaster, connected to a lake. "You remind me of why I wanted to possess your vessel in the first place. Obtaining Leonardo while residing in *your* body? Mmm. But" —her eyes flit to a darker black— "you cannot be claimed."

Lowering her head, she reeks of the devil as she locks her gaze on mine. "So, I shall make you suffer. And for that, *child*, you absolutely cannot blame me."

Running her fingers over Leo's chest, his head, his neck, it's like she's remembering their touches of another time. "I do think there is a great pleasure to be had from forcing you to watch as I take what is mine."

My stomach squeezes, but I refuse to back down or look away.

Her smoky fingers grope his collarbone as she purrs, "What is even more delicious is that you, a girl who prides herself on being so smart and wise, never once foresaw what I planned the entire time."

Tethering my attention, she gazes at the platter of fruit and the people once again. "*Real* power comes from becoming an original sire, *Frosty*. As I am sure you are aware, Beauregard has never tapped into who he could be." She strolls to the basket on the podium. "Once any human partakes of the fruit, they become a creature, yes, but they also have the ability to siphon as much power as they like."

That's what Mr. Harris had been saying about Lindy.

"Like the Great Whore of Babylon, I am doing what any Blurred One should have been doing all along: I am building a sire army. And, as siphons, we shall be virtually limitless in our power, possessing sire bodies."

The cold, hard truth of what she's planned washes over me. I can't stop all this. I thought I simply needed to prove my grit, but there's too many of them, and siphons? Sires? Where's Eva and Raylan? I need my team!

"Leonardo," she purrs. "It is time."

Reaching up, Alora pulls her thin, black veil over her stony face.

Despite all that's wrong, including the fact that I'm still ninety-seven percent sure I am a terrible person who deserves to die, this feels right. This is what I've been training for. Killing baddies. We're killing a lot of baddies.

Raylan and I are as in sync as if we'd choreographed and rehearsed. Back to back, we clean up a mess of unruly banshees, dart blowin' witch doctors, and more creatures I don't know the names of quite yet. If it's aiming to get to the tree, it dies.

"How are you on ammo?" Raylan calls between blasts, his dark green shirt covered in chunks of slime.

"Mmm, I'll probably need to resort to my wicked bare hands pretty soon," I say as I kick a two-legged somethin' er other in the ribs. The ribs crack, and the creature screams in pain. I swing the handle of my gun down on its head, and the creature quiets. "At least there's no buzz saw."

"Buzz saw?" Raylan asks with an adorable quirk of an eyebrow.

A powerful roar like a freight train vibrates across the

field, and I swivel to see who's making the sound. I've seen a lot of weird things today, but this one takes the crazy cake. Frost had warned me, but . . . massive wings, whiter than if they were made out of a bunch of fluorescent light bulbs, stretching as wide as a school bus, spread from a mammoth of a man in a flowing, white robe.

"Makes you feel like you're on the right side, right?" Raylan says, his face resolute. I feel a twist in my gut, like I'm an imposter, but remind myself I'm just here to help the good guys win.

The seraph, Uriel, fights with the speed and strength of ten of us humans. He bends, dodges, throws, and punches like a gorilla ninja. Yep, that's about right. But a hulking Blurred One twists a spear in Uriel's shoulder, making a splotch of scarlet appears.

"Let's give the angel a hand," I say to Raylan and sprint toward the brawling being. Won't hurt to catch a glimpse of that tree, either.

"I am no angel," Uriel shouts, punching the enormous Blurred One forty feet into the air, where it gets snagged in one of the few remaining electricity lines.

The bugs under his skin dance as he sizzles like a hot dog.

"My bad." I grin at the heavenly dude. "Don't have my celestial terminology down quite yet." I unload my four last bullets into a one-eyed ogre that's inchin' too close to the enormous crack in the ground. "I'm guessing the tree's down there?"

"Don't ask him about it," Raylan says, dodging a knife thrown by a witch doctor. He grabs the doctor's arm and twists it back until the knife plunges into his own chest. "Makes him mad." Raylan laces his fingers together, like a step for me, and nods. "Let's help the guy out."

So chivalrous, that one. I run for a head start, then use his hands as a stepping stool and leap onto Uriel's back. I hold tight to his tree trunk of a neck with one hand and pull the spear out with the other. Uriel howls, but then turns so Raylan can help me back down.

"There ya go, Uri," I say with a grin, and since we're close, I give Raylan a peck on the cheek for good measure.

"Eva," a tenor voice shouts over the raucous. Quickly, I scan for any immediate threats, and not seeing any, I look around for the voice. Christian, in his pale red shirt, now dark with sweat, comes barreling toward me. I get my machete at the ready.

Immediately, Christian throws his hands up in an act of peace, but his face is determined. "I was wrong," he says. "Well, right *and* wrong."

I raise my brows. "I don't have time for this," I say, eyeing a Blurred One trying to sneak up on a hunter with a ton of new tattoos. Raylan loads up the menace with rock salt.

Christian rushes closer, a pillar of earnestness. "I was right that there is more. That I am called to more, but it's *you*. Not Alora. *You've* got the light." He puts a slender hand on my shoulder. I promptly shrug it off. "That's why I felt so confused before. Your light must have been mixed with the Despairity's, but once you left, they felt nothing but empty."

I scoff. Man's confused, all right. "Dude, go get your mom and go back to Louisiana." Speaking of which, another Blurred One's getting awful close to the crater. Maggots convulse across a bowling ball of a man's head while he holds Raylan frozen. Uriel pounds the ground as he heads toward him, but there's a half dozen on the other side of the massive hole.

"I got it," I shout to Uriel, pointing behind him. "You get those."

I finally get to pull out my handy dandy, pocket-sized drill. Take away their power, trap them in the body, only slightly maiming the host. Alora disposed of my wing nut necklace a long time ago, though, so I dash to Raylan and fish one out of his pocket while Raylan tries, fighting against the hold, to shout all sorts of niceties at the Blurred One.

"Well," I say to Christian's pretty green eyes, "give a girl a hand, then."

He brightens. Chin set, he rushes to my side. I toss him the screw.

Now, how to get this nasty guy to hold still . . . he's using a lot of concentration to hold Raylan, so as fast as my completely human self can, I run behind all four hundred pounds of him and jump-kick both his knees forward, so he falls flat on his back.

"*Now!*" I shout to Christian.

To his credit, he is right there within a half a second, screw placed on the philtrum. I jump around the Blurred One's body and onto his chest, plowing my knees in as hard as I can, then place the drill and pull the trigger. The Blurred One screams as the screw sinks into his philtrum, but it's done within five seconds.

"Good work, man," I grudgingly tell Christian.

"Who the hell are you?" Raylan yells at him, back in the fight, but grumpier for his momentary defeat.

"Someone who knows how powerful your girlfriend is," Christian says with a guileless smile.

"Well, then, that makes two of us," Raylan bellows back, chucking his empty guns down and grabbing his nail-studded baseball bat. "It's about time."

"I think I know how we can start to take back that power," Christian says, starting to jog back from where he came.

"The fight's right here!" I yell.

"Both of you." He motions, jogging backward now, to both Raylan and me. He looks like he belongs on a college campus, not a killing field. "Come see what your old friend Dom has been up to."

"Christian," I hiss. "Where on Earth are you taking us?" I tap the side of the oldest church in Bloodcreek with the bloodied rifle I picked up off some motley corpse on the way over here. "I'm all about prayin', but I think now's a time for acting . . ."

"Where's Dom?" Raylan barks, not impressed that we've been lured away from the fight. Man, I've missed his straightforward way of life.

Christian jerks his head like he aims to just take us on a stroll around the grounds. "He's around back. Your sister's inside."

I jolt, and Christian throws his hands up to slow me down. "Eva," he says, his voice aggravatingly calm. "She's in trouble, but we have to stop Dominick to help her. Please, trust me."

Raylan and I exchange grumbles and a look.

"Why are we listening to this guy?" he says, wiping his ten-inch bowie knife on his pant leg.

I rub my face in thought. "My gut?"

Raylan levels the look of a four-star general at Christian, who nods like he's just trying to talk us into eatin' some gator legs 'cause they're chock full of nutrients. Raylan sighs in acceptance, and I love that he speaks in "sigh" with me.

"Okay?" Christian asks.

"Okay," I agree. "But if this is a trap, we're gonna mount your head on a stop sign."

Christian draws his mouth down, acting like he's thinking for a second, then grins broadly. "Deal." He turns to go around the church.

"Hang on," I say, and hold my hand out to Raylan, gesturing for him to hand me his knife. He does without hesitation.

I flip the handle of the long bowie knife and turn my right arm over. Biting my lip, I hastily drag the blade along the soft inner skin of my forearm.

"Eva." Raylan gasps and tries to grab the knife.

"No, stop," I bark, twisting and turning the serrated edge into an intricate pattern, trying to do as little damage as possible, but also knowing there's not much time. I hiss with pain, but soon, I have a triquetra that's not going anywhere. It may look like a kindergartener drew it, but it's there. Ain't no way I'm getting possessed again. "*Now* we can go." I nod to the men.

Raylan gives me a grumpy shake of the head as I hand his knife back to him.

Christian takes off, bounding with his long legs around the church with Raylan and I following, gun and knife at the ready.

Muffled voices escape the church, and my fingers twitch for action. We reach an entrance at the back, probably to the pastor's office. The door's already ajar, and fragrant herbs waft toward us. Dom must be here, all right. Dude's got more herbs than a reggae concert.

One hand on the door, Christian looks directly at me. "If it's all right, I'll go in first. He won't expect anything from me."

After just a bit of hesitation, I nod, to which Christian cracks his boyish smile. "He'll be up in the loft. Follow me in just a few seconds." And he's off.

"Three, four, five . . ." Raylan counts off, then storms into the church.

We bound up the rickety wooden stairs as quickly as possible while trying not to sound like a herd of elephants. I let Raylan go ahead of me since the stairs are narrow, and let's face it, at this point, he's still the stronger . . . well, everything.

As we near the top, Christian's calm voice drifts down toward us. "Just thought I'd see if you needed anything." All I can see is the back of his dark head.

"You get outta he-ah," a raspy rattle that could only be Dominick replies. "Before I drink a mix of you' fluids for replenishment."

The sound of Dom's voice makes me want to scream louder than a thousand sirens. *He* is the reason I was able to get possessed in the first place. If it weren't for *him*, *I* wouldn't have killed Mags. We wouldn't be in this situation at all. He needs to *die*.

Raylan must sense my fury. He holds his left hand up at me, urging me to wait. I sort of want to stab his hand, but he's right. I train my eyes on the bright red rug and imagine Dom's blood soaking right into it, blending in.

"Okay, sir." Christian's head bobs. "But, perhaps you'd like some of this instead?" He disappears from view, and we hear a loud *thud*. I suppose that's our signal.

Raylan and I burst into the loft, where Christian stands with a giant Bible over a barely conscious Dom.

"I hate to use a Bible like that, but . . ." Christian says.

Dom slumps over in an unnatural position on the floor, dreadlocks trickling with blood. Something falls out of his lap, onto the rug.

Christian moves out of the way, wiping the Bible. Raylan darts to Dom with his knife, but before he can get to him, before Dominick can even register who we are, I shoot him between the eyes.

CHAPTER 47 - FROST

The chupacabra drags a weasely, robed guy from an alcove on the far right side of the room, and as the clergyman starts reciting matrimonials, all I can think is, *no way* is Alora taking Leo from me.

I grab the salt spray from my front pocket and spray like she's Ebola and I'm the CDC.

Seizing Leo's lifeless hand, I *pray* I can break through his witch doctor spell and convince him to come with me, but it's like walking through still-drying cement. My mind hits a wall of slippery deadweight.

"*Leo, come on!*" I plead, but his consciousness won't budge. And his eyes don't so much as flicker beneath the black stitches. *Leo*! It's like seeing him in Tess' basement all over again.

From the salt spray, Alora's essence is scattered, but it doesn't take long for all her powdery bits to reconvene.

She's like a quickly-thrown-together sandcastle. No soul or care or substance. She's willing to rule over Leo with no regard for his feelings.

With the flick of her hand, Alora throws me to the

nearest bench. My skull smacks oak without mercy. And as I strain to lift my head from the smooth lacquer, it takes everything I have to not pass out or cry. That time I urged Leo to feed on me? You know, so we could beat Knox when he was too powerful because he'd fed on too many people's misery? I'd do that again, but Leo's as lifeless and vacant as snakeskin.

How to break through the spell coiling around in his mind?

Everybody knows I'm fond of throwing knives; I toss two in Alora's direction—not because I believe I'll hit her, but because I wouldn't be sad if they hit the priest. Not that I actually want to kill him . . . but he's performing *Leo and Alora's wedding*.

"*Ad quos eieci te ad infernum,*" I recite, my childhood line: "I banish you to hell."

A flicker of a smile twinges on Alora's lips as she coolly watches me.

Holy water!

That'll slow her down—for all of three seconds—but I have to try anyway. I'm just reaching in my back pocket for the vial when the back doors bang open.

In walks a dark-haired beauty in a crumpled-up Depeche Mode T-shirt and torn jeans.

"Eva!" I'm excited to see her but warn her with a scream.

She's flanked by Raylan, eyes warm, but he's ready for a fight, and . . . Christian, in his red shirt, looking sweatier than before. When did he leave? He doesn't look quite as focused as Raylan, but the guy does keep an eye on my sister—as if deferring to her authority.

Eva limps a little as she slowly walks forward and glances from her accompanying boys to the people sitting on benches, covered by sheets.

She raises an eyebrow. *Sheet people? Really?*

I shoot Eva a grin of my own, 'cause apparently, we *can*

communicate without speaking. I haven't been imagining it all this time! I send her a wisecrack. *Alora never got to dress up as a ghost for Halloween.*

Eva's already-delirious eyes stretch even wider as she laughs. *Nice!*

I giggle while Raylan, Alora, Christian stare at us, completely clueless as to the conversation we're having. I can't get over how, all along, I thought I was making it up that Eva and I could read each other's thoughts, but it was Leo's gift working in me.

The priest has gotten to the part about sickness and health, and Eva abruptly stops midway down the pews.

"Alora, you didn't invite me?" Perching on a pew, Eva pats whoever she's sitting next to on the shoulder. "Howdy." She then leans over and nods at each and every sheet-covered person on the bench. "Hello. Hello." To the last one, she wriggles her fingers in a wave.

Alora's shoulders go so rigid, it's like she wants nothing more than to rip the veil from her face. But appearances matter now more than ever. She really does want to take everything from me. "So you managed to climb out of your pathetic little mind. I thought you would be lost in there forever, amidst all the mountains of insecurities and shame."

Eva growls, jumping to the balls of her feet. Reaching down, she pulls her favorite .9mm from a holster on her thigh. "It's kinda hilarious that you had to voodoo your way into getting Leo to marry your cockroachy face."

Alora's peppery hands ball into fists, and I half wonder if she's going to attack the priest for being in the wrong place at the wrong time.

Feigning boredom, Eva tosses a softball-sized doll to me. "Wanna bring Leo back to us, Frosty?"

Just as my hands connect with the cloth doll, Alora sends

it to the back of the chapel, where the arm slams into a candle and catches flame.

Leo's arm lights up with fire, too, and I yank my holy water out of my pocket, but the vial's totally empty.

Aaah! I used it all up on the gremlin before I was brought here!

Luckily, Raylan goes all ninja, sprints up to Leo, and dumps his own vial on his best friend before ducking and rolling away. But he should have doused the doll, because all that happens is Leo's skin crackles, sizzling further, as the flame licks his skin and shirt away. Leo continues to face straight ahead, unseeing.

As I spin to grab the doll from the table in the back of the church, Alora sends it flying to the ceiling.

It catches on a decorative, wooden lip, getting stuck about twenty feet high.

I need a rope, a ladder, a freaking quadcopter to get the thing.

If I could get to Leo, he could move it after I use my tiny screwdriver to pull that screw from his face.

Or do I have to douse the doll first?

I don't have time for these debates!

Surely, there's some holy water on that priest, but when I take a couple of steps toward him, Alora lifts a twiggy hand and sends all the sheets covering the people in a fancy flutter —like doves taking off for their first ceremonial flight.

"Christian," Alora demands, "you are working for the wrong side."

Apparently, Christian's been patting one of the people's faces to make them wake. He straightens guiltily, lingering near the person, and scans the room. Is he looking for exits? Just the front and back doors, plus an open window. I can hear more witch doctors chanting outside.

Christian raises to his full height. "I've always been

looking for something more. Problem is, without Eva, you have nothing."

Alora lifts her palm and telekinetically throws Christian headfirst into the Lucifer statue. There's a loud *CRACK* as Christian thuds to the base.

He doesn't get up, and the people in the pews continue to blindly stare straight ahead, transfixed on the fruit of the tree. I recognize some of them. The tall, well-groomed farmer who runs the tractor supply; a checker from Brookshire's; a familiar-looking woman in a bright green dog shirt, and a lady who looks like she could be her BFF—a frizzy-haired, big-bangled woman with large sunglasses on her face. "Mrs. Sanders?"

I thought she went back to San Antonio to be with bass guitar guy, but, apparently, she's back. We need to get her out of here.

Eva, Raylan, and I glance around the chapel to form our best strategy.

Should we split up? One of us take care of the witch doctors outside? I think to Eva.

She snarls into my mind, *"I'm definitely staying inside."*

One by one, the people in the pews stand and file to the front of the church. They're still emotionless and controlled, but Leo's the only one with stitches on his face.

The people are going to eat the fruit. Become twenty or so beasts.

Plucking up the prettiest top fruit from the wicker basket, Alora opens her disgusting mouth even before her nuptials have ended to take a healthy bite.

A black smudge of smoke tears from a muscular-looking guy's teeth.

The guy slumps a little to the side as the Blurred One— not one of the Despairity—hurls itself toward Alora in a messy streak.

It rips the fruit from Alora's hand and says in a voice like rusted ball bearings, "MINE!"

This new Blurred One's mouth stretches, contorts, and doubles in size. She's a slip of a person—a terrifying stretch of water that threatens to drown us just by looking into her eyes.

Alora knocks over the podium. "ZILLAH!"

Her crony hucks the entire spherical fruit into her own mouth . . . only to burst into an exquisite explosion of dusty grains.

Everyone—everything—in the room draws silent. From the unconscious Christian lying on the floor to the people who are all standing in line to the suddenly quiet priest. Even from several paces off, I can feel Alora's terror; it gallops and leaps, twists and writhes up her incorporeal spine.

She can't eat the fruit?

She can't eat the fruit!

Her soul, her very being, flexes into complicated knots—writhing. Angry. This has been the crux of Alora's plan from the beginning.

How could God or Lucifer trick her? I'm sure she's thinking.

"NOOOOO!" Alora tears her veil from her face. In a violent spasm of rage, she grabs what's left of the fruit and flies through the air to seize the priest's collar. Her essence flickers, clicks, and clashes. "*Eat!*"

The priest's dull, vacant eyes flutter to black as twin beetles scuttle from each one of his nostrils to his cheeks. Oh, so he's possessed. I hadn't realized.

He doesn't want to eat it. He doesn't want to die.

Quicker than lightning, Alora raises the fruit and smashes it straight into his face. His front teeth break off as the crucifix rattles behind him with a *clang*. From the priest's lips, a demon shrieks a million protests in pain.

Black powder shoots in fireworks from his eyes.

The spirit *and* the body are now a big, giant, wasted pile of nothing.

In a fit of hysteria, Alora spins and hurls herself toward the quiet chupacabra at the back.

The chupacabra . . . where her sister resides.

Thick, black smoke flutters from between the armored monster's fangs when Alora leaps into the air and crams the fruit up the divots in the chupacabra's nose. Its eyes flash deep black—before it, too, becomes another sheepish pile of musty grain.

It's all so unexpected.

I can't help laughing.

The fruit turns even the monsters into dust if a Blurred One's inside?

What if a Blurred One's not inside?

Looks like more science experiments await!

The roar that comes from Alora's mouth is so loud, the base holding up Lucifer crackles, separating. A fist-sized piece of the base rolls off and knocks Christian on the head.

He actually wakes.

"WE CAN'T EAT THE FRUIT!" Alora screams. She lifts the muscly guy who housed Zillah, throws him halfway across the room, and impales him through the chest and back on one of pointier parts of Lucifer's wings.

"WE. CAN'T. EAT!"

She sets her evil, demonic eyes on Mrs. Sanders, and there's no way she's hurting such an innocent lady.

Raylan, Eva, and I jump to block Alora on her rampage. But she spins and jumps, forcefully stepping on Brookshires' checker's head, and dives into Mrs. Sanders' lips as her eyes stretch wide.

She's inside Mrs. Sanders.

She's inside Mrs. Sanders.

We lower our weapons, Eva, Raylan, and I.

Christian's just finding his feet, but there's nothing to do now but wait.

We could screw or drill her, but Eva and I look to one another; we're not so sure Alora would let Mrs. Sanders survive.

Blackness flashes in Mrs. Sanders' eyes as she gracefully lurches to her feet. Alora pops her neck in an obvious display of authority. "We can still rule the sires," Mrs. Sanders' middle-aged voice cries. "It shall just have to be by proxy."

I inch toward the pile of dust where the priest used to be to secure his holy water. Still need to get Leo free. But Alora lifts her hand, causing each and every piece of fruit to fly to all twenty-some-odd people who are primed to join her army.

"Eat the fruit." It's so wrong to hear Alora use Mrs. Sanders' voice. "*Eat the fruit*, and show your allegiance to me!"

A few of the humans nod. Some, like the woman in the dog shirt, look absolutely terrified. A pocket of black smoke shoots from one human's lips and darts for the open window; guess he or she doesn't want to be confetti.

Eva grabs a piece of fruit that's nearly reached Brookshire's checker guy and tosses it from hand to hand like the softball we've needed all this time. "I say we cram a piece of fruit down Alora's throat and call it a day."

But our tractor supply farmer's already got a piece of fruit, and he's taking a hasty bite.

He's not turning into dust.

Because he's not possessed. All Blurred Ones will stay very far away.

His nose darkens to black and elongates, and hair sprouts from his neck and face.

A werewolf?

Bleh, I hate werewolves.

This is not what we want happening.

Things are getting hairy. Some people, literally. Frost is looking pretty beat up, Leo's slowly becoming smoked brisket, and I'm not real stoked to see Alora hitchin' a ride in Mrs. Sanders here. No time for fear, though.

Raylan, ever the soldier hunter, is already grappling with a gorgeous, nearly-naked lady with a cow's tail, a newly-formed hulder. The knife doesn't do much against it, so he's gone to hand-to-hand. So many creatures are changing, but we don't know if they're all evil. They could be victims just as much as we are. They don't all need to die.

"Christian." I grab his arm, relieved his skull isn't caved in from that toss by Alora. "Get as many people as you can into the foyer and lock them in." I gesture to the enclosed foyer at the front of the church. Maybe that can buy us some time.

He gestures toward the group. "My mom," he says, eyes worried for the first time. He bolts toward the group, putting a supportive arm around the small woman. She's coughing but doesn't seem to be growing horns or scales, so hopefully, her transformation won't be too intense.

He starts coaxing all the less-transformed people to follow

him. Aside from his mother, only three more follow, grasping their throats, resisting the change. "Tell them to hold on," I call to him. "We don't all have to be Alora's playthings." I shoot a dirty look at Alora, but then I catch of Leo's freaky eyes again and Shorty hovering next to him. Like she's actually concerned about him.

"We need the doll," I plead with Shorty, pointing to the small magical object in the rafters. "Wake up and do the right thing."

She jerks back like she's offended but doesn't attack me. Could Christian have softened her up a bit?

Frost storms up to the basin of holy water and grips the entire thing like she's going to throw it on something, either the doll or Shorty.

Alora sidles over to us, and I brace myself, 'cause let's face it, I haven't had a whole lot of luck fighting her. I blast her with my last four rounds of salt rock. She shrieks in pain, but it doesn't dissipate her for long.

"Come on, woman!" I scream at Shorty, who stares at Alora. "Help us. What does doing all this get you besides being super miserable all the time?"

Shorty responds by lifting a wispy arm and snapping the doll to her like a fly to a frog. She holds it close, flames doing nothing to her. Frost lugs the basin of holy water to us, ready to dump the whole thing on Shorty if she gets extra diabolical on Leo. But Shorty plunges the doll into the water.

Steam erupts from the doll and Leo beside me, and the fire is out.

Frost sets the bowl down and races to Leo.

You've got this, I think to Frost, knowing that removing the screw will be painful for both of them.

Christian, who's shoved a pew against the foyer doors, runs back to us, panting, but Shorty must be having second thoughts, 'cause she raises me up by my throat.

"Taryn," Christian says, voice soaked with compassion. "Let's do this right this time."

She doesn't move for a moment, like she's actually considering switching to Team Awesome. Her smudges for eyes seem to blink, and her head tilts slowly, almost ninety degrees.

She drops that python jaw and screams so loud, the windows throughout the church shake. The beautiful stained glass lilies shatter, and she flies away.

Alora, seeing her sister bail on her, storms up to the hulder Raylan's still awkwardly grappling with. She inhales, sucking in the creature's essence, crackling with power. It's like seeing Mrs. Sanders with roid rage. Leo, now free of the screw, throws a charred hand out to freeze her but is only partially successful.

"I think we're going to have to screw Mrs. Sanders," Frost says, shaking her head, drill in hand.

Alora rolls her shoulders back. "I do believe I'll just go ahead and make myself some more friends." She bursts from Mrs. Sanders' lips and starts to fly out the window Shorty just vacated, but Mr. Harris comes scrambling through the door from the loft, shouting a spell. Alora stops in the air and shakes like she's in a distortion field.

"This won't keep her," he shouts. "But Beau is ready, and I suggest you all come now."

CHAPTER 49 - FROST

Outside the church, we spot the rural Mardi Gras witch doctor who was spelling the sheet people. He's got a crazy, horned mask, and he's sprinting for the woods, but I'm not in the mood to chase him down. He's just a symptom of the problem. So I sneak the drill back into my pocket and examine Leo's damaged face. The ripped, fleshy hole in his upper lip is starting to mend, but it'll be a few hours before he heals completely. Not to mention his eyes.

We should sprint to the car—check on Beau ASAP—but I *have* to take the time to make sure Leo's okay.

I wrap my arms around his sagging shoulders before he can tell me to run or explain he has a car nearby; he doesn't exactly respond, but he doesn't pull away, either. Just like when Maggie and Raylan used that drill to make sure it could slow down a Blurred One, he is still very weak. I don't care. I have him. I love him. I breathe in the musky sweat on his shirt and cling to his arm and shoulder muscles. I don't *ever* want to forget what this feels like.

When his arms tense, I think he's finally going to hug me back, but instead, he says, "You should hurry."

You.

Why isn't there an "us"? Or even a "You and I"?

Leo has to know how desperately I've wanted to free him of Alora's clutches and ditch this stupid chapel.

"You just about got hitched to Alora," I joke. "Don't tell me I should run along and hurry."

Leo flinches like my very words are scalding, but I didn't mean to hurt him, so I reach up and grab his face. "Hey!" His cheeks are unusually scratchy as I try to force him to look me in the eyes. "*Hey!*"

But the way he's hanging his head makes his face heavier than an anvil. I loosen my grip. "I said that I'm *happy* to see you, Leo. Aren't you happy to see me?"

Leo shakes his head, shaggy bangs hanging in his face, but it's not a "no, I'm not happy to see you,"—more of a "you don't understand."

I *hate* the chasm he's pointing out between us like it's the Great Divide. Weeds snap beneath his shoes as he backs up. He swallows what sounds like a painful lump in his throat, *still* refusing to look at me.

"I am sorry—Frost—but . . . it has to be this way."

I grab his arm, refusing no as an answer. "She let you go! You need to snap out of it! We need to find Beau before he does something *really* insane."

Leo reaches up and grabs a piece of the church's thin wooden siding, and it crumbles under his touch. His voice is almost inaudible. "I am not going with you."

Why's he lying?

"You've seen what I was—what I . . . allowed her to do to me. I need to stay behind and end her the way I should have in the beginning."

No, *I* was there 'in the beginning.' *I* was with him on that bridge when he gave up and fell in the water. To think how guilty we both felt when he hurt that beautiful butterfly.

Looking up, Leo takes the time to gaze at me long enough to absorb my face. I can feel the tears building up in my eyes. But I can't let them drop, because that would mean he's not going with me.

I reach out to him, praying he'll see the sense in staying with me, but his face goes so ashen, I'm worried he's going to pass out. His lips are blue, and his entire face is trembling. Grabbing the chapel wall harder, he growls, "How could I *possibly* believe I deserve to be with you? I've killed people!"

I pound the siding. "So have I!"

"To defend yourself."

"Just like you!"

"*You* are not a cold-hearted killer, Lenee . . ."

My heart all but shrivels up. I didn't know it was possible for it to literally evaporate. Never in the history of the world would I have believed Leo would be so cruel as to use my given name.

Leo gave me Frost.

I am Frost.

He can't just rip that away.

I don't know which is worse—that he actually said it, or that he's obviously thought of using it long enough to speak it aloud now.

My head spins a million miles an hour. I must have bitten my tongue, because everything smells and tastes like batteries. My chest rises and falls; rises and falls . . . before it gives up the ghost—and caves.

"But we belong together . . ." A stupid, single tear falls from my eye.

Leo looks like a shell of the person I met in San Antonio last spring. His eyes are sunken and bloodshot, and I don't even know what sort of spell the witch doctors did to lock him away from my mind.

"I am a demon." He grits his teeth. "You are a virtuous, *beautiful* young woman who deserves to be happy."

"But *you* make me happy!"

His jaw clenches; he squeezes his eyes shut, but he's *not* leaving me.

Turning around, Leo grips the church wall so hard, more pieces break off and crumble. "We have been deluding ourselves to think it could be any other way."

No.

He doesn't know what he's saying.

We are still worth fighting for. Next to Eva, he is the single reason why I keep fighting.

I tense for him to turn around—he'll at least kiss me goodbye!—when he stalks back up the porch into the chapel.

He didn't.

He couldn't.

Another piece of the church wall crumbles like plaster to my feet.

*W*ay, way on the other side of the field from the tree, Beau scrambles to set up a long, rectangular table with his siblings. They're in the center of a spray-painted devil's trap, so no Blurred One or monster would want to be physically inside—but that doesn't stop the fire darts and other weapons from flying into the circle.

In his fanciest clothes, with tasseled shoulders and a rope tie, Beau looks like he's about to enjoy a banquet, but that can't be what he's about to do.

He's setting up their final meal to die.

Two of Beau's sisters, wearing cowboy boots and pretty little red and blue dresses with matching handkerchiefs, carry the dinnerware in wicker baskets. There's a table runner, candlesticks, fancy golden chargers, and red plates. Three of the other siblings scramble to straighten the checkered table-cloth from Sasquatch n' Koi. In the center, lies a large plate of fruit. *The* fruit.

Why is everyone so willing to sacrifice themselves when I'm sure we could find another way?

A giant with a head the size of Mississippi throws a few spears into the trap, narrowly missing the youngest of Beau's siblings.

"BEAU!" I scream. He needs to stop this. His little brothers and sisters are going to die. Their family has become a pillar in our community. We can't lose them, no way.

The giant grabs another spear and lobs it. I grab a random car door from the field and block it just in time.

"I was thinkin'," Beau shouts to be heard over the giant's roaring, "takin' everybody out when we go is kinda John Wayne."

I want to grab him by the shoulders. Talk some sense into his muddled mind. But a second giant with a flat face comes stomping up, injudiciously setting off two C-4 mines. They rip off a hand, but he keeps coming.

I throw a knife into the giant's heart—kind of a Hail Mary. He stops dead in his tracks, pulls it out, and licks the blood like it's newly harvested honey.

Swinging to retrieve my knife from my sleeve, I yell, "Beau! Get your brothers and sisters somewhere safe. End this foolishness. You don't have to die!"

Sadly—I'd almost say fondly—Beau looks around at his brothers and sisters, who are perched around the well-ordered table with the best childhood manners I've ever seen. "Ya know that book?" Beau smiles up at me. "*The Girl Who Could Fly?* There was a part in that story I really liked." He gets this far-off look in his eye. "'I have seen the coming of the dawn. Unconcernedly watching the passing of the day. I will not stay silent. Like the birds, I *will* fly.'"

I don't want to hear him reciting quotes about death and flying. "But Grendel, Awan." I nod at the girls in their cute red and blue dresses. I don't even know all his siblings' names. "They're just kids, Beau!"

Another spear shoots through the air—these freaking giants!—and I glance around for my knife, which the other giant discarded like a rubber toy.

I sprint to the car, where I'm pretty sure I saw an AR, left behind by neck tattoo guy. It's not in the best condition, with a lot of scratches in the paint, but the clip's not empty.

Heaving the weighty machine, I pull the trigger and fill the giants with so much rock salt, we'll be able to de-ice all of Missouri.

I try to pretend it doesn't feel good.

Both Leo and Beau are set on leaving me.

By the time I make the flat-faced giant's head look like cottage cheese, the other giant's grown bored. He stumbles off to feed on a banshee or something.

Tossing the AR—clip's empty—I turn to Beau, unable to believe I have to say this. "*Please* don't die."

Beau fluffs out a cloth handkerchief. Laying it across his lap, he pretends like it's our second ever date. "Froster, you an' I both know my brothers and sisters and I've lived longer than our share o' lifetimes."

I dislodge and grip another knife. "But you were stuck in boxes! You didn't really get to live your lives!"

Beau chuckles, surveying a pile of sparkly fruit on the plate. "Uri donated these." Tucking another napkin in his collar, he says, "All my brothers and sisters really wanna do is see their daddy." He winks at me. "He's actually a good guy! *An'* they'll get to reunite with him on the other side."

I wish I had some wise words—something that would

change his mind—but all I can come up with is, "For an ex-ghoul, you have an awful lot of faith."

"I've learned from the best." Beau juts his freckled chin at me. "Plus, it'll all be worth it to see you an' Eva-lou happy."

A band of vampires tears after us from behind the car while two hunters with matching black vests make quick work of removing their heads with matching bowie knives.

"Hey," Beau says as his brothers and sisters reach for their own pieces of fruit. "I heard A-lora can't even eat the fruit of the tree! That right there, Froster, is somethin' that should put a big, wide smile on yer face!"

I say in a warm hush, "There has to be another way."

What of the sweet, simple cowboy I met at the diner? The one who helped me with the dishes after a long day.

What about the time he chased me down the road in his pickup after he proposed to me? Saved me from his mom, even though he had to fight through her ironclad control, all to protect me.

Beau shrugs like he's never done anything significant in all his time. "Not everyone gets to live the storybook kinda life. Heck, I'm jus' real glad I got to be part of somethin' special after you, Raylan, Leo, 'n' Eva-lou stopped Mama from bein' such a killjoy. Know how nice it's been to set up my own diner? Be free of her saucy ways? Froster . . ." He holds out his hands, begging. "Yer *worth* fightin' for. You've given me a slice of the happy life. And, I gotta say, I agree with Leo that, no matter what happens, it's *yer* time to live an' love. He an' I made a pact, see. It's *yer* an' Eva-lou's time to be the girl in that book. *Yer* time to rise, take flight."

Reaching out, he plucks up a big, white fruit, smiling broadly at his brothers and sisters to do the same.

"But they're *so* young!" I cry.

Tears shine in Beau's mud-colored eyes. "Know when ya invited me over, n' I saw you n' Raylan n' Maggie fixin' that porch? You played it off that it got hit by a semi. Well, I knew right then n' there that I had found my people. Thanks for findin' a friend in me."

He opens his big, flirtatious lips and takes a ginormous bite.

"BEAU!" I cry as a beat-up Toyota Corolla comes barreling down the field, driven by a dark-eyed beauty.

Eva.

Maybe Mr. Harris can reverse the effect I'm sure the fruit is having on Beau.

Eva hits a hole—an empty C-4 mine—as she leans out the window in time to see Beau slumping in his seat.

He doesn't explode in a pile of dust; his skin slowly fades to the weathered stone of a castle as trees and debris hurtle through the devil's trap.

The same thing happens to another sibling. And while the heavy stench of smoke lingers in the air, fire billows and rages in the nearby elms and cedar trees.

The effect of the fruit takes Beau's stouter brother, and I hate that I don't even know his name.

The field goes unnaturally quiet.

No more giants stomping the ground; no screaming vampires or banshees.

The hunters in the black vests look around.

So do I.

The bloody field sags with a hundred different supernatural bodies with stony skin like Beau and his siblings—a gremlin holds the AR I dropped; the giant who stomped away appears to have lost an arm to a C-4 mine.

All of them—all of these suddenly motionless bodies—are dead. Must be the byproduct of Beau and his siblings eating the fruit of the tree.

He did it.

He did it.

The turd *didn't* have my blessing.

As I turn around to face Eva—to explain—a long, sleek arrow that looks like it belongs in The Before flies straight for the top of my chest cavity.

I'm out of weapons.

And I don't think Eva's going to be quick enough to block it this time.

One dark arrow, loosed from Alora's bow, flies. It doesn't shake, swerve, or hesitate before forcing its way into Frost. It certainly didn't ask permission.

Frost's eyes shoot wide, like the nightmare she just woke up from is actually real. Did she dream that I shot her, and now this thing that has been me for so long really did shoot her?

Please, let her remember it wasn't me. She staggers once, as if the arrow shoved the strength right out of her like a greedy little pest. Some blood sprays from her shoulder. A few inches over, and it could have been fatal.

Leo races past Alora to Frost's side, and then Frost's shooting a look at Leo as if she's scared for *him*. Oh, Frost, will you ever learn to admit when you're hurt?

The fruit, *Eves,* she says in my mind. *To kill the Blurred Ones.* Right. Let's end this beast.

Raylan's two steps ahead, already bolting for the table and what's left of the fruit from Beau and his family's sacrifice. Alora freezes him, though, so I launch myself at the table. Just a few pieces lay there, and I'm just five feet away.

A lampad emerges from the woods, holding her torch aloft. We meet each other's eyes, then both look at the fruit. She lowers her torch and heaves a giant breath at it, engulfing the entire table in flames.

I hurl myself to the side, knocking into Raylan, praying we're far enough out the flames' reach. We land on the ground with a *smack*, and I look to the table. Within seconds, the fruit is nothing but goo and ash.

We'll get more, I call back to Frost's mind.

She's grabbing a shovel, of all things, arrow protruding from her and all. I think she's going to try and whack Alora upside the head with it, but she slices the dirt near a smooth stone at her feet instead.

"They buried salt grenades," Raylan explains, plunging his bowie knife into the dirt. "Hopefully enough to slow down the last two Despairity."

"Till we get more fruit," I finish for him.

"You got it, babe," he says with a grin.

A Blurred One, ripped flannel draping his body, flashes to Raylan's side, and I unload two salt slugs from my freshly loaded Berettas into the maggoty face. It feels real good.

Leo's hair falls into his eyes as he continues trading mental blows with Alora. Behind him, Uriel tirelessly whips and tears the Blurred Ones away from the tree. What could they possibly want from it, if it will kill them? And with no supernatural creatures left—bless you, Beau, and your siblings—I guess it's time to start over and feed the fruit to us poor, puny humans.

Over my newly vacated body.

Raylan uncovers an oval container in the ground about the size of my hand, covered entirely with runic etching. I know a salt grenade when I see one.

I snatch it right from him and barrel toward Alora. I'm gonna be the one to cause her as much misery as possible.

A different dark form rushes in front of me. "Shorty?" I ask. "What do you want now?" But I don't wait for an answer, 'cause she's doing her wide jaw thing.

"Taryn!" Christian's voice bellows with a new conviction, and he steps away from the ashes of the table he was inspecting. The table where Beau just ate his last meal. Christian finally uses his height to be commanding. "You can do more!"

Shorty ain't listening, though. She lunges at me, and as angry as I am to use this grenade on her instead of Alora right now, I chuck it into her gaping mouth.

She shrieks, flashes with her dark, pain-fueled energy, and dissipates.

Raylan will find more grenades.

Behind us, Christian sighs, like there aren't ten Blurred Ones within fifty feet of us, and more and more are trickling out from the woods.

Frost uncovers her grenade. But she can only shoot eye daggers at Alora instead of throwing it because Mr. Harris is coaxing the arrow out of her shoulder. With his trembling hand on the shaft and the faint glow emanating from her, I imagine it's part nerves, part magic he's using.

Frost's fingers twitch on the grenade, ready to launch.

"All right, babe," Raylan calls, sprinting to the nearest smooth stone on the ground. "Let's go. Think he'll try to stop us?" He jerks his head toward Uriel.

I wink back, doing my best to feign confidence. "Sure, it's just the fruit of the Tree of Amazingness . . . right?"

Raylan grins his sexiest sideways grin, like he's equal parts in love and in disbelief. I'm dying to kiss his scruff.

He pops up the rock and grabs the grenade underneath. I'm running to join him so we can head to the tree together, but Shorty, aka Taryn, solidifies right in front of me again.

Half a second later, I'm sailing thirty feet through the air, and I land at Alora's wispy, nasty, ancient feet.

Stunned and with the breath knocked out of me, I try to scramble to my feet, but Alora is right there. She throws another assault at Leo, and he's knocked back a few feet, boots skidding along the muddy ground.

Alora rears up to her full height, preparing to do a beautiful swan dive. Into my body. I try to get back on my feet, but another Blurred One holds me down with just her gaze. I've got my new handy-dandy triquetra, so hopefully, Alora can't get back in, but I still wouldn't love her trying.

Raylan chucks the grenade at Alora. It explodes, and she blinks out.

"Leo!" Raylan yells. "Frost! Get the fruit! We'll hold them off."

I love it when he gets all commander-y. But true story, I'd do this anyway. I need to get this chick out of my freaking life.

Frost, sans arrow, and Leo take off to the crater.

Christian jogs to my side and holds out a hand, but he's looking around.

"Taryn," he calls to the air. "Come, let me be your vessel again, and we'll do better things. Our Father wouldn't want you to suffer like this unless you choose to."

Dude's seriously trying to talk sense into a Despairity?

At least ten Blurred Ones are working their way toward us, slowed down only by the scattered spells and traps surrounding the field, and I know Alora will be back any second.

Frantically, I search the ground for another stone that looks like it could be hiding a salt grenade. I see one a few yards off, so I try to crawl to it. Darn it if my ankle doesn't want to cooperate right now. Must've happened when I got thrown like a kid's backpack after school.

"Eva," Christian says, stepping in front of me.

I don't love the way he's between me and my next salt grenade. Hopefully, Raylan's grabbing another.

Christian's eyes turn black.

I throw myself at him so that, by any luck, I can gain some distance to the stone covering the grenade. Christian simply raises his hand and freezes me in place. But then I feel that familiar, tiny tug I felt before, way back at the canoe shop.

"We'll help you out," he says with a smirk, and his eyes go back to his normal autumn green.

Christian and *Taryn* flip up the stone I was trying to get to with a twitch of the wrist so I can grab the grenade, then charge into the oncoming Blurred Ones. One by one, they chuck the bad guys like they're just little sacks of potatoes. By golly, he actually got her to change sides.

Alora blinks back in front of me. She ain't changin'.

CHAPTER 51 - FROST

A few summers ago, Maggie took Eva and me to see a cave. Legend said that a family of trolls lived down there, and thinking it was a bunch of hogwash, Maggie took us along without mentioning anything.

We camped out under the stars. We'd gone down "to look for fossils" when Mama Troll jumped out on us and tried to eat Maggie's ear right off her face.

That's one of my earliest supernatural memories.

Maggie occasionally got us into scraps, even though she tried to keep us in the dark while fulfilling her hunter duties.

I still can't believe she didn't go down fighting for Eva.

Can't believe she's not the person I thought she was all this time. All this time . . . man, we just don't have time!

Half the cavern's collapsed—no wide-open spaces—and I wish we'd gotten the fruit from Beau's table or even from the church.

We're still one step behind.

Well, that's about to change.

As I survey Uriel's old haunt, I'm happy to say that the half-collapsed crater above us has forced everyone to be more organized. There's only enough room for people to pass through one skinny tunnel in a single file line, and despite what Leo might think, it's the perfect setting for us to work together. To remind him who we are as a couple, because I'm not sure I can keep going without him or Beau in my life. We'll seize the fruit, hand-deliver it to Alora and the other Blurred Ones, and, with a little luck, finally find peace.

No one's running out of the tunnel this way, so either everyone's still gathered around the tree, or there's a way out on the other side . . .

Hopefully, that's not the case.

Leo strides up to a stringy-haired, pasty guy with a Nirvana shirt and bloodshot eyes. Seizing the boy by the shoulder, Leo looks directly into his eyes.

What kind of human are you? he asks, digging.

Bloody images of the guy killing cats and dogs flit through my mind, and I sucker-punch the guy in the jaw. He spins fast and knocks into the cave wall so hard, he drops, unconscious.

Leo turns to face me with an appraising gaze.

"Beau taught me to do that after he lost his powers." I shrug. "Thought it would come in handy."

"Beauregard . . ." Leo whispers, his gaze surveying the other side of the cave's ceiling.

"He and his siblings died for us, you know."

"For *you*. And Eva."

I grab hold of his arm, wishing he'd fully come back to me. "He told me about the 'pact' you made. Leo, as far as I'm concerned, if you aren't here, I don't want my life."

His eyes darken. "Don't say that."

All at once, the hunter with the fresh neck tattoos scrambles down the rope ladder we made.

He carries a steel crossbow that looks an awful lot like Maggie's . . .

"Thought I could help you guys!" the guy says, holding the crossbow backward and practically tripping over his own feet.

Slowly, never more stoically, Leo appraises the guy. He examines the red, swollen tattoos, and the fact that his belt's not even on straight.

When Leo steps closer to the human, I think he might lecture him or send him back to fill more salt grenades; but instead, Leo gently reaches over and settles his hands on the guy's hands, which are trembling. Rearranging his hands so they're holding the crossbow properly, Leo says, "Guard the hole." He nods at the rope. "Anybody who ignores a warning call, shoot."

Leo glances at me as if to see if I have anything to add, and I shoot him a smile of support.

"When you run out of arrows," I add, "tell us so we can supply you with a new weapon."

The man nods, the cowlick at the back of his head waggling.

The boy examines the way Leo just placed his fingers on the crossbow when a string of elderly women's voices echo from about four meters above us.

"*I* get to eat the fruit first!"

"*No, me*!"

"You would be a terrible vampire, Marsha. You get squeamish when we go to the blood bank."

Neck tattoo guy aims his crossbow at the older ladies, who are each wearing floral jackets and carrying large handbags dangling from long strings. "Hey! Don't come down here! Or . . . or you'll be mincemeat!"

"Helen," Marsha, the one with bigger hair, complains. "I *told* you this was a terrible idea. Let's go to that estate sale in Brumley."

There's a quick scattering of gravel as both women climb back out the other side.

A great rustling ensues as the women fight over who gets to drive while Leo clamps a hand on the hunter's shoulder. "If anyone doesn't turn around, shoot. They could be possessed, even though a Blurred One headed down here would have to be insane."

"Kind of like you?" I offer.

Leo's eyes twinkle just a little bit before he looks away.

Part of me worries that Alora was able to change gears so fast by allying herself with the monsters, even though she and the other Blurred Ones can be killed by the fruit. She must *really* hate us if she's willing to risk being within ten feet from the fruit. What did she say? *I need you to hate me almost as much as I have hated you since the beginning.*

"She has nothing on you," Leo quietly says, and oh! It shouldn't wig me out that he can so easily read my mind.

I push the image of Alora holding her bow with exactness out of my mind. The wound in my shoulder still twinges a little, but there are benefits to being allied with Mr. Harris, who's already patched me up a second time.

A furry troll with weeds for hair comes barreling down the tunnel, and it's *exactly* like the one that attacked Eva and me when we were little.

With a casual flick of his hand, Leo throws the troll and knocks her out on a stalactite. She slumps to the ground, and I guess she just ate the fruit and was newly created since Beau and his brothers and sisters took down all the sires already.

"Show off," I mutter as a tad more light shines in Leo's eyes. "Some of us can't throw things with our minds."

Green drool dribbles from the troll's mouth as we stroll by, and Leo ducks his head in shame.

He doesn't have to take me so literally.

"Don't feel bad," I say. "We're doing great things! We're down here to stop any more monsters from getting away after eating the fruit—and shove some into Alora's pretty little face."

Leo laughs as a human girl with long, auburn hair crouches on the ground ahead of us by just a few feet.

Not sure what she's doing here all alone. Maybe the troll was her escort to the tree?

Timidly, I pat the girl's shoulder. She looks to be about Eva's and my age.

She springs around with one of *my* daggers in hand, aiming directly at the wound where Alora shot me.

She's one of the girls from my school. Former friend of Jenny's . . .

As our hands connect, I sense the type of girl she is today.
Locks people in the janitor's closet.
Bullies kids into doing her homework.
Cheats in AP History.

I totally didn't expect to see into her mind. This girl needs to be reminded of the utter bleakness of the dark side.

Leo wraps his hand on mine and sends the girl a chilling image of what he could look like.

Scores of bugs—roaches, maggots—devour his face. He reeks of death. He actually looks like he belongs in a Japanese horror movie with his sunken eyes, cracking lips, and gray, cataract-covered eyes.

Leo grins as the girl lets out a gut-wrenching scream.

Returning to his true form, Leo lets her go, and so do I.

She scampers for the hole, and, for the good of humanity, my Blurred One's never been sexier.

"What was that?" I have to ask.

"Just a little trick I learned when I spent some time in the Serengeti."

"'When I spent time in the Serengeti,'" I mock him with a lower voice.

He doesn't mean to smile, but I can see the light of

amusement shining in Leo's eyes. He *has* to see we belong together, even if all his accomplishments can be a little hard to take.

Another boy comes barreling from the tunnel—this one with long, sharp fangs—and Leo effortlessly tosses him to the ground. "It's a pity he threw away his life."

I boost a shoulder as I adjust the satchel I forgot I was holding. "He made his choice."

Leo's gaze skips to mine, and I already know what he's going to say. *So have I.*

"The difference between you and him is, you have an *amazing* girl who's fighting like crazy to keep you in her life."

"He could have that." Leo nods at fang-boy.

"*Plus,* you regret your choice."

"If he lives long enough, I guarantee you, he will regret his choice."

I grab Leo by the shoulders and spin him so that he has to look directly into my eyes. "Okay. You got me. Not everyone's lucky enough to have a Frost Abram in their life. But *you do,* so . . . be thankful, sheesh!"

Leo's gaze glitters and dances as he absorbs mine. A sandstorm of heat wafts between us; I could kiss him right now if I didn't think we were about to be interrupted by a trove of trolls or zombies.

Slowly, I release his shoulders, my fingers feeling like they've fallen asleep. "Okay?"

"Okay."

Another roast of heat threatens to loosen all my limbs and make me liquefy, but I can tell that's all I'm going to get out of him—that's all he's going to say—so I change tactics as we scurry down the tunnel, not another soul in sight.

The cavern dips, winks darker; I grab the flashlight from my belt and shine it down the path so we can see. Still, there's one big, colossal issue I haven't been able to bring up until this point.

"When Alora tried marrying you . . ." I remember our big fight. "Leo, were you awake?"

As we tread closer, I can sense the glow of the tree, and even now, Leo's nerves pop and sizzle as he glances at me.

"I was there, but I could not control my vessel."

"Then there's nothing to be guilty about!" Just like she did to Eva, Alora controlled his mind.

Honestly, I can't imagine enduring that helpless feeling, not to mention Alora's dark and twisted methods, so I take his hand. "I'm sorry."

Leo accepts my hand for about five seconds before a pasty, skinny figure comes scampering up the tunnel and—yikes. Kid looks like he's barely hit puberty. He's missing half his face.

Leo and I each grab an arm as he lashes out at us with his teeth. I try to settle him down. *Relax, we are not the enemy.* But the zombie boy's shirt rips and tears as he thrashes.

There's a loud *crack,* and then I'm left with nothing but his arm.

Leo looks at me with a twinkle in his eye as the guy squirms on the floor. "Your power . . ." he nods at the arm I didn't mean to take. "You harness it so effortlessly."

"Only because you gave it to me." I shake the arm at Leo before realizing the gesture's ridiculous, so I drop it at the boy in a heap. Wish we had time to help him or something, but the tree's iridescent glow lights up my face—a magnet on my soul. A pull that makes me dizzy. I want to close my eyes, bask in its power and essence, but instead, I dutifully pull off my satchel and start grabbing fruit and cramming it inside.

"You do not feel its influence?" Leo asks.

Ah, Uriel had been surprised that I could withstand the temptation of eating it.

"I'm a barrier." I shrug, batting away the tree's power. "Again, evidence of the *good* you've done for me."

With guarded eyes, Leo watches me. The fruit feels kind of like tennis balls, only *way* prettier and slightly less fuzzy. I tuck them in, one by one, just grateful that this part is easy.

"We'll find a way for you to be human," I promise him.

Raising an arm, Leo telekinetically makes a few more pieces of fruit fall into my bag, filling it to the brim. I couldn't carry more if I tried.

"We *will* find a way," I say again while he hesitantly reaches out and brushes the side of my face.

"You," Alora seethes, looking a little frayed around the edges, even for a Despairity. "You are going to be my vessel for the next hundred years. And every time you are the least bit noncompliant, I will remove one of your sister's appendages."

"You know what, *Alora?*" I spit her name, still trying to crawl to the grenade. "I will be the most noncompliant creature in existence. Frost can take care of herself. I think she just showed you that."

I reach the grenade and throw it at her, but she deftly dodges it. I spy Raylan from the corner of my eye, searching for another grenade. How many did they bury, though?

Alora huffs. "Frost is the most pathetic creature in existence, after you."

Four more Blurred Ones enter the field from the other side. Christian/Taryn are still throwing down, but we're so surrounded. Seeing those two completely turn allegiances like that gives me one solitary, wholly asinine thought. It could be the distraction that will be my ultimate doom, but there's no way we can keep holding off Alora, no matter how amazing Raylan and I are together.

I look at the incoming Blurred Ones as I try to pull myself back to my feet.

I try to look past their nasty, cockroach-writhing faces, to the souls of my brothers and sisters I used to live with in heaven. Before. I search to see any glimpse of them. It's not easy to see, but I search for that same tug I felt with Christian. I assume that's what the tug is. A remembered loyalty. And just maybe, I knew one or more of these souls in The Before, too.

Alora backhands me like I'm her troublesome servant. "Let me in," she says. I fall to the ground, head landing with a crack on the stone that was hiding the grenade. Although her blows are like taking a shovel to the face, I think she's wearing out. Plus, I can't give up when this just might work.

Raylan lands a salt grenade right on her, and she disappears again.

One Blurred One, her vessel gorgeous with a straight nose, sun-kissed skin, giant almond-shaped eyes, and honey-colored hair, hesitates her advance for just a second. She tilts her head a smidge and looks at me. I search for the pull and, oh my goodness, it's *there*. Even stronger than Christian's.

I work my way back to my feet, ankle throbbing, head pounding and dizzy. Oh, look, I taste blood. But the Blurred One gives me a shy smile that lights up her entire face.

"I think I know you," I say with what I hope is a friendly grin and not a freaky Freddy Krueger one. 'Cause who knows what my face looks like right now.

She smiles a little broader, accentuating her heart-shaped face, and bobs her head. "I think you're right." Her voice is high, boisterous, and smooth, and I instantly like her.

I focus as hard as I can on that pull between us, hoping that as I feel it, she'll feel it, too. The pull feels so natural, so familiar. Like something I knew a long time ago but had forgotten about. Like influencing people for good is actually kinda my thing. Maybe Alora was taking that and twisting it?

"Wanna start doing some good?" I ask her.

She turns to the nearest Blurred One, an older man with yellowing skin. He sneers at her, and she tosses him onto a fence pole.

"He was pretty unredeemable," my new friend says, and I don't bother to hold back my chuckle. She turns to take on the third, but he is ready. They start exchanging blows, so I focus on the fourth.

I do feel a tiny pull. My heart soars with hope. But as soon as I feel it, it's gone. Severed like a hatchet to a cucumber.

"I know who you are," this last Blurred One spews. "And I'll help end you."

"Raylan!" I holler. "Can you give me a hand?" I charge at the Blurred One, pulling my drill out between strides.

"Right here," Raylan says, coming up right behind me, wing nut ready to go.

Our new friend throws the baddie down, and I pounce. We have him screwed up tight within ten seconds.

"Thanks," Raylan says, looking at the nice Blurred One with an inscrutable expression. "And not that I mind, but, why are you helping us?"

The girl tosses her hair back, and although the bugs scuttle under her honey-colored skin, I'm amazed how beautiful she is for a Blurred One. She kinda glows.

"I knew Eva in The Before," she says, her voice way too cheerful to make sense as a Blurred One. Like she's spunk incarnate. "I almost listened to her, but doubt got the best of me," she adds with a casual shrug. "Maybe this is my second chance. Either way, hers is a good side to be on."

Amidst this insane field of battle and so much death, my

Raylan looks completely resolute and happy, for just an instant. "It's nice to find people to help *me* help *her* get it." He gives her a light punch in the shoulder.

"But you admitted I'm not that good," I say, wanting to whisper it because this new idea of confidence is as wobbly as a newborn giraffe.

"Are you crazy?" Raylan scoffs. "You're the best person I know. Don't know why you can't believe that."

"What about what you said in my head, back at the camp?" I *want* to believe, but I also don't want to be crushed like a dandelion under a gorilla.

"Eva, I love you, but I honestly have no idea what you're talking about."

Our new Blurred One friend bounces from foot to foot. "Guys, less chit chat, more fighting!"

I think about all the different influences that have been bombarding my mind. How now my sister and I can even talk telepathically, and something clicks.

"Raylan, you weren't stuck in my brain with me? No buzz saws or drowning?"

He laughs, open and loud. "No buzz saws or drowning."

Oh, my freaking heck, *ALORA*.

Another Blurred One charges me, but I ain't got time for this. I look at my new friend and ask, "Hey, what's your name?"

"Kathryn," she says boldly.

"Get this fool for me?"

"With pleasure," she says with her magnetic grin, then slides between the charging Blurred One and me.

"Kathryn the *coward*," Alora bellows. Wench is back.

"What's more cowardly?" I say to Alora with the driest expression I can muster. "To own up to your mistakes, or hold onto them for *eternity* and stay miserable, just so you can pretend you know what you're doing?"

She jumps at me like a freight train, driving her soul into me with so much power, I feel like I'll spontaneously combust. She growls savagely, and when Raylan and Kathryn turn to fight, she throws them off like they're Beanie Babies. I think I hit a nerve.

"I know that wasn't really Raylan! And you're just pissed Leo wants Frost and not your miserable self," I say through gritted teeth.

She pushes with all her might, clawing at the crude triquetra on my forearm, like she can overpower my body through sheer resolve. "Everyone thinks you're some kind of hero," she hisses in my ear. "A leader. But all you did was what you were told. And that's all you've done since. You're nothing but a puppet."

She could be right. I mean, she didn't come to earth and forget. She really knows what I was like. But, isn't it what I choose to do with my life that matters?

Kathryn goes toe to toe with Blurred One after Blurred One. Raylan fights like the dickens to get back to me, but more and more Blurred Ones are converging on him. They know he's unstoppable.

Christian and Taryn are over on the other side of the field, single-handedly fighting at least fifteen attackers.

"You know what?" I grind the words out through the concrete determination she's exerting on me. "These people are here because of me. That Blurred One, that *Despairity,* is fighting here because of me. Because I didn't give in to your poison."

"But you did," she says with a smirk and an arrogant laugh.

"I had a momentary lapse of judgment because I had a very, very sick creature living inside me, and years of being told I wasn't good enough."

So, I'm talking a really big talk, but the fact is, she's still on me, and there's not a whole lot I can do about it. I'm praying Frost and Leo get back soon with the fruit, but who knows what kind of opposition they're facing down there. What the heck am I supposed to do?

And then it hits me, and I let out a little giggle.

I force my right hand into my pocket for my smallest pocket knife. I manage to slide it out, and, through the hurricane that is Alora, I push my right arm over my body, reaching for my left. Grateful for the hours Mags, Frost, Raylan, and I sat around familiarizing ourselves with our knives, I easily find its weak spot and flick it open.

As soon as the knife's secure, I slice through my triquetra, tearing my arm open. Breaking the seal.

"Come on in," I tell Alora, but she's already pouring into my head like a whirlpool.

She's not getting the upper hand this time.

Instead of fearing her, fighting her, or closing myself off to protect myself, I relax as she flows completely into my body. Then I remember everything I've come to realize is me.

I focus on this new connection with Kathryn, the bond I have with Christian. My amazing boyfriend, Raylan, and all the faith he has in me. Frost has always believed in me. Leo. Even Beau. The fact that, given a *choice,* I would always try to do the right thing. Mags and Dad were . . . wrong.

"I can't kill you," I tell her, *"but you can't corrupt me. And you definitely cannot use me anymore."*

She's madder than a wet hen, but I have complete control of my faculties.

I rise to my feet and dust myself off.

Wouldn't you know it, Frost and Leo are chugging across the field with that glorious, white fruit in Frost's hands. When they see me standing alone, amidst the field of fury, they stop, questioning. Leo's hand raises for a fight, and Frost looks like she could tear me in two with her bare hands.

"It's okay, y'all," I call to them, waving for them to come quickly. "Get your fruit ready."

"Alora," I say aloud. "This is for Beau."

I don't remember The Before. I don't know for certain if I was good or bad, but fighting for these people feels so right. It's who I want to be. And I can tell you, I'm done seeing myself as others see me, whether good or bad. I'm gonna be me, and that me is gonna be amazing.

I want Alora out, so I will it so. Gathering my will, stoking in the hottest, blazing fire, I let it flow. I force Alora out of my body. Throw her out like I'm a nuke and she's the freaking mushroom cloud. Because I can, and I'd do it again.

Frost, with a grin more wicked than the devil himself, shoves a piece of fruit the size of a softball down Alora's throat.

$\mathcal{A}$lora gagging and gargling on the fruit is the most glorious sound I've ever heard in my life.

She chokes; spasms. Eyes flicker to gray before she puffs into a glorious cloud of confetti.

We killed her.

We. Killed. Her!

I spin to kiss Leo, but, uh, my hands are covered with the fruit juice, so I wipe the syrup off on my pants. Last thing I need is to pass it off to Leo accidentally . . . or eat it and become a wendigo or something.

I crouch to the grass to wipe off my hands, and Eva giggles. "Sorry, Martha Stewart. Fresh outta hand sanitizer."

I shoot Eva a grin before throwing my arms around her, giving her the biggest hug of my life.

"We did it!" I shout. "Hey, how did you chase her out? Did she let slip how amazing you were in The Before?"

Eva cocks an eyebrow at me while Raylan wraps a protective arm around her waist.

"Right, of course not," I say. "Well, *Eva,* you were pretty much the most hardcore person I've ever seen in my life. You shot guns with fireballs and could pretty much do Jiu-Jitsu and MMA."

Raylan smiles wider than the field. "Well, of course she did."

A cloud of black smoke shoots into the lips of some poor, unsuspecting eighty-year-old guy near what's left of the gazebo.

A whistling sound comes from the sky, and when Eva, Raylan, and I look up, the bust of a statue whirs through the air—directly toward us.

The eighty-year-old just chucked that, and I've no idea who that is, but I don't need another Blurred One targeting Eva today. So I run the few paces to my discarded satchel, pluck up another piece of fruit, and cock my arm to launch it right at the guy's face.

Blurred One? He vacates the body, and the eighty-year-old guy's left in peace.

"Frost . . ." Leo's calming presence is a balm for my jumpy nerves when he joins my side. "The seraph has proposed an idea."

"Whatcha got, Furry Uri?" Eva whoops as a fan of feathers slaps the air.

Uriel perches on the ground with a thud they could probably feel in Kansas City. "THE BLURRED ONE RULER HAS BEEN CONTAINED."

Eva rolls her beautiful eyes. "'Ruler,' 'psychopathic tyrannical bully.' . . . I don't know, *I* would go with 'Caligulora'—if we're going to jot something down for posterity."

Leo takes a protective step between Uriel and Eva and me. "Tell them your idea."

Uriel thrusts out his chest with righteous indignation. "LUCIFER'S PROGENY SHALL *NOT* TELL ME HOW TO BEHAVE."

Only mildly terrified that Uriel will throw me like he

threw Beau across the cave, I tentatively reach up and pat the muscles on his arm. "What's your plan, Uri?"

Uriel eyes Leo before once again settling his ageless eyes on me. "I SHALL INFUSE THE AIR WITH THE ESSENCE OF THE FRUIT OF THE TREE. ALL I MUST DO IS SHAKE IT. NO BLURRED ONE SHALL REMAIN CLOSE BY."

"That would actually work?" I gasp. "Why didn't you mention this before?"

Uriel narrows his eyes at me. "*YOU* WANTED TO DESTROY THE TREE."

I guess we didn't exactly start out under the most trusting of circumstances, so I nod.

"AND THE THOUGHT HAD NOT OCCURRED TO ME."

Eva hugs me from behind. "Do it!" she shrieks, and I let out a little laugh, tears threatening to spill from my eyes.

"Do you think you could find a way to prevent more humans from eating the fruit, too?" I ask, feeling shy. "You know, so we don't have any more monster siphons."

"THAT, I CANNOT GUARANTEE. YOU SHOULD KNOW HOW OUR FATHER CHERISHES AGENCY."

Eva and I exchange frowns. A Blurred One, overhearing our conversation, vacates a middle-aged man in his fifties.

"HOWEVER, I SHALL BURY IT EVEN *FARTHER* THAN THE COWBOY BURIED THE TREE. AFTER INFUSING THE AIR WITH THE FRUIT, CHASING AWAY LUCIFER'S PROGENY, I SHALL BURY THE TREE AS FAR AS THE CORE."

"The . . . core?" Raylan pipes up, wrapping an arm around Eva's waist.

The muscles along Leo's jaw flicker as he smiles slightly. "Where the temperature is ten thousand degrees."

Eva glances around like she just got caught with beaver

nuggets in P.E. before patting Uriel real quick on the back. "I like the way you think."

The seraph gives us a curt nod before tensing his arms to take flight. I surprise even myself by grabbing his shoulder before he can fly away.

"Uriel." I force myself not to be anxious and push my nerves aside. "Did you know that the fruit would kill a Blurred One?"

The seraph doesn't look all that pleased by my question, but neither does he pull away. His wings flap just once when he says, "I DID NOT, THOUGH IT PARALLELS OUR FATHER'S PLAN FOR MANKIND. HE WISHES FOR HIS SPIRIT SONS AND DAUGHTERS TO BE BORN. THE FRUIT MADE HIS FIRST CHILDREN ON EARTH HUMAN. LUCIFER'S PROGENY ALREADY REFUSED THE FRUIT AND THAT CHOICE."

"God knew Alora's big, bad plan was screwy to begin with," Eva quips.

"A tender mercy . . ." I agree.

But if God is that aware of who we are, and *He* planted the tree, he had to know there would be exceptions—a soul who would regret his choice. A being who would later want to be born so badly that he would do *anything* to make it right.

"Do you think . . ." I avoid Leo's eyes. "Is it possible . . . that the fruit wouldn't hurt Leo? Because he fights for the good side?"

The seraph's wings send a fresh wave of cool wind to my face. "IT IS POSSIBLE. IF HE HAS *TRULY* REPENTED. THOUGH CONSIDERING THE LIFE HE HAS LED, IT IS EVEN MORE PROBABLE THAT HE SHALL DIE A VERY PAINFUL DEATH. AS IF BY YOUR SALT GRENADES, HE SHALL BE REDUCED TO NOTHING. VERY POWDERY."

Sensing all the grief Leo must be feeling, I shoot the seraph a cringing smile. "Thanks." I turn to Leo.

*But it won't hurt you, because **you are good**.*

I do my best to explain, but all the insecurities rush to Leo's eyes. He rubs the back of his neck and begins to pace.

Leo, you have to believe me. I take his hand. *God knows you're worthy of being saved!*

He digs his hands into the back of his hair, but as Uriel flies off, I can't help feeling the hope of keeping Leo. He *won't* die.

"No way am I missing out on seeing *the tree*," Eva says, grabbing Raylan's hand and dragging him away.

Raylan yells, "We can't see it! The cherub's burying it to ten thousand degrees!"

"Shhh!" Eva waves her arm like she's stopping traffic. Then, like she's explaining to a four-year-old, she very slowly points to Leo and me. "See how they're about to have a moment?" she says between gritted teeth.

Raylan's eyes widen, and Eva giggles as she drags him toward the crater, blasting a few smoked Blurred Ones along the way.

Eva's belief that there's no need for goodbyes should prove that I'm not crazy. Raylan watches us from about forty feet off, but he doesn't come back. He's not coming back, because *he believes*.

"Beau chose to be a martyr, but you don't *have* to," I say to Leo.

The ground rumbles as Uriel moves the fallen rock blocking his path to the tree.

I retake Leo's hand, because it seems he's pulled away. "What is life, if we choose not to believe?" I never realized this about myself before, but it's who I am. Belief—hope—is a large part of who I am. "I believe in you and Beau and Eva and Raylan and, if given the chance, I would have tried to convince Maggie to *never stop fighting*."

Leo doesn't say a word as the ground rumbles, golden flecks from the fruit scattering up from the cave. Taking a step forward, Leo tries to smile as a hurricane rages in his eyes. His gentle fingers cup the side of my face. "You know you are my sole reason for existence."

"And you are mine." *We're going to build a life together. Study flashcards. Travel like crazy!*

You know that isn't possible.

I reach up and grip his hand next to my face. *It is.* And I kiss him, tears pricking my eyes.

Leo's lips are both smooth and soft. Tender yet hungry. He kisses me back, and I want to swallow him whole; push him away, because *this* is his attempt to say goodbye.

But we aren't saying goodbye.

My arms wrap around his shoulders, clinging to his back.

"Don't leave me," I whisper. *Don't leave me.*

He holds onto my waist like a lifeline, and as the gold powder of the fruit floats closer, we kiss and kiss again.

His lips are fire; luminous. Hot! Scalding.

If the powder's going to take him, it's going to have to take me, too.

Leo ducks his face into my neck as I shiver with fear. "I will love you until the end of time."

The powder of the fruit wraps around Leo and me. We're in a nebula, full and terrifying. Mist licks at my neck and face. Will it turn me into a monster? I forgot that could be an outcome of Uriel's plan, but I don't see anyone's spines breaking apart as their skeletons change shape.

Will the powder take Leo away?

His hands are still real; I keep kissing his face, and the powder hits his jaw, his brow, his hairline . . . nothing happens, except the butterflies in my stomach are literally going to make me implode with anxiety.

Leo clutches my back.

I tense—he tenses—we wait.

The mist licks at our backs once again before traipsing to another Blurred One. The man in his eighties is possessed again—and, instantly, he's a powder keg.

Black dust shoots up and down, left and right, and Leo's still here.

He's still here!

I laugh so loud, I nearly don't hear his laugh.

Nearly.

I straighten the canvas of my freshly finished painting, then lean back into Raylan's waiting arms to study it and its corresponding piece. It felt so good to paint again, and even better to let out an ounce of the pain I feel for the loss of its subjects.

I did my best to capture Beau's wit and charm, along with his impossible innocence. I didn't really know his siblings, but I included them as best I could, loving and surrounding their big brother.

Peaking behind Beau's canvas, I glimpse my other new piece. It was the harder of the two to paint. Mags. It's a painting for only those closest to me to see. I painted her in somber tones, her face in a shroud. I'd loved and trusted her, but she couldn't see past her preconceived notions to the real me. Frost found a stack of her journals, and when I'm ready, I'll read them and try to sort it out. I'm sure it'll take years to sort out that mess of feelings.

It hurts to see the painting, but it helps me process everything. Especially since I would never have wanted to kill her. But I did. I didn't fight it, anyway.

It seems so recent that we were gathered here at the house for Dad. So much death in just a year.

With no bodies, there are no caskets, so this doesn't really feel like a funeral. More like a party where the guests of honor just plum couldn't make it, especially with the cowboy sushi—Frost's idea—and lasso-throwing contest we had out front a few minutes ago—Mom's idea. Plus, of course, lots and lots of pie.

"Can I have your attention, please?" Frost's assured voice cuts through the conversation in the living room. Our group is small—Leo, Raylan, Mom, Mr. Harris, Kathryn, Christian, and his mom, but we've got a lot of love among us.

Side note, thanks to being force-fed the fruit, Christian's mom now seems to have developed the ability to breathe underwater. Guess she was pure enough that, like Leo, she didn't die with the evil peeps.

"I wanted to honor Beau and his siblings," Frost says, standing next to a table with something covered on top. Her voice softens, but it's strong. She looks like some powerful, rich, ranch-running woman or something, poised with grace, her eyes carrying the depths of oceans of experience. I guess having a lifeline to an eternity of memories can teach a girl a thing or two.

"I skimmed through the mountain of books Beau read in the last month," she continues. "I think he was ready to learn everything under the sun. And instead of doing it through textbooks or documentaries, he wanted to do it through the art and experience of literature." She stretches a hand out to Leo, who hands her a ratty copy of a paperback book, then leans back against our green sofa's arm, looking at her with, as impossible as it seems, even more love than when we were all back here last summer.

"He was reading this when he died, and he'd written a quote in the front. 'Literature is strewn with the wreckage of men who have minded beyond reason the opinions of others.'" He was always going against the opinions of others. So, I carved this tree, using the knife skills Beau taught me and utilizing a weapon as a tool for beauty instead of destruction. To represent what he and his family did for all of us."

She uncovers her creation, and our group takes a collective breath. An intricate tree carved from wood, full of dark and light highlights, twists of branches reaching out a good foot and a half and roots sprawling across the table. It's absolutely stunning. She even carved tiny, delicate leaves with fruit on the branches.

She shifts a bit, the tiniest crack in her confidence showing.

"They would absolutely love it, Frosty." I extricate myself from Raylan so I can put an arm around my sister. I give her shoulders a squeeze and savor the moment of just being with her again, without an intrusive house guest in my body. I hate talking in front of people, even just a group this size, but I owe them.

I pull my arm from Frost's shoulder and angle toward her gorgeous tree.

"Thanks for saving the world, Beau," I begin with a big breath. "And your sweet brothers and sisters. I didn't get to know you long, but I reckon we'll be reminiscing about you for the rest of our mortal lives. Thanks for not being afraid to live your life big and on your own terms."

I feel my eyes welling up and look to Raylan for strength, but he's got tears streaming down his amazing cheeks. I cry a laugh and let the tears flow, unashamed. "I can't believe we're all standing here." Frost reaches for my hand, and I grab hers hard. "Thank you for fighting for me. Thanks to them, and thanks to all of you. I aim to do y'all proud."

"Here, here!" Leo shouts with his kind smile, and the

group claps, which makes me cry harder, but it feels really good.

CHAPTER 55 - FROST

In the beginning, I never thought Leo's and my relationship would last. After San Antonio, I thought he was going to be born and be a baby eighteen years younger than me.

It wasn't until we were hiding from Tess and Dom at that lake house that it really hit me that Leo would do *anything* to keep me safe.

And I felt the same way about him. I needed him in my life.

When the powder of the fruit hit Leo and me, I knew, I just *knew* that everything would be all right. Sure, I got scared for maybe about thirty seconds, but that's life. It's normal to have doubts and not feel brave all the time.

I will never forget that moment. Gold powder hit Leo's face, and nothing happened. It was the most beautiful thing in the world, watching the glorious truth that he was going to live dawn in his eyes.

We stood hand in hand. It literally felt like God was smiling down on us as the stars shined.

"Do you ever watch the stars, Frost?" Leo had asked last

summer when we climbed that tree at Maggie's. *"I used to lie on my back and stare at a tent's ceiling. I swore to myself that I wouldn't allow myself the luxury of looking at the stars again until I made things right."*

And that is what Leo did for the rest of his life.

He hunted with and helped Raylan.

He helped us take down Knox.

He survived Tess and combatted jealousy.

He fought against *all* his old demons, seeing through the hollowness of Alora's lust that she so freely gave.

You know, if I hadn't ever seen who Eva was in The Before—who we were and exactly what happened—I don't think I'd appreciate just how lucky and blessed we are to be alive.

And now, as we coast on a raft over water too blue to be real, with the promise of more stars to come out—dim or shining—I can't help laying on Leo's shoulder and pretending, just for a moment, that we never faced any monsters in the beginning.

We've begun our trek to travel the world.

Money's a non-issue since Leo stashed enough away to last us three lifetimes. Now? We can spend days and evenings like these, basking in the sun and starlight.

"Are you going to age with grace?" Leo asks, skimming his fingers along my jawline.

I automatically shiver and smack him on the chest. "You have *way* more wrinkles than me, and you're not even twenty-five."

Oops, I shouldn't have brought up his age. He still hasn't fully sorted through hijacking his vessel's body, but we both know the original owner wasn't a good guy.

He was an overdosing junkie. I poke his side. *Remember how we can't go to Canada? The guy practically ran the drug trade up there.*

From what I can tell, that's why Leo targeted the guy in the first place, but it's not something he's ever talked about. Maybe he'll share with a little more time.

Sticking my toe in the freezing water, I splash him with some of the Mediterranean Sea. "Hey, you always said this body and your spirit have an uncanny resemblance. Maybe that was God's intention all the time." When I saw Leo in The Before, he looked almost identical to this vessel.

His fingers skip along my wrist, my forearm, and all the way up my shoulder before rubbing it affectionately. "I am afraid this vessel will not last as long as yours. *I* fear I will not age with grace."

I roll over so that I can look up at him, elbows propping me up as I rest on my tummy. "I will love you even if you sprout a third eyeball and buck teeth."

"Right."

"Well, maybe not the buck teeth, but we could get you braces . . . or Invisalign."

"I knew you only liked me for my body."

I swat his arm. "That's not what I'm saying. What I'm saying is, I will love you whether you grow warts or wake up with throat cancer. If you need to get a mole removed. If you go blind."

The teakwood raft skates across the water as Leo scoops me up in his arms, which smell like the wild oranges we plucked in Sicily. "Same."

We lay like that for what feels like hours, the sun warming our faces unlike anything I've ever felt in Bloodcreek. We certainly did put on sunscreen.

Leaning down, Leo nuzzles my face. "Marry me?"

My veins burst with equal parts of ice water and flames. "Wha—?"

He chuckles into my hair. "Then we can start staying in

the same room since I am growing tired of being a respectable boy."

My face and chest practically burst with joy. Someone get me a fan; some A/C. True, Leo and I have had a few heated make-out sessions, but we've made rules, and we never step over the line.

I'm ready for the next step. More than anything in my life.

Wrapping my arms around his shoulders, I whisper, "I will marry you . . . as long as you agree that I have all the power. And we get to keep my last name."

"We?"

"You don't even have a last name."

Leo sinks into my arms. "We name our first son after me."

"I thought Tess was the only narcissist we knew. Maybe we should run to city hall first thing in the morning."

Leo chuckles at that. "Appointment's at six a.m. in a little church just up the coastline."

I blanch, stunned. "ARE YOU SERIOUS?"

"I can cancel it." He shrugs as if he doesn't care.

"Don't you dare! We shouldn't stand up a priest!" Then, thinking how pissed Eva will be to miss this, I think maybe we could include her and Raylan via Skype. Definitely not ideal, but hormones . . . better for forgiveness than permission, right?

Puffy clouds stream past us as happy tears sting my eyes. Alora thought she got what I wanted, but I'm getting *way* more than she could ever dream.

"What are you thinking?" Leo's fingers graze my hair, my eyebrows, and the always welcoming length of my cheek.

"Just trying to figure out if I should dunk you or . . ." I kiss the scruff on his chin. *Show me one of the good things you've done in your life.*

I'm still buzzing with the excitement—maybe we should

dive right into this water and swim to the church he promised me—but I need to take a page from Eva. Chill. I got this. Go back to the habit we've established these last few weeks.

Almost unbidden, the memory of an abnormally tan Leo enters my head. *His muscles ripple from inside his shirt, and sand clings to his wet legs.*

Even from inside his head, I can feel my lips smiling.

Leo clutches a surfboard like it's his lifeline, and his chest hair's sun-bleached.

The sultry waves move in and out before they disappear, and when Leo tucks the surfboard under his arm, he drifts through the mist to a Greyhound headed for Springfield, Missouri.

The bus ambles on, and he takes another . . . to a small town with a newly built tractor supply. A Brookshire's. Anteeks 4 U. A sad little trailer with a beige man who dutifully tends the high school library.

When Leo goes for a very, very long walk, he pauses in front of a house with a seemingly innocent creek and a large sycamore tree.

A woman has just parked her car. She grabs her keys and wanders inside.

Leo cups his eyes and peers into the car's backseat.

Beads of sweat glisten and gather on the forehead of a baby. She wears a pink bow, and with her light skin and thin features, she looks like . . . me.

The baby—I begin to cry. And, pulling on the pink tulle bow on my head, I attempt to squirm out of my seat. But I'm strapped in, and it's got to be ninety degrees.

Leo telekinetically unlocks the door, lifts the handle, and pulls me out.

Carries the car seat.

Passing the giant arm of the sycamore tree, Leo gingerly opens the front door of the house and slips the carrier inside.

It isn't until he's strode a quarter of a mile away and vacated his vessel, his essence floating above the sycamore, that Mom opens the door, big fat tears streaming down her face.

She glances around the yard, and, seeing nobody, whispers, "Thank you," to the trees.

Heart in my throat, I lean up to kiss Leo. I caress his lips. "You saved me."

"I would say you were the one who saved me, but we both know how you're on a mission to prove I'm a saint."

He holds me closer, wrapping me in his arms like I'm his oxygen. I adore the flutter of his heart, the way he's resolved to take me to every beautiful place he's ever seen.

I whisper, "You *are* a saint." And I touch his skin, his dry, sun-kissed hair, memorizing this moment for the rest of my life.

Remember how we like, saved the world a couple of weeks ago? And now Frost and Leo are off canoodling who knows where, and I'm stuck here in *high school*, aka makeshift trailers, until they build a new one since the old one burnt down. Raylan is so stinking stubborn that he got Mom all fired up, and they're bound and determined that me not graduating would be as bad as all the Blurred Ones coming back to Bloodcreek.

Well, I dare those Blurred Ones to try.

I scratch the light pink skin on my forearm, where Mr. H helped my carve-job to heal. I will the bell to ring, but it's more stubborn than Alora. But, hey, I've got a really cute boyfriend waiting for me outside, so there's that. I still can't keep the stupid smile off my face when I think about him.

The bell finally gets a clue and rings, so I scramble out of my desk and wave a hearty goodbye to all the other seniors around me. Four more months. Then what? Who knows, really?

I burst through the school doors and hustle myself to the parking lot, where Raylan's leaning against his truck, waiting for me. It's his birthday today, and I aim to spoil him rotten. Twenty. Old man. Good thing I'll be eighteen soon. Any time Mom gets a little snippy about him being older, it's real nice to be able to play the Leo card.

I throw my arms around his neck and kiss him. Sometimes it takes me right back to that alley in San Antonio, where he seemed so mysterious and dangerous. But now, he kisses me back, and there's no ploy.

"Happy birthday, baby," I murmur onto his lips. His light scruff is just what I need to wake up after the eye-burning boredom of calculus.

"Thanks, baby," he says, taking my backpack from off my shoulders. "Trudy and Christian just called to tell me they're sending up some Cajun snacks, whatever that means."

My heart swells at the news. For someone with such a rough childhood, I just adore that Raylan's making up for lost time and making so many amazing relationships. He keeps trying to talk Christian into being a hunter with him, but Christian's determined to help people slay their inner demons instead. Turns out, he's a therapist. Figures. And Trudy dotes on Raylan like he's her own son. Good.

"Excellent," I say. "Now, you ready to celebrate?"

"You mean going muddin' with my ol' lady?" he says, voice pitched in an awkward accent. He pokes me in the waist.

I slap him playfully. "You tryin' to be Wade? You're gonna have to grow out your hair." Poor Wade. He's mostly recovered but goes white as a sheet any time we're within fifty feet of each other. Hopefully, if I keep buying him Beaver Nuggets, he'll forgive me eventually.

"Yes, let's go. But first, Diet Coke, stat!"

"Yes, General Eva," he says with a tiny salute and loving grin.

I blush and squirm. Still getting used to that lil tidbit of information Leo and Frost shared.

We climb into Raylan's truck and drive. I text Mom to let her know we're on our way. She's been way more interested in keeping tabs on where I am since she found out that the last time I was "at Maggie's," I was actually hosting a pretty wicked parasite.

I slide over and grab Raylan's hand and sigh in contentment. I know we won't be content in Bloodcreek for long, but while I'm finishing school, it is pretty glorious to just get to live our lives. Especially since no Blurred One dares set foot anywhere near here anymore.

Maggie willed her place to Raylan, so he's gonna sell it . . . when we're ready to deal with it. For now, he's renting a cute house in town. It's one of the few buildings left unburnt, but it's still cheap 'cause somehow, people aren't keen on moving to Bloodcreek now.

He's also taking classes at the University of Missouri, majoring in math and fine arts. I had no idea he could be such a nerd. It's pretty sexy. He does his homework in our basement while I paint, and Mom comes down with a question to ask us every ten minutes.

Raylan turns on our new favorite album, Odesza's *A Moment Apart,* and cranks the volume. "I love you, Eves," he shouts, even though I'd be able to hear him just fine since I'm so close. "You're the greatest girl in the universe."

I squeeze his hand in reply. "I love you, and happy birthday. Now, let's go live happily, forwards and backwards."

Bloodcreek road twists and squirms like the water moccasins in our creek back home.

Usually I have to watch the road to not get carsick, but not today. Today we've got a mission in the crosshairs.

Seeing Eva and Raylan after forever.

After Leo and I finished our European tour—and dipped into Africa to see a wildebeest migration in Tanzania—he took me to Japan to show me where he lived—a little coastal village. While there, he showed me the very monastery that supplied Leo with that tent where he resolved to wait for me to look at the stars.

So far, everything about Leo's and my life has been pretty surreal. And while I know we can't always be on a worldwide tour, I do believe future trips will be a key way for us to stay close to each other.

"Turn left here," I tease Leo, as if he doesn't know where we are. He's a human compass, so I always make a point to pretend he has no idea.

As we rumble past black-eyed Susans and purple cone-flowers, I can't help feeling glad that we've come back to

Missouri when the wildflowers are out. Somehow, the hills seem bigger—freer—and the green landscape with its swaying oaks doesn't seem as stifling anymore.

The old convertible with the bikini-clad mannequins is gone. The new high school's built in a better location, surrounded by towering cedars. There's even an outdoor cafeteria, and if Eva and I had that, maybe we wouldn't have been so stuck on despising our school.

When we amble up to Maggie's house, instead of seeing a cute '30s house that needs a little TLC, all I can see is a shack that either needs to be sold or blowtorched. None of us have decided. None of us wants to bother. It's why we've chosen this location to meet up.

The loose nuts and bolts strewn around in the grass have been there ever since I can remember, and I *still* can't believe Maggie turned on Eva. We were a team. Even Beau could see that, and he'd only been with us a few months.

Reva's old Nissan Rogue is parked squarely in the driveway. I throw open my door even before Leo has stopped the car and leap to the weeds and gravel.

"Frost!" he shouts.

Husbands . . . "I'm all right!"

Hopping around a Yeti cooler, a ginormous ant pile, and a new, strappy-looking weapon that roughly resembles a grenade launcher, I can hardly believe it's been five years since we said bye to Beau and good riddance to Maggie.

Eva tears across Maggie's front porch like she's one of those wildebeests in Tanzania, and just as fiercely leaps into my arms.

"Frosty!"

We both shriek and giggle. She pats the knife I keep tucked up near my elbow—when I'm not passing through airports—and I keep toying with her long, silky-smooth hair.

"Where's Raylan?" I ask as we break apart.

A squeak on the porch tells me my sister's other half's not far behind.

"Eeee!" I sprint up the steps to give Raylan the biggest hug, since he's the best hugger ever. His muscly arms hold me with superglue, and he feels like he's been lugging around cement blocks for fun.

Eva throws her muscly arms around Leo, too, and somehow, all of us have ended up on the grass in a four-studded circle.

"Not letting up on the hunting regiment, I see." Leo observes Raylan's bulging traps and stacked shoulders.

"Blurred Ones won't kill themselves," Raylan practically growls, and Eva gets this starry-eyed expression that tells me their romance isn't dead at all.

I think they spent the last month in Reno. We don't have Zombi, and we're out of the fruit from the tree, but Eva and Raylan's method of "killing" Blurred Ones is akin to what we did to Knox—screw them, then dump them in a deep hole.

Eyeing the sky and how the sun's slipping through the trees even further, I snag my sister's arm. "Ready for our walk?"

Eva nods—it's something we've planned to do together the last few months. It's not that we don't trust the boys with anything we have to say, but after all this time, we simply need a sisterly recharge.

I give Leo a quick peck on the cheek. "See you in maybe five hours."

He winds his fingers through mine and pulls me to his lean chest, sending flurries all the way from my stomach to my toes. Ooh, and his wife has rather excellent taste in Irish cologne . . .

Eva groans like we've taken way too long; Leo trails his fingers along my waist before kissing my throat.

Waving goodbye to our boys, Eva and I set off amidst

rabid mosquitos that nip at our legs and arms. We tromp around Maggie's shoddy house—thistles *everywhere*—and wander through the shooting range with its broken root beer bottles and bullet-ridden cans of Diet Coke.

It's all so strange, like time stood still.

"You sure Leo won't be offended we don't include him while we talk?" Eva sidesteps a cobweb dripping off a silver maple.

"Since when has Leo ever been offended by anything?"

Eva barks a laugh. "Hey, you never know! Raylan keeps telling me, I need 'girl time.'" Eva's imitation of Raylan's voice is spot on, but the humor fades from her eyes all too soon as we pass Maggie's old hunting shed. To think Maggie finally took us in after we coveted seeing it for years.

When we come to the fire ring where we had all those long talks and cooked s'mores, I think Eva might want to stop, but she keeps trucking on.

"Let's not pick a destination," she murmurs. "Just wander."

It's been our motto the last couple of years. While she and Raylan covered the east and west coasts, Leo and I hit as many great travel spots as possible. He even showed me the beach where he learned to surf. And, in between all our tours, we've been taking online classes for college.

We're learning that we're an obnoxiously competitive couple.

Arm still hooked inside Eva's, I say, "So, I have something cool to tell you. Next year, I'll actually be able to graduate."

"No way!" She swats my arm. "You're flyin' through college!"

"It's pretty convenient, because I'm actually due in October."

Eva stops in her tracks, the most dumbfounded and prettiest smile stretching over her face. "No. Freaking. Way."

She blinks real fast to hold back the tears, which is why I wasn't sure how to tell her. Ever since she and Raylan tied the knot three years ago, they have been hoping for a kid of their own.

"It'll happen for you." I squeeze her arm.

Eva smiles, but, with the way she falls silent, I can tell this isn't something she wants to discuss right now.

"Are you gonna tell them?" she asks as the sun shoots sparks of orange light over the horizon. "Your kids, I mean."

"About the Blurred Ones?"

I know I've hit the mark, because she doesn't say a word.

I toy with an errant branch from a nearby redbud with its pink blooms. *Does* it make sense to tell my future child that his daddy was once on the devil's side? Should repentance include forgetting the past or being open about what has gone on before?

If we told our child about who Leo was, wouldn't he or she just want to go out and find some Blurred Ones to learn more? If we don't tell the truth, we risk our child doing the *exact* same thing Eva did when we went to San Antonio.

"I don't know . . ." I try to be honest and clear. "It's not like I can ask for advice from anyone who's gone through what he has."

There's always Taryn, the other Despairity . . . but not sure we want to go there.

Breaking away from my arm, Eva moves off a few paces to absorb the orange-ribboned clouds. "I'm happy for you."

"And I am happy for *you*." I take a tentative step toward my sister. "You and Raylan have exorcised more Blurred Ones than any hunter we know."

"We're pretty hardcore."

I laugh, my voice rattling like a tambourine through the cedars. "What are you going to do next?" I graze my tummy with my pinky and thumb.

Eva shrugs, spinning round and round, arms held wide. "Who knows?" She lifts her arms high above her head. "Conquer the world!"

I didn't notice before, but we're on a higher patch of ground than the rest of Maggie's land. We can see all of Bloodcreek from up here, and while everything hasn't grown in since Alora set the whole county on fire, it *has* started to come back, but clean. Greener. And we've been able to grow more varieties of trees than Bloodcreek has ever been able to grow before.

What's more, Mom finally found a great job she loves. She tends the plants in a nursery she set up to receive all the shipments sent to our town. I've never seen her so independent and fulfilled; it's almost like the fire was a cleansing agent and burnt away all her grief, her sorrow.

"I'm not sad we went through it," Eva says, scanning the pink tips of a sweetgum. "Even Maggie."

That's not what I expected to hear at all.

"If I didn't have to doubt myself so completely because of her, I never would have known for myself that I can be pretty awesome."

"Well, aren't you a veritable Gandolph?"

Eva cracks a smile. Though we've exchanged postcards over the years, she's never once said anything about Dad, Tess, Alora, *or* Maggie. Postcards are not the natural place for that sort of thing. I didn't know how she was handling it.

"Finding out about the Blurred Ones made us who we are," she says, tracing the lines and contours of the .9mm strapped to her belt.

My eyes twinge and burn with tears. "I still wish Beau could be here, though."

Eva smiles grimly before changing to a full-toothed smile. "Did you know the town rebuilt Sasquatch n' Koi?"

"No!"

"It's not exactly what Beau envisioned—you have to call ahead to make reservations 'cause it's black tie—but it's nice. There's even a picture of Beau and his brothers and sisters on the wall. Put there by the new owner . . . Wade."

I bust up at that. "'You oughta be my ol' lady.'" I mimic the pickup line Wade once used on her, and while my sister hasn't fully healed from everything that's happened, she's close. Really, do any of us fully heal from past wounds? I believe in forgiveness and redemption, I do, but what is a memory? A perfectly clean, white spot on the wall, or a newly constructed rung in a step ladder that climbs on and on?

All I know is, Eva *is* stronger. She's arming herself with the shield of faith, proving how she's the most dauntless girl I know.

Laying her arm across my shoulders, she casually asks, "Think Beau would be proud? You know, since we're still hunters?" She nods at the small, rounded headstone we placed for him alongside his brothers and sisters'. Of course, we placed the whole family near twin blackberry and raspberry bushes, because *everyone* knows Beau Jones' razzleberry pie was to die for.

I take charge of my emotions by clearing my throat. "Eva, you could do no wrong."

"Neither could you." She stares at the inscription I asked the etcher to put on Beau's stone—the hope he shared right before he died: *Rise, take flight.* That's all we can do, isn't it? Stand up, dare to bloom, brave *every single* demon that crosses our paths—until we return to our Heavenly Father's arms.

At the top of Beau's stone, the etcher carved a pair of angel wings and cowboy boots. Uriel might have something to say about my choice, but that's what Beau was—the booted angel who took down the majority of the monsters of the world. We still have Blurred Ones, but none of them can come to Bloodcreek with the essence of the fruit lingering in the soil—not enough to affect a human—and what would be life if we didn't have *any* monsters?

When Eva lowers her arm, I link mine through hers. Together, we watch as the sun dips below the horizon, flaring violent streaks of pink and orange. Bluebirds warble and chatter their gorgeous, low tones, and I don't know how to say it—I don't think there are the "right" words—but the warmth swelling in my chest tells me we can handle whatever crosses our paths.

Mostly, I'm glad I get to do it with my fearless, reckless, gorgeous, hilarious, cool-as-a-cucumber demigod of a sister.

ACKNOWLEDGMENTS

Mary, thanks for always having my back and for making this trilogy possible. I most literally couldn't have done it (and a lot of other things) without you. You're my partner in so much crime and dang, I'm lucky. - Cammie

Cammie, thanks for letting me have the privilege of entering Eva's mind and reading about her strengths, struggles, and wicked awesome sense of humor. You are exactly what Frost said about Eva on the last page of this book. Thanks for being the talent in this duo! - Mary

Thanks, hubbies, for not thinking we're evil when we're giggling while plotting tragic demises. Thanks, kids, for being the best cheerleaders and letting us ignore you once in awhile. Kevin, there's no way Eva could have found her power without you. So many thanks.

Thank you to our amazing writing colleagues: Sara, Vanessa, Katie, Tamara, Paige, and Janet. Cheers to many more projects and successes!

Thank you to Dan Smith of Bastille for helping us nail Leo's thoughts and viewpoints. Also, the writers of Sam and

Dean Winchester, for showing that we can fight, win, lose, have fun, cry, be vulnerable, love, and still be the truest heroes.

Most of all, thank you, Father in Heaven, for giving us this life, in which we can create beauty out of darkness.

ABOUT THE AUTHORS

Mary Gray balances dark and twisty plots with faith-based messages. Some of her best ideas come when she's lurking in the woods, experimenting with frightening foods, or pushing her kids on the tire swing. She is a contributor to The Faithful Creative Magazine, a co-owner of Monster Ivy, and the membership chair of Indie Author Hub.

Cammie Larsen loves all things creative, especially something that tells a fantastic story. She's doing what she can to bring more beauty and insight to the world while building her own life's story. For now, that includes helping run Monster Ivy Publishing, volunteering at her local church, and hanging out near and far with her hubs, kid, and two giant dogs. She's an editor, graphic designer, and contributor to The Faithful Creative Magazine.

To learn more about our publishing company, please visit: monsterivy.com.

ALSO BY THE AUTHOR(S)

HUSH, NOW FORGET - two sisters team up with a pair of hottie hunters to unveil the truth about the Blurred Ones and what they really are.

SLEEP, DON'T FRET - the Abram sisters head out to New Orleans to contend with some witch doctors and Raylan's ruthless sister.

THE RIPPER OF MONKSHOOD MANOR - never go into Monkshood, unless your goal is to meet your Maker...

OUR SWEET GUILLOTINE - a young executioner falls for the daughter of a woman he had to kill...

HER DARK FANTASY: A PREQUEL TO OUR SWEET GUILLOTINE - A short story prequel to French Revolution-era novel, OUR SWEET GUILLOTINE. Young Tempeste witnesses an executioner break apart her mother's feet in an attempt to extract a confession.

THE DOLLHOUSE ASYLUM - a group of teenagers are granted asylum from the apocalypse, only to be forced to reenact some of the most famous, tragic literary couples... or die.

THE DEVILS YOU MEET ON CHRISTMAS DAY - a short story anthology about the outliers, the murderers, the misunderstood, and the forgotten.

HOW TO WRITE FAITH-BASED MESSAGES FOR A SECULAR MARKET - for secular writers who hope to incorporate messages of hope and faith.

HOW TO WRITE CLEAN YET SCINTILLATING ROMANCE - bodice rippers are some of the most lucrative books in the industry. So what if you write books that aren't as steamy?

HOW TO WRITE DARK AND TWISTY BOOKS TO SHOWCASE THE LIGHT - in this brief nonfiction booklet, Mary discusses a psychological and scriptural basis for tackling darker books, some of her favorite techniques for mastering the craft, and how to show the strength of God's light.